P9-DVU-180

There are moments
when I question why
we so willingly put ourselves in danger,
but then I try to imagine life
in some of the homes I've glimpsed
in my trips across the river
and think how sad it must be to
live only for oneself.

Prudence Willard
Marietta, Ohio
September 9, 1857

Secrets of Wayfarers Inn

Family Secrets

Family Secrets

BECKY MELBY

Guideposts
New York

Secrets of Wayfarers Inn is a trademark of Guideposts.

Published by Guideposts Books & Inspirational Media
110 William Street
New York, NY 10038
Guideposts.org

Cover and interior design by Müllerhaus
Cover illustration by Bob Kayganich, represented by Deborah Wolfe, LTD.
Typeset by Aptara, Inc.

Printed and bound in the United States of America
10 9 8 7 6 5 4 3 2

Chapter One

"Cobblestone!" LuAnn Sherrill sat in the back seat pressing her forehead against the window—more like a five-year-old in front of a candy counter than a woman who'd just taken the senior discount at the Buckley House. Beneath the tires, red cobblestones murmured of days gone by. History and its untold secrets never failed to ignite her curiosity, but today she had other things on her mind. "We won't stay too long, right?"

"Right." The half-hearted answer, coming from Tessa Wallace, her longtime friend who sat in the passenger seat, wasn't reassuring. Tess pointed at an empty space, and Janice Eastman, LuAnn's other forever friend, parked facing the river.

LuAnn got out of the car and stared at the building, from its crooked basement windows to the missing shutters on the top floor. Her breath caught in her throat. How had a building this rich in story come to be in such need of repair? The real estate ad in the *Marietta Times* classifieds had described it as a warehouse, but clearly it had once been something else. Four stories high, the building must have been a hotel at one point.

She turned around, drinking in the sight of sunlight sparkling on the water and docked boats bobbing gently along the edge of the river. Since she'd arrived in Marietta this morning, everything around her, from the hauntingly familiar smell of the Ohio River to the trill of song sparrows, seemed to welcome her back and remind her that, this time, she was safe.

Tess and Janice had already crossed the street. She joined them at the massive arched front door. Tess pointed to a dirt-covered yellow sign. "The For Sale sign looks like it's been here about as long as the building."

"That may mean I need a different Realtor." LuAnn glanced at her watch. "He's late." *Come on, mister.* Didn't the man know she had a life to get on with, a purpose to figure out?

Janice shook her head. "No more setting your watch five minutes ahead. You're not on teacher time anymore, girlfriend." She high-fived Tess, honoring the promise the three of them had made four decades ago: "We will never be boring or bored, and we will never act our age."

LuAnn stretched the stiffness out of her neck. She'd graded her last paper just over a week ago in Clarksburg, West Virginia, and sat at the head table at a banquet honoring her thirty-five years of service. She was done working. Retired. Three weeks had passed since her mother's funeral. No more daily visits to the memory care facility. Her time was her own now, but she still couldn't shake the constant feeling she was supposed to be somewhere. Once she found a place to live, she could start figuring out what life beyond teaching was supposed to look like. And then she'd relax. Maybe.

Out of habit, she looked at her watch again. As she opened her mouth to mention that this time the Realtor really *was* late, something caught her eye. A bronze plaque, almost obscured by a thick mass of woodbine.

WAYFARERS INN—BUILT IN 1826—
GAVE SHELTER TO RIVER TRAVELERS AND WAS AN
IMPORTANT STOP ON THE UNDERGROUND RAILROAD.
THIS PROPERTY IS LISTED ON THE NATIONAL REGISTER OF
HISTORIC PLACES BY THE UNITED STATES
DEPARTMENT OF THE INTERIOR.

Janice shook her head, sending unruly platinum-tinted curls dancing. "I remember seeing this building from the deck of a sternwheeler, but I never knew its history."

Tess touched the knocker at the center of one door. "Imagine what this looked like when it was first built. I bet it was a bustling place. Can't you just see the steamship captains smoking their pipes and flirting with girls in hoopskirts?"

LuAnn stepped up to a window. Cupping her hands, she tried to peer beyond the dusty, wavy handblown glass.

"Greetings!" The deep voice came out of nowhere.

LuAnn's pulse skipped a beat as she turned to see a silver-haired man with shockingly blue eyes. He wore a gray summer-weight suit and carried a clipboard and a For Sale sign that did not match the one nailed to the doorframe. "Hello. We were just—are you the Realtor?"

"Brad Grimes. Grimes Realty. Just took over this listing." He set the sign down and held out his hand. Firm shake, unwavering eye contact. He shook hands with each of them and followed each introduction with "Pleasure to meet you."

As her students would say, the guy was old-school. And a bit too slick looking for her taste.

"Let me tell you about this magnificent structure, ladies. It was originally called the Riverfront House, but around the time of the First World War, a new owner renamed it after a poem called 'The Wayfarer.'" He closed his eyes as he recited the lines. "'Is it the hour? We leave this resting-place made fair by one another for a while. Now, for a god-speed, one last mad embrace; the long road then, unlit by your faint smile. Ah! The long road! And you so far away!'" He opened his eyes and directed his gaze at LuAnn as he continued. "'Oh, I'll remember! But...each crawling day will pale a little your scarlet lips, each mile dull the dear pain of your remembered face.'" He gave a slight bow.

Janice and Tess cheered and giggled. LuAnn simply stuttered, "R-Rupert Brooke."

He arched one brow. "You know your literature, ma'am."

"She'd better," Janice chimed in. "She taught English for thirty-five years."

LuAnn needed to get the man off romantic poets so he could give them a quick tour before moving on to the houses she hoped he'd found in her price range. When they'd seen this listing in the paper, she was as curious about the building as Tess and Janice. She'd told the receptionist exactly that when she called. Just curious, not in the market. She didn't want to waste anyone's time. Especially her own. Before she had a chance to tell him they only wanted a short tour, Tess jumped in.

"How many rooms?"

"At one time the inn had twenty-four guest rooms and a tavern on the main floor. Unfortunately, some of the walls on the top floor were knocked out. But the others are relatively intact." He unclipped a single key from his clipboard. "You'll find she's been a bit neglected, but"—he unlocked the door—"as they say, she's got good bones."

He switched the lights on and swept his arm out like a circus barker. LuAnn could easily imagine him sitting in this room in the 1800s, swindling someone over a game of poker.

The room was dirty and cluttered with empty cardboard boxes, but she was thrilled to see no one had tried to camouflage its character. Wide floor planks, deeply scarred and with square nail heads visible in spots, whispered of frenzied dances and barroom brawls. The outside walls were white-painted stone.

"Look at the ceiling," Janice whispered, her voice as hushed as if they stood in the Sistine Chapel.

Pressed tin. LuAnn felt a surge of adrenaline as she looked from the peeling paint on the tin ceiling to the curved stairway that led to a balcony.

"You're a history lover, aren't you, LuAnn?"

He remembered her name? She couldn't think of his. Grimes Realty. But what was his first name? "I also taught American History." She walked to the staircase and put her hand on the mushroom-shaped newel cap, feeling the smooth patina of the wood.

Tess squealed from across the room. "Look!" She pushed aside a stack of flattened boxes, revealing an antique gold cash register.

"I'm told that's original. Came with the building," Grimes Realty said. "This was an antique store for many years before it was used for storage. It's been empty for quite a while, sitting here with all this potential. What a waste, don't you agree?"

All three women nodded.

Janice stood at the bottom of the stairs. "Can we go up?"

"The fourth floor is boarded up, but I can show you the second and third. No electricity up there, but we've got daylight. I'll lead the way."

Of course you will. LuAnn hung back, wishing she were alone and had hours to explore each corner, giving rein to her imagination as scene by scene flickered like an old movie reel. She pictured a player piano in the corner by the hearth and a young woman with a peacock feather in her hat singing "Miss Nancy Paul" and "The Sailor's Grave." In the opposite corner, she could almost hear a whispered conversation between two clandestine lovers, or see the hotel manager squinting through wire-rimmed glasses as he balanced his books. She could easily conjure jangling music chords floating over a haze of smoke and the backdrop of coarse laughter. The smell of freshly caught fish, the blast of a riverboat horn...

"Lu?" Tess gave her a quizzical look from the balcony.

"Coming." For forty years, she'd been the one at the top of the stairs, nagging her friends to keep up, urging them on to their next adventure. She was the trip planner, the reservation maker, the list maker. But retirement had given her blank pages instead of lists, and she wasn't good with empty squares on her calendar.

They started with the first room to the right at the top of the stairs.

"This is the only suite, probably a sitting room and bedroom at one time," Mr. Grimes explained. "The handblown glass in the windows is original, as is the woodwork."

LuAnn took out her phone and used the flashlight app to illuminate a hinged iron light fixture on the wall. "Gaslight," she said under her breath, picturing shadows flickering over a padded settee and four-poster bed and reflecting off the high ceiling. On one wall, a marble hearth surrounded a fireplace that seemed to be made of the same bricks as the pavers on the road.

Room after empty room sent shivers of possibility dancing up her spine. "Someone needs to restore this."

Janice chewed on the corner of her lip. "What a shame."

As they descended the stairs, Mr. Grimes said, "My brother advertised this as a warehouse, but I'm hoping to find a buyer with vision. Can't you see this as a boutique mall or filled with little vintage shops?" The guy's voice rose just slightly. Probably amping into sales mode.

"Or a bed-and-breakfast." Tess looked at Janice, then LuAnn. "We should buy it."

"We should *what*?" LuAnn started to laugh but was cut off by Janice—looking stunned but clapping her hands.

"We should!" Janice's voice held a pitch of excitement LuAnn hadn't heard in well over a year. "This would absolutely not be boring."

"You're not serious." LuAnn felt her eyes widen as she looked from Janice to Tess.

"Serious as a shark attack. Think about it. We are perfect for it, and it's perfect for us." Tess turned to the Realtor. "I taught hotel services classes, and Janice taught domestic arts. And LuAnn is the best cook and talker-to-people I've ever met."

"Oh, really?" He handed them each a spec sheet, LuAnn's tension growing by the second. "Who knows what fascinating secrets this old place holds, ladies? If the legends are true, there may even be a long-deceased guest traipsing around on the fourth—"

"Do you *see* this price?" Tess's eyes bulged. "It's doable. And to save money, we could live on the haunted floor and turn the rest into guest rooms."

LuAnn expected to hear the *Twilight Zone* music at any moment. "*Live* here?"

"We could." Janice ran her hand along a swath of vines carved into the bar, then stared into the dusty mirror that covered the wall behind it. "We could do this."

Tess tapped her lip with one finger. "Think about it, Lu. When, in the forty-plus years we've known each other, have we ever been this freed up? We're all retired. I'm tired of renting, Janice's daughter is getting sick of her, and you're homeless! How perfect is that?" She grinned. "Lu, you are moving back to Ohio so we can do things together, have more adventures, right? What if this is what we've been praying about, our 'what's gonna happen next'?"

LuAnn glanced down at the spec sheet. Bradley Grimes—that was his name. And Tess was right about the price. The building was a foreclosure, currently owned by the bank.

When she looked up, three faces stared expectantly at her. These two incredible friends who'd brought her through the worst moments of her adult life—finding out Phillip, the first man she'd fallen in love with, was actually married, and losing the love of her life, Jesse, to an undetected heart valve defect, two weeks before their wedding—were looking to her for answers.

She and Janice had been in kindergarten and first grade together here in Marietta, before LuAnn's world turned upside down the first time. They'd reconnected in their freshman year of college and met Tess in the school choir.

How could she voice objections when she saw something in her best friends' eyes she hadn't seen in far too long? These sweet friends who had lost their husbands needed something to look forward to. And so did she. It had only been three weeks since her mother's death, a week since the end of school. She suddenly had room in her schedule and her heart that needed to be filled. But still, logically...LuAnn took a step back. "Let's be sensible. We haven't even seen the fourth floor. We don't know if it's structurally sound or a wise investment. We need an appraisal and a business plan and..."

The smug grin on the man with the clipboard said he knew the sale was a done deal. And, despite her protests, she knew it too.

You had me at secrets, *mister. And* potential. The dreams those words could spin. Could this really be the answer to her year-long prayer for purpose after retirement? Every inch of Wayfarers Inn captivated her, but she couldn't let on yet. Like the imaginary poker players in her imaginary time machine, it wasn't smart to show your hand before striking a deal. "Can we see the basement?"

"Absolutely. Follow me. Might want to use the flashlights on your phones again. There are a couple of bare bulbs, but that's all." He led them behind the bar and pointed at a swinging door. "That leads to the kitchen." Then he gestured toward the wall beneath the stairs. He smiled at LuAnn. "After you."

After me, what? She squinted at him.

"Step closer and push just to the left of that seam in the wallpaper."

The seam was barely visible in the pinkish-tan paper covered with faded magnolias. She pushed. And gasped. A door sprang open toward her.

"Careful now. Hold the railing."

The stairs creaked, wood straining against the constraint of rusted nails. The railing was smooth. She walked slowly, feeling the worn dent in the center of each step. Holding her phone high, she imagined it was a kerosene lamp and she wore a long muslin nightgown and a lace-trimmed cap as she snuck down to the cellar for a glass of cider.

She stepped to the left when she reached the bottom. Thin light filtered through dusty windows that were tall enough to allow sunshine to enter if they were cleaned. A monstrous furnace occupied the center of the cavernous room, octopus arms stretching in all directions. A cistern occupied one corner, part of its wall crumbling. She motioned to Tess and Janice. "Room enough to install a hot tub in here. I saw it on Pinterest."

Tess tucked a wisp of copper hair behind her ear. "Modern comfort meets rustic past. I like how you think."

LuAnn pointed to an arched doorway. "This is so much nicer than I expected. High ceilings, beautiful brick..."

Janice nudged her shoulder. "Is that a yes?"

She ignored the question. "Get that furnace out of here and—"

"You could open this up as a banquet hall," Bradley Grimes interjected.

Exactly. Everything she'd been afraid to dream about could happen right here. A place to cook, to care and connect, to listen and pray and minister. All while maintaining the historical integrity of this amazing building.

"Let me show you something fun." He pointed to the archway and started walking. "It appears at least some of the hotel staff lived here, or at least it was made to look that way." He led them through the arch, then turned right, down a hallway lined on both sides with white-painted six-panel doors. Four on each side. "Each room has its own custom touches. Feel free to look."

Janice put her hand on a doorknob. "You're sure the long-dead guest lives on the fourth floor?"

Bradley gave a ghostly laugh. "One way to find out."

LuAnn walked to the end and opened the door on the left. The empty room was minuscule, maybe six by eight, barely large enough to hold a narrow bed and a small washstand. The end wall was brick, the two side walls paneled in white beadboard. There were five hooks spaced about a foot apart on the wall to her left. On her right, a stool about two feet wide was attached to the wall, painted white to match. No window. At night, this room would be the kind of dark that seemed palpable. Imagination in overdrive, she closed the door and turned off her phone. Blackness engulfed her. Except for one tiny point of pale light. Under the stool. Below ground level.

How was that possible?

Inching forward in the dark, she lowered to her knees and reached out and touched the spot, two inches above the floor, on a recessed line in the beadboard. She fumbled for her phone, turned on the flashlight. She rapped on the wall above the stool. It made a solid sound. She tapped the board beneath it. Hollow. Taking a deep breath, she put both hands on the stool and pulled. And almost landed on her backside.

LuAnn gasped as murky light and the musty smell of damp earth wafted into the room.

"Tess! Janice! Come look at this!"

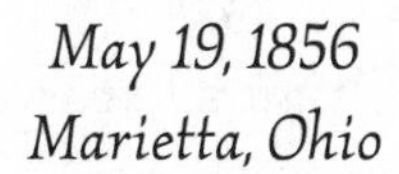

May 19, 1856
Marietta, Ohio

"Stay close, Patience, we have much to do this morning." Prudence Willard laughed at the white goose that waddled in front of her, head held high, surveying the farm she thought she owned.

"What shall we do first? Gather the eggs or check on Charity?" The horse was ready to foal. This was her first, and Prudence wanted to be by her side. She knew the fear of giving birth alone and wouldn't wish it on anyone, even if that someone was a cantankerous draft horse. The thought brought back the stab of loss. It had been almost a year since her daughter lay in her arms. She'd taken two breaths in this world, just long enough for Prudence to scoop her up and kiss her. Twice. Once for hello. Once for goodbye.

Enough. Father, my precious girl is with Thee. She thought of the words of King David. "Can I bring him back again? I shall go to him, but he shall not return to me." Would Hope still be an infant when they met in heaven?

Patience the regal goose led the way to the chicken coop, and Prudence dutifully obeyed. After collecting eight brown eggs and thanking her faithful hens, she peeked in on Charity, who seemed to be fine, and headed back to the house. Rather, she *followed* back to the house. Patience knew the routine.

Jason would be in from feeding the pigs and tending the cows and would be ready for breakfast.

As always, Prudence lingered near the hitching post and stared at the house. Originally part of the Campus Martius fortification built sixty years earlier, it had been moved here by Jason's great-grandfather, who had served under General George Washington, when the fort was dismantled. Prudence loved every inch of it, from the twelve-pane windows, wide-planked floors, and brick hearth, to the four-poster bed covered in the Ohio Star quilt she'd made herself. She'd watched the progress of Melvin Clarke's opulent home on Fourth Street—all red brick and spires, with a turret that belonged on a fairy-tale castle—and hadn't once felt a twinge of envy. Would a house that size ever feel like a home?

Before stepping onto the porch, Prudence looked toward the river, squinting in the sunlight at the twisted oak.

A chill scampered up her spine. "Oh, Patience, it looks like we will be having company tonight." The strip of green gingham that fluttered on the wind almost blended with the new leaves. Almost. She ducked into the house and set the eggs in the crock on the sideboard.

Jason sat with his Bible open and his bad leg propped on a stool. Five years ago he'd been shot while helping two slaves escape a plantation across the river and, oh, how he hated feeling less than the man he'd once been. If only she could convince him he was a hero in her eyes. She kissed her husband. "I will just be a moment." She gave a sigh woven tight with trepidation. "We have a message."

"Be careful." Jason held her hand as she took a step away, his fingertips grazing hers until they were separated.

She nodded and walked out. Jumping off the porch, she waited for Patience to take the lead again. A farm wife and her pet goose—who would ever think they were up to anything more than a morning stroll? She bent, picked a wild petunia blossom, and ordered her feet to saunter. Excitement and fear tangled together like a roiling stew at full boil. The excitement came from knowing she and Jason were here "for such a time as this," but fear was ever present.

With one last look, she slipped through a mass of foxglove and goldenrod and into the underbrush that surrounded the woods along the Muskingum. Her hand trembled as she reached into the hole in the trunk of the old oak, lifted the rock, and found the slip of paper.

Two packages and an envelope. Pick up tonight after dark. Please ship out in two days. Postage high.

Her shoulders sagged. Two adults. One child. How old? Twelve, like she had been when she escaped? Younger? They would be in her care for two days. Forty-eight hours—to feed and bandage and console and pray over their guests. Decoding the last two words set her pulse galloping.

Danger high.

Chapter Two

"What is it? A secret room?" Next to LuAnn, Tess crouched in front of the two-foot-square hole.

Janice knelt beside her. "It's a tunnel."

"I wonder where it comes out?" said LuAnn. "The city has probably registered the other end as a historic place also." She looked over her shoulder at Bradley Grimes, and in that moment she knew from the look on his face that the man was as shocked at her discovery as she was. Could it be possible that the Historical Society didn't know about the tunnel?

LuAnn's emotions swirled within her. Why hadn't she bottled her curiosity until after they'd signed papers? This find could change everything. Even in the dim light, she could see the dollar signs multiplying in Bradley Grimes's eyes. The price could double. Or it could end up off the market, donated to the Historical Society. Not a place to minister but a place to cordon off with velvet ropes and Do Not Touch signs.

"Lu! Look at this." Janice motioned for her to come closer. "The opening gets bigger. And it's lined with bricks."

LuAnn shook off her shock and set the stool aside. On her knees, she dipped low, aiming her flashlight into the hole. "It goes under the road, right?"

"Right to the river." Bradley shook his head. To his credit, he appeared more in awe than calculating profit.

Fully alert now, LuAnn sat back on her heels. "We need to check it out. Make sure it's not visible."

The others stared at her, ghost-story light glowing eerily on their faces. Janice furrowed her brow.

Do you ladies not know what we've stumbled upon? This is huge! And it could be ours if we play our cards right. She kept her self-serving thoughts to herself. "We need to make sure it's protected. Not everyone respects history."

Tess nodded. "Let's go take a look." She motioned toward the opening and grinned at LuAnn. "You first."

Janice shuddered. "You're not serious." Her fear of small spaces would make that a terrifying thought.

Looking down at her white pants, LuAnn shook her head. "Not dressed for it." Though every fiber in her history-loving being wanted to slither through that tunnel just the way a freedom-seeking runaway may have done more than a century and a half earlier, they would need to have it inspected first. *They.* Once word got out, would they have anything to say about the next phase in the life of Wayfarers Inn? Was this building their destiny, or would they, like ordinary tourists, need to stand in line to buy tickets to view the incredible piece of history she had just uncovered?

Bradley led the way up the basement stairs, giving LuAnn time to whisper to Tess and Janice. "Play this cool, okay? If we act too eager to buy, we'll lose our negotiating power. If we have any chance at all."

"What do you mean?" Janice gave her another quizzical look.

LuAnn explained. "The bank owns the building, but I don't think they know about the tunnel. And if they did, they might decide to just donate it to the city. But this would be such a great draw for us. A B&B with an actual Underground Railroad tunnel? Crazy."

"Okay." Janice ran her hand down her face, and her usual bubbly countenance turned somber. "This is my 'we're only moderately interested' face."

Tess laughed. "Perfect."

LuAnn squinted in the sun as they walked from the dim light of the building onto the sidewalk. She glanced at the corner of the building. Who had dug the tunnel beneath the narrow road to the river? They'd jumped to the conclusion that the passageway had been used for slaves fleeing to freedom, but there were other possibilities. "You know, we're making assumptions that might be way off. The tunnel might not be nearly as old"—*or historically significant*—"as we think. It could have been built as an entrance for bootleggers in the 1920s or maybe even more recently for drug smugglers."

Bradley shook his head. "Pretty sure it was built when this was still a dirt road. I'm guessing it was dug from up here." He pointed at the ground. "How else would they have lined it with bricks and shored up the top well enough that it's still intact?"

"How would they build a secret tunnel out in the open?" LuAnn countered, trying to throw him off from what she suspected was the truth.

"A foot at a time in the middle of the night...or they could have made it look like part of the regular construction. Remember, there may not have been any other close buildings back in 1826."

The words were condescending. The voice wasn't. This man was really starting to irritate LuAnn.

On the river side of the road, Bradley held his hand out and helped Janice and Tess down the bank. "Careful, ladies. Wouldn't want the future owners of Marietta's finest bed-and-breakfast getting injured."

So he was still considering them as potential buyers. But the decision wouldn't be his to make. It would be up to a board of bank officials and maybe a group of Historical Society members. LuAnn looked down at the proffered hand. No ring, though a slight groove on his finger made her wonder. Was he one of those salesmen who took off his wedding ring when dealing with a female client? She accepted his offer of help, putting her hand in his, then stepped onto the sidewalk.

"I can't find it." Facing the riverbank, Tess bent down next to a frenzy of brush dotted with wildflowers. "It has to be here. This is the straightest shot from that corner of the building."

LuAnn stood next to Tess and looked back toward the inn. And blinked. For the space of a breath she was sure she saw movement, a blur of white, behind a second-floor window. She stared a moment longer. Nothing. Just a reflection, no doubt. Or her imagination taking over again. She looked down. "It must be—" She stopped. Two skull-sized rocks, caked with thick mud and chunks of sod, sat just to the right of Tess's sandals. "Where did those come from?" She stepped around Tess.

From that vantage point, she noticed two broken tiger lily stems. In front of them, the brush appeared trampled. She eased into the tall grass. There, totally camouflaged by brush and flowers, was a small, weathered wooden door. A tightly closed door. But she'd seen sunlight through the tunnel... which meant someone had been here and closed the door in the last five minutes.

Below the door, on an old, rotting board, sat an earring, gold and clean and gleaming in the sunlight.

Without a word, she picked it up and slipped it into her pocket.

LuAnn bent casually and grabbed one of the rocks. "Let's cover up the door."

"Isn't that like tampering with a crime scene?" Janice wrinkled her nose.

Tess laughed. Janice's view of things had been a constant source of good-natured teasing since the three had met. "There has to be a crime to have a crime scene. We're not tampering, we're covering. We're archaeologists protecting historical treasure."

LuAnn cringed. "Well, maybe not *treasure.*" She gave Tess a "remember?" look.

"Yeah, you're right. Maybe they used the tunnel for a drainage ditch or something."

Bradley laughed. "Pardon my frankness, but...not a chance."

Rude man. LuAnn managed to smile instead of glare. They needed him on their side.

His eyes narrowed. As if thinking *shrewd woman.* Had they, like in spy movies, been "made"? Had he figured out their intentions in downplaying the importance of the tunnel? LuAnn held up her arm and made a show of checking her watch. "We really should get going. We still want to see the kitchen before we move on to look at the houses you found. And then. . .we just might be ready to talk about making an offer."

A bit of color washed from Janice's cheeks. Bradley's eyes lit up. It seemed to take Tess a moment before she could remember how to use her lips. "What she means is, we'll take a couple of days to research what it would cost to renovate the place." Tess glared at LuAnn. "Right?"

Right. That was exactly what she should have said. But for once she wasn't acting out of logic and practicality and the need to plan every detail before making a decision. For once, she was simply listening to her gut.

So very *un*-LuAnn.

Tess grabbed her arm as they walked up to the front door of the inn. "What were you *thinking*?" she whispered.

I have no idea. "That was just a placeholder. No loss if we decide we don't want to do it, but once we put in an offer they can't raise the price on us—no matter how much our new find has increased its value."

"Oh. Good thought."

"I have them once in a while." She fingered the gold hoop in her pocket and stepped behind Bradley as he unlocked the door. The four of them walked in, and stopped.

An ivory lace scarf hung, swaying gently, from the ceiling fan above them.

Janice covered her mouth with her hand. Her eyes bulged. "W-was that there before?"

A tiny spasm jiggled the skin below Bradley's right eye. "It was probably up there all along and the wind moved it when we opened the door."

What wind? No one voiced what LuAnn knew they were all thinking. She shrugged. "Yeah. Probably the wind. Let's go see the kitchen." Her voice wavered on the last two words.

Beside her, Janice whispered, "There's no such thing as ghosts, right?"

"Right." *No such thing.* "Let's go." LuAnn stepped around Bradley and led the way to the swinging door behind the bar. If they stood beneath the swaying scarf a moment longer, one or all of them was likely to run. It was just the wind. She pushed open the door. Her foot slipped out from under her, and she grabbed the doorframe just in time. She looked down. The floor was strewn with peanut shells. "There is, however, such a thing as mice."

"*Eeeeww.*" Janice hid behind her, peering around her shoulder. Then, mice apparently forgotten, she sighed in awe and gave a squeal of delight.

The room was huge, with space for a ten-foot-long harvest table if they wanted an eat-in kitchen. Ceiling-high white cupboards and a once-white tiled floor that looked like it could be restored by a good cleaning, re-grouting, and replacing a few squares. There were no appliances, but it was easy to see where a commercial stove and fridge and dishwasher could fit. With better lighting and a new sink, it would be a perfectly functional B&B kitchen. LuAnn twirled in the middle of the vast space, then stopped herself. "This is... adequate."

Bradley laughed. He was definitely onto them.

"I don't know if I trust him," Tess said as she hugged a cup of English toffee latte and nibbled on her bottom lip. They'd claimed a white pedestal table with mismatched chairs next to an exposed brick wall at Jeremiah's Coffee House on Front Street. The ambiance was perfect for strategizing. They'd already discussed the pros and cons of each of the homes Bradley had found for LuAnn. She'd liked the bungalow, built in the 1930s, on a street with stately old oaks and well-kept lawns. But she couldn't think seriously about a house until they made a decision about the inn.

Janice sighed. "But he has such beautiful blue eyes."

"Not a reason to trust someone." LuAnn winced inwardly at the truth of her statement. Bradley Grimes was a charmer. Men who recited poetry and appeared to read a woman's mind were not to be trusted. She'd learned that the hard way. "We need to get him on our side or find a way to work around him."

She took a sip of toasted pecan coffee and added another packet of sugar. She'd always done so well at healthy eating during the school year, then let herself splurge during the summer when she could bike it off. Would retirement become just one long binge? She'd have to sell her car and bike everywhere she went.

"How would we go around him?"

"Hmm." LuAnn read the scripture verse on the wall above them. Jeremiah 29:11—*"For I know the plans I have for you," declares the* L*ORD*, *"plans to prosper you and not to harm you, plans to give you hope and a future.* Then she offered up a quick prayer for wisdom. "What if we were to go to the Historical Society before Mr. Grimes has a chance to meet with the bank? If we tell them our intentions, we might get them on our side and they might have an influence on the bank."

"What *are* our intentions?" Janice, with her usual beautiful simplicity, posed the question they should have asked before they began scheming about ways to get around Bradley Grimes. And, as usual, LuAnn felt gently chastened. Where would she be without these gracious women in her life to tame her quicksilver reactions?

"Good question." LuAnn dug in her purse for her old-fashioned three-ring planner. She was a paper-and-pencil girl, and no amount of available technology was going to change that. "Let's make a list of possibilities." Another one of her favorite words. "Whatever we decide, are we in agreement that it needs to be a place of ministry?"

"Absolutely." A stray curl danced across Janice's forehead. "I can't imagine the three of us finding joy in anything else."

Tess nodded. "Agreed. It's who we are. And with that in mind, I vote for B&B." She took out her phone and tapped her list app. "Sorry, ladies, but I have the whole thing laid out and decorated in my head. It will take another latte and a serious amount of very dark chocolate to get me on another track."

LuAnn wrote "B&B" on the first line under "Wayfarers Inn Possibilities."

"Bradley mentioned a boutique mall."

"What about a coffee shop?" LuAnn wrote the words as the thought came to her. "Except we're only a block away from Jeremiah's."

Tess leaned forward, whatever she was about to say already dancing in her eyes. "I've always wanted to open a place that offered only one kind of food. Like that potato bar we used to go to."

LuAnn felt a spurt of adrenaline accelerate her pulse. "I always thought it would be fun to just make soup."

The light in Janice's eyes matched the look on Tess's face, and they both nodded. "I love, love, love making soup. We could offer coffees too, and desserts, of course. But we'd be known for our specialty soups."

"But what about the rooms upstairs?" Tess raised one eyebrow. "You know I'm not backing down from this. Can we do both?"

LuAnn gave a slow nod. "I don't see why not." She flipped a page. "You two figure out the color schemes for the rooms, and I'll start the menu." She put pencil to paper and began to write. *Cheesy Broccoli, Tortilla, Split Pea, Navy Bean, Chili, Minestrone, Cauliflower, Baked Pota—*

"Do we really want to do this? Even if it means a fight?" This time the logical question came from Tess. "I really, really want to do this, but are we prepared for a battle? It might not just be a fight to be able to *buy* it. The Historical Society could put restrictions on what we can change, or the neighbors might not like the increase in parking, or who knows what we'll run into. And what about cost? What if it's nothing but a massive money pit? These are supposed to be our adventure years. Do we really want to take the chance of getting in over our heads?"

Janice looked at LuAnn, who looked at Tess, who looked back at Janice. LuAnn cleared her throat. "How boring would life be if we didn't regularly get ourselves into jams only God could get us out of? Right?" She flattened her right hand in the center of the table and two hands landed on top of it with a duet echo of "Right!"

"Then let's head over to the Historical Society and stay one step ahead of Grimes Realty."

"Yes!" Janice pulled her hand away. "But, guys?" Her gaze darted from Tess to LuAnn. "There's no such thing as ghosts, right?"

"Ghosts don't wear scarves." LuAnn stuck her hand in her pants pocket and pulled out the earring. "Or jewelry."

May 28, 1856

"We cannot continue, Prudence." Jason lifted the basket of greens onto the table. Collard, mustard, turnip.

"We have pie plant, more than ever before, and the radishes are as large as apples this year."

Jason's stern countenance melted, and he smiled a smile that weakened her knees. "My sweet girl, how I despise arguing with thee, but man cannot live on pie plant and radishes alone."

"Of course not. We have the Word of God to nourish us."

He groaned. "Does thee not hear my belly rumble? We have barely enough put by for ourselves until harvest. How can we continue to feed so many more mouths? And I fear for thy safety, my sweet."

Jason had never known true hunger. For that she was grateful, but because of the comfortable life he'd lived, he did not share the pain of those fleeing to freedom as she did. "Might I suggest a compromise?"

"Might I stop thee from suggesting?" Lamplight danced in his eyes.

"It would be in thy best interest to hear me out, Mr. Willard."

Jason rested his elbows on the table and his chin in his hand. "I am listening."

"Thee has a legitimate concern." She had watched the Quaker woman who adopted her use this approach often—bring out all of his good qualities, and there were many, and then she would play on his sympathies. "Thee is the head of our household, and thee knows I will respect your wishes, but thee is also a man with so much God-given compassion for others. If only I had met someone with thy kindness and generosity on my way north. As I shivered alone with only the dark of night to hide me, nibbling on blades of grass to stave off hunger and—"

Laughter thundered against the cabin walls. "All right! Tell me about this compromise."

She shifted closer to him on the bench and rested her head on his shoulder. "What if I were to find another place to offer food and shelter?" She had a place in mind. Rumor had it the pro-slavery activist who owned the Riverfront House was growing restless and looking to head west. To God be the glory. She had never been one to label a man evil, but she could not avoid it with this one. How beautifully ironic if the hotel he built came to represent a haven of safety for the men and women he actively sought to ensnare.

"Thee is saying we will no longer be involved?"

"No." She lowered her voice, knowing her words would burst the hope in his. "I would continue to pick them up and ferry them back across the river, but instead of bringing them here, I would deliver them somewhere else."

The shoulder she rested on dropped. She stared at the flickering flame in front of them for several long moments before he spoke. "This calling of thine…I cannot fight it, can I? If thee can find another place to shelter them, I will hold my tongue."

"And thee will eat."

He kissed the top of her head and tugged at her braid. "And *we* will eat."

Chapter Three

The two-and-a-half-mile ride to the Washington County Historical Society took them past a manicured riverside park and clapboard houses built in the nineteenth century. LuAnn sat in the passenger seat, once again in time-machine mode as she imagined the area in the 1800s. Women wearing ankle-length dresses—plaids and deep blues and greens—with bell sleeves, high-necked collars, and fitted bodices.

Before the Civil War, the riverfront economy may have been booming. But while new businesses were being built to accommodate the people living in the new houses that lined Front Street, an unseen drama was being played out in secret stairways leading to hidden rooms.

What would it have been like to be a freed slave, safe in Canada, knowing God was calling you to return, to cross the Ohio River once again, to reach family members and friends and guide them to safety? What kind of courage did it take for abolitionists to risk reputations, businesses, and even life itself, to be a link in a chain of caring people who believed in freedom and equality for everyone?

What would her role have been had she been born more than a century earlier? She could imagine herself doing exactly what they had discussed today—offering shelter, listening, serving. And making soup.

Just before turning in to the redbrick complex that housed the Historical Society and the Health Department, they passed an exquisitely landscaped lawn surrounding a three-story stone mansion with a wraparound porch. A copper weather vane gleamed in the sunlight atop an old carriage house. Another building with a history she'd love to discover.

The woman who met them in the lobby and introduced herself as Margaret Ashworth appeared to be the same vintage as some of the artifacts on display. She shook their hands and led them to her office. "You're interested in the old inn. I can't tell you how thrilled I am. Some of us have been lobbying for the city to take it over, but the funds just aren't available."

LuAnn flashed the most brilliant smile she could muster. They'd decided this would be a relationship-building mission with the goal of getting into Mrs. Ashworth's good graces. "We're all history buffs, and we're just eager to hear anything you can tell us about the building."

"Oh my. What a checkered history that building has." Mrs. Ashworth rubbed knobby-fingered hands together. "Intrigue, mystery, debauchery, heroism, a lovers' triangle, murder…everything a true history buff thrives on."

LuAnn leaned forward. "Tell us about the lovers' triangle."

"I'll tell you the facts and then the legends, okay?" She sat back on her cushioned chair and folded thin arms across her chest. "Back in 1857, the Riverfront House changed hands. Howard Bickerton, a young, idealistic man from a wealthy

London family bought it, sight unseen. Bickerton's father was one of the founding members of the British and Foreign Anti-Slavery Society, and Howard apparently wanted to leave his mark in the movement. After the passage of antislavery laws in England, he began supporting the fight in the States. He hired a contractor to build a house in Marietta, and a business partner to come with him, and sailed to America." Mrs. Ashworth stopped and asked if they would like coffee. All three declined.

"I assume you've seen the little rooms in the basement?"

Tess nodded. "They're not hidden, though."

"Quite brilliant, isn't it? The work of Mr. Bickerton. Bounty hunters would search for secret passageways and hidden rooms, but Bickerton likely hid them right under everyone's noses. If the need arose, the fugitives could have donned uniforms and pretended to be hired freemen, not that that would always protect them, of course."

"So... the lovers' triangle?"

"That's where the facts—" A slightly stooped woman with thinning white curls, even older than Mrs. Ashworth, walked in without knocking.

"Excuse me, Margaret." She pushed up blue-framed glasses that looked far too large for her face and magnified her eyes. "This is quite pressing."

Margaret's face pinched. "Irene. I would appreciate it if you would knock before—"

The woman waved away Margaret's words with a slip of yellow paper. "It's about the inn. Did you know the bank—and my nephews—have listed it? There are a few people who are quite—"

"Irene, I'd like you to meet these lovely ladies. Irene, this is Tessa Wallace, LuAnn Sherrill, and Janice Eastman. Ladies, this is Irene Bickerton Martin."

"Nice to meet you all." She smiled. The quintessential sweet little old lady.

Nephews? Bickerton? Stuck on those two words, LuAnn struggled to stay present in the moment.

Margaret held her hand out for the slip of paper. "You have a message for me?"

"Sure do. They're calling a meeting for tomorrow night at Midtown Bank." Irene gripped the paper with her fingertips as Margaret tugged on it. "Seven o'clock. They're asking if you can put a message on the Face page and Twitter it."

If Margaret's face pinched any tighter she'd start losing circulation to her lips. "I will announce it."

Irene let go of the paper. "This could mean a fight. Some people feel mighty strongly about messing with our landmarks."

LuAnn couldn't help jumping in. "Surely people are in favor of buildings being restored to their original glory and repurposed so the community can once again enjoy them."

"Well, there are those. And then there are others who think the best way we respect our history is to leave the buildings alone. And speaking of leaving alone, I'll do just that for all of you right now. Toodles." Irene waved with arthritic fingertips and padded out of the room in ballet slippers.

Margaret cleared her throat. "I think it best if we not let anyone know your intentions at this moment."

"But we can attend the meeting, right?" Janice wiped her hands on her skirt. "It's open to the public?"

"Yes." Margaret dabbed her top lip with her fingertips. "My. Such drama. I wouldn't expect more than a handful of people to show. I suppose the inn is a landmark, but not one we've been able to showcase. There just aren't funds available to restore every old building, and I can't imagine that many people even care." She gave a tight smile. "So, back to the lovers' triangle. As I was going to say, that's where things get a little fuzzy.

"All we have to go on is what appears to be a love letter found in a cookbook at the inn. It was on display, but it disappeared years ago. I don't remember it all, but I clearly recall one line. 'My Darling, just say the word and I will leave my husband and stay with you.' It was signed, 'Yours forever, Charisse.'"

"Who was Charisse?"

Margaret's Cheshire Cat smile irked LuAnn. Her dramatic pause only irritated her more. "Charisse...was Howard Bickerton's wife." She waited, as if expecting a triad of apoplexy. "The message was written on letterhead from the steamboat *Elizabeth,* so clearly it was written after they left England. And a note in the inn's guest ledger states that Mr. Bickerton's business partner would not be coming, so his room would be available." She bent toward them. "Now"—her voice lowered to a hush—"did the partner, whom we assume was her lover, return to England, or did he stay in America and they continued their affair in secret? We may never know, but Howard and Charisse went on to have twin sons and live long lives. Whether happily ever after or not, we may also never know."

"Wow..." Over coleslaw and baby back ribs at Bar-B-Cutie, Tess summed up the day with a sigh. "All we were going to do today was house shop."

LuAnn yanked a paper towel from the holder and blotted barbeque sauce from the corners of her mouth. "As Steve Jobs said, 'Everyone here has the sense that right now is one of those moments when we are influencing the future.'"

"I wish Jeffrey were here. He had such good business sense." Tess pressed her thumb and forefinger against the bridge of her nose. "We made all of our big financial decisions together. I just don't trust my judgment when it comes to something this big." She shrugged. "But I trust God and you two, in that order."

Janice nodded. "Lawrence handled our finances. The church covered all the parsonage maintenance and most of our utilities. I handed him my checks and just trusted him to take care of the few bills we had. I wish now I'd taken a more active role. Not that he would have welcomed my input." She arched an eyebrow.

LuAnn understood. Lawrence Eastman's opinions of the role of a wife hadn't always sat well with Janice. "This is such a wild, crazy idea." Janice twisted sauce bottles in the wooden holder in the center of the table until all labels faced the same direction. "Crazy, but honestly I haven't been this excited about anything in years. We have no idea what we're getting ourselves into—financial ruin, shunning from the community, ghosts who wear lace scarves and gold earrings—who knows? But it just feels like something we have to do, doesn't it?"

It did. LuAnn's heart warmed at the joy on the faces of her two friends who'd known so much grief in the past few years. Tess had lost her husband four years ago. Janice's had died just over a year ago.

Tess set her fork down on the red checkered tablecloth. "Can we just stop right now and pray?" She didn't need to wait for an answer before bowing her head. "Lord God, You know we want to honor You above all else. We want to do Your will. You've given us freed-up time, and health, and a desire for a new adventure, and a sense of purpose in this season of our lives. Is buying the inn Your plan for us? Please make it clear and please help us to be grace-filled and kind to every person we meet, even to those who might come against us. In the beautiful name of Your Son, Jesus, we pray. Amen."

"Amen." LuAnn grinned. "'If God be for us, who can be against us?'"

"A lot of people, actually." Janice smiled and shrugged. "There might be a battle. But God will prevail."

Tess lifted her water glass. "Here's to putting on the full armor of God and marching into the fray."

LuAnn laughed. "Here we are gearing up to face Goliath and we'll probably walk into that meeting tomorrow night and there won't be a single per—"

"You're the ladies buying the inn." A young woman in a green shirt with pale skin and tattoos—flowers, vines, and barbed wire—circling her upper arms like bracelets, stood next to their table with her arms crossed over her chest.

LuAnn swallowed hard. "We looked at the inn. It's a lovely old building, don't you agree?"

"It's a building. And it was built in a place it never should have been built. Do you realize that every structure erected on the riverbank increases the possibility of flooding and adds to the already rampant pollution in our nation's waterways? Do you know how many species of mussels are listed as threatened or endangered because of what's being done to our river?" She held up a purple-nailed hand laden with silver rings. "Rabbitsfoot, purple cat's paw, snuffbox, pink mucket, northern rifleshell..." She sighed and closed her hand. "Please reconsider." She stared at each one of them in turn, then left to rejoin two women and a man in matching green shirts. The man, tall and lanky and long-haired, put his arm around her and kissed her on the cheek.

"'My. Such drama.'" Tess quoted Margaret with a perfectly pinched expression.

"What in the world are we getting ourselves into?" Janice nibbled on the corner of her bottom lip. "I feel my blood pressure rising."

LuAnn motioned to the boy who'd brought their orders. "Could we have three boxes, please?" When the young man walked away, she said, "We all need some rest."

Their server returned with three Styrofoam containers. And a worried look on his face. "I just heard you're buying that old hotel on Ohio Street. Is that true?"

Tess sputtered. "We *looked* at the building. That's all. Just looked. We're not the bad guys here."

"Yeah. Okay. I get it." He pulled on the gold stud in his earlobe. "But if you did buy it, how soon would you, like, start working on it?"

LuAnn put her hand on Tess's arm. *Don't say another word.* "We have no idea if we're even interested. Do *you* have an interest in the building?"

"Me?" The boy stepped from one foot to the other. "Why would I care? I'm not into history or anything." He set their check on the table, muttered, "Have a nice day," and walked away.

Tess let out a pent-up sigh. "Why would anyone in this town care about that old building? But it seems everyone does."

Chapter Four

LuAnn had stayed here often in the house Tess rented since she'd sold the home she and Jeffrey built, but the guest room bed had never looked so inviting before. LuAnn kicked off her slippers and sat on the overstuffed blue and white plaid chair next to the window. The room, with its butter-yellow walls, white trim, and blue accents, was an oasis. Especially tonight. She yawned, curled her feet beneath her, and picked up her to-do notebook. She leafed to the list she'd made before locking the door of her West Virginia condo for the final time.

Get PO box
Find Realtor
Sympathy cards
Check volunteer possibilities

She drew a red line through the top two items, stared at the next thing on the list, and, as tension built in the back of her neck, jumped to "volunteer possibilities." She needed something to fill her time, especially on those days when Tess and Janice were busy with kids and grandkids. She opened her laptop. And her phone rang. Who would be calling her at nine forty-five at night? A number in Marietta. Margaret? Or had the green girl or the shifty server somehow gotten her name?

"Hello?"

"Mrs. Sherrill?"

"It's Miss, but, yes."

A slight pause. "This is Brad Grimes. I'm just calling with some follow-up information. And an invitation."

Invitation? Should she be intrigued or worried? "Okay."

"My great-aunt told me she had the pleasure of meeting you today." Amusement danced on his words.

"Yes?"

"Irene."

"Ah, yes. Sweet little lady. You didn't mention you have family connections to the inn." It came out like an accusation, and in a way, it was.

"Well, way, way back."

"Sounds like you have some indiscretion in your family tree, Mr. Grimes."

He laughed. "I've heard the stories. Not sure they're true. My aunts have a picture of my great-great-grandparents. They look as happy as anyone in those old photographs ever did."

As if you can tell anything by a picture. She'd had a number of happy-looking pictures taken with Phillip, the second man who'd stolen her heart and stomped on it. And people could be very happy one moment and devastated by unfaithfulness the next. She edited the thought. "Maybe they were."

"I sense some hesitation in your voice, LuAnn. May I call you LuAnn?"

"Yes, certainly."

"I'm no stranger to loss, and I'm guessing you've had some hurts yourself." His voice, low and gentle, made her head feel foggy.

"Haven't we all?" She wasn't going to allow this conversation to turn personal. Her "hurts" were none of his business.

"My wife died three years ago. Cancer. I'm just beginning to feel like, I don't know, like maybe my life didn't really end when I lost her."

Oh. There was false charm, and then there was this. Transparency. Did men know how disarming that could be? "I'm so sorry for your loss, Mr. Grimes."

"Thank you. And please call me Brad."

"I appreciate your honesty, Brad. It's so easy to get stalled in the past."

"I take it you've experienced that firsthand."

The man was fishing. Why? To connect with her as a person, just simple human empathy? Or was this another sales tactic? She'd had a neighbor who was a car salesman and he'd shown her the training material about "bonding" with potential clients. "I imagine everyone has experienced that a time or two if you've lived long enough. You said you had some information."

"I do. Aunt Irene said you were there when she gave Margaret the notice about the meeting."

"Yes, we were."

"Well, apparently this thing's gone viral. Not only are there people from town who are up in arms, but word has reached the state historical society and they will be sending representatives. And I heard a rumor there will be TV cameras."

"Seriously? For one measly building that's been sitting empty for a decade?"

"You know that old line from a song, 'You don't know what you got till it's gone'? Kind of the same principle at work here, I think. It sat there in disrepair all these years and no one cared, but mention the word *change* and you stir up a hornet's nest."

LuAnn wrote the meeting time on the calendar in the front of her daily planner. "I'm not fond of change myself. I can understand that reaction. What do you think will happen?"

"I have no idea, which is the main reason I called. If you ladies are sure you're interested, I think we should see if we can expedite this sale. I know that makes me sound like a pushy salesperson, but it would be in your best interest too."

He did sound like a pushy salesperson. But he also made sense. "By 'expedite,' I assume you mean an offer in writing before the meeting."

"That's what I mean. The bank may be less likely to cave to community pressure if they have a reasonable offer on the table. The other option is that you three plan on getting up at the meeting and quelling fears by explaining your vision for the inn. Assuming you have a vision, of course."

Oh, did they have visions. LuAnn glanced down at her notebook. List after list—colors, recipes, things to change, things to buy, and diagrams of room arrangements. Over dinner they'd done price checks on commercial appliances and woodwork and floor refinishing. They'd checked Angie's List for the best local builders, electricians, and HVAC contractors. "We need to see the fourth floor before we make any decisions."

"Absolutely. I'll talk to the bank and see what needs to be done to make that happen. Are you free in the morning?"

"We will be. Janice's brother-in-law, Marv Williams, is a retired architect. We'll find out if he's available and see if we can find a building inspector on short notice."

"Good. So that's the information part. About the invitation..."

"Yes?"

"Aunt Irene and her sister, my aunt Thelma, request the honor of the presence of all three of you and their amazing nephew, as opposed to the one who is less amazing and currently on vacation in New York, for supper at their house tomorrow night before the meeting."

"That sounds wonderful. I'll talk to the girls, but I think that will work."

"Great. Five o'clock at the stone house just south of the Historical Society."

"The mansion? With the copper weather vane?"

Brad laughed. "That's the one."

The phone rang at 6:16 in the morning. So much for sleeping in, the main perk of retirement. LuAnn grabbed it and glared at the screen. Janice. The woman wasn't an early riser. "What's up?"

"I called Marv last night after you called. God's hand is all over this, Lu. Marv is having coffee with a couple of friends from his church later this morning. One of them is a building inspector. How not coincidental is that?"

LuAnn grinned. "Can't get any more not coincidental. Can they meet us?"

"Yep."

"Are you coming for breakfast?" LuAnn threw off the covers and swung her feet to the floor.

"Be there in about ten. All showered, dressed, and made-up. Is Tess up?"

The smell of hazelnut coffee pierced LuAnn's grogginess. "She's up. Bring your camera."

"Will do."

LuAnn staggered into the bathroom and, by the time she entered the kitchen, dressed for the day, her mind was buzzing with additional items to put in her notebook. "What about zoning? It's zoned commercial. Does that cover a B&B?" She didn't bother with morning greetings. "And we have to form a legal partnership, probably a corporation. I'll look up some attorneys, unless you..."

Tess sat in her favorite chair, Bible on her lap, phone in her hand. Her face matched the dove gray walls behind her.

"Are you okay? Tess, you don't look good."

"I just got the strangest phone call."

"Really? Who was it?"

"I don't know. A man. A deep voice. All he said was, 'Sometimes the past is best left in the past.'"

The air of excitement they'd had when they entered the inn less than twenty-four hours earlier was gone. And so was the lace scarf.

"Thanks for taking that down." LuAnn smiled at Brad. "It was kind of creep—"

"I didn't take it down." Brad turned in a slow circle, scanning every inch of the floor.

"I've always wondered what this place looked like on the inside." Marv motioned for Janice to take pictures of the ceiling. He turned to his friend Joe. "Ton of potential, huh?"

Joe nodded. "As long as the ghosts are okay with you being here."

Five faces turned to stare at him.

"Hey, I don't believe that stuff. But I've heard stories since I was a kid, and more just recently. People claim they've seen candlelight flickering up on the top floor." He gestured with a claw hammer. "One guy said he was sure he heard organ music. Funeral music, he said."

"Okay then…" Tess gestured toward the stairs. "Let's go—"

"Hey, folks"—Joe pointed toward the bar—"has that always been there?"

Janice gasped. Words, scrawled in neat, straight letters on the gold-framed mirror read, "LEAVE ME ALONE."

LuAnn stepped closer. "It's written in lipstick. And there's a handprint." She looked closer. "Not a whole hand and no fingerprints. It's too smudged."

Janice's brittle laugh echoed in the empty room. "Ghosts don't leave prints."

"Okay then." Tess turned her back to the mirror. "Let's have a look at the haunted space where we're all going to live." She aimed a ghoulish grin at Janice who answered with a faux glare, squared her shoulders, and led the way up the stairs. Footfalls echoed off pressed tin and cracked plaster as they walked along the second-floor balcony to the stairs leading to the third floor and then the fourth.

LuAnn glanced beyond every open door as they walked, creating scenarios in her head. A weary traveling salesman stopping at the inn, finding rest for body and soul in a plush bed, warm soup, and conversation pointing him to God. Newlyweds, renting the second-floor honeymoon suite, decorated in an English garden theme, welcoming sage advice from three older, wiser women. If she closed her eyes, she could hear laughter in the walls—voices of future guests mingling with echoes of past visitors. An almost imperceptible chill shimmied down her arms. She hadn't had time to process the words on the mirror and the disappearing scarf. Combined with Tess's bizarre phone call…

"Don't touch the railing." Again, Joe pointed with the hammer.

She let Tess and Marv pass her on the stairs and waited for Brad. "Did the bank send someone in here to inspect the fourth floor before we look at it?"

"Not that I know of. I think the biggest concern was the broken railing. They were fine with us going up there as long as Joe was along. Why?"

"Just trying to make sense of the message on the mirror and the disappearing scarf."

"I know. Me too."

Joe and Marv wrenched the piece of plywood blocking the top of the stairs, and they stepped into a wide-open space.

Brad gave a low whistle.

Almost half of the upstairs walls were gone. There were rectangles without floorboards where fireplaces had been and spots where walls had been torn down and the ceiling plaster of the third floor was visible.

Three doors opened on each side of the hall. Tess walked into the first. "I get this one!"

Janice entered the door across the hall, then peeked out. "We can each have two rooms, right?"

Marv scanned the space. "This could work." He looked in one of the end rooms. "One of you would have to have these two at the end. We could take out the doors and make this a passageway between bedroom and sitting room, or office or whatever you wanted it to be."

"I guess that would be me." A strange feeling swept over LuAnn as she stood in the corner room overlooking the river. She took in the crown molding, wide baseboards, and walls papered in faded green and purple flowers. She rested her hand on the dusty nine-pane window and looked down at the river. What would she have seen if she'd stood here back when the inn was new? Standing here next to a four-poster bed covered with a hand-stitched quilt, warmed by a fire in the fireplace, maybe sitting at a small desk, penning a letter to family back in England or a beau who'd gone west to search for gold.

"We'll have to add closets and bathrooms." Marv's voice brought her back to the twenty-first century. "The open space could pretty easily be convert—"

"*Eeeeww*!" The scream came from the room Janice had claimed.

They ran to the doorway and found her standing on a rickety stool. "A mouse. It went into the closet."

LuAnn laughed. A nervous but relieved sound. Only a mouse. She opened the beadboard closet door. "We'll need bigger closets, but these old ones might be cute for book… shelves." She swiveled, not wanting anyone to see what she'd just seen. "Don't you love the old windows? It's so cool how everything looks kind of ripply. Let's go look at Tess's room and see—"

"Hey, what's that?" Brad pointed toward LuAnn's feet. "The closet floor is tipped."

Tess crowded in next to him. "Look. A handle."

She was right. On the raised edge, a thin strip of leather was nailed to the wood.

Brad nodded at LuAnn. "I think you should do the honors, Miss Sherrill. Since you clearly saw it first."

Insufferable man. He knew they wanted to play down the historical significance, and here he was calling her out. LuAnn stared down at the board, wishing, once again, she'd been able to divert attention. If she uncovered any more secrets, the Smithsonian would descend and transport the whole building, piece by piece, to Washington. Pulse tripping, she knelt and pulled up on the strap.

The closet floor lifted.

Chapter Five

Brad dropped to his knees in front of LuAnn, and Marv laughed. "Want us to step out while you propose, Grimes?"

LuAnn scrambled out of Brad's way, feeling her face flush. All the times in her life when an embarrassing moment made her wish for a hole to open in the floor so she could crawl in, and it finally happened. If only she could slither through it and away from the laughter her supposed best friends were magnifying.

Brad rolled his eyes at Marv, then helped LuAnn lift the heavy board. A hook had been placed on the left side of the closet to hold the strap. They looked down. And down. Into a shaft about four feet square. A ladder, built onto the outside wall, appeared to lead all the way to the basement.

"Any reason we shouldn't go down?" LuAnn looked to Joe for the go-ahead.

"Yes!" Janice answered first. "It's steep and it's straight down and you have no idea how safe those boards are and you could break your neck. And there are mice."

"I'll go first." Joe crouched and scooted over the hole, feet dangling into the abyss.

"So glad you offered." Marv patted his ample middle. "You'd be calling 911 to unwedge me if I tried."

"That's my excuse too." Janice put her hands on hips that were not much wider than they had been forty years ago. No one expected Janice, with her claustrophobia, to venture into the tight space.

Joe eased forward until his feet touched the fourth rung. He took hold of the top rung and smiled over his shoulder. "Appreciate prayers. I know where I'll go if I die today, but I'd rather not miss my tee time this afternoon."

LuAnn leaned over the hole. "Yell if it's okay for us to follow."

"You really want to go down there?"

She had to admit, the disbelief in Joe's voice combined with the surprise on Brad's face was a bit of an ego trip. "Oh yeah." Determined to be ready for slinking through tunnels or whatever obstacles they encountered on the top floor, she'd worn jeans, a T-shirt, and hiking boots. She wasn't afraid of heights or confined spaces. Or mice. As long as there were no snakes, she'd be just fine.

"Okay. I'll yell."

The boards looked strong enough. They listened with collectively held breath as Joe stepped on each rung.

"Same kind of closet on the third floor," he called up. "The trap door is hooked up."

Ten more creaks and he yelled that he'd found another closet on the second floor. LuAnn bent as far over the opening as she dared.

"I'm in the basement, I think!" Joe's voice echoed up the shaft. "It's safe."

LuAnn sat on the edge, her feet swaying in midair, and did exactly what Joe had done. Grabbed the top rung, scooted forward, planted feet on the fourth board. Once her backside left the floorboards, she glanced down and experienced a moment of panic. One slip and she'd fall four stories to her death. And then she remembered Joe's "final" words and smiled. "Appreciate prayers. I know where I'll go if I die today, but I'd sure hate to miss supper at the mansion." She moved her hands down and took a step, and the fear left.

Forty-nine steps later her feet touched solid ground. "I made it!" she yelled, and turned to high-five Joe.

But Joe was gone.

Brad landed beside her before she had time to take in her surroundings. They were in a passageway, about four feet wide. She couldn't tell, in the darkness beyond the circle of struggling light at the base of the ladder, how long it was. The outside wall was exposed stone, the inside gray, unpainted wood. "What is this?" she whispered.

"I don't know." Brad tapped on his flashlight. "Where's Joe?"

"I don't know." She stepped away from the ladder. "Joe? Where are you?"

"Right here." He popped up behind them. "There's a door leading to the rest of the basement. I'm going to check out those rooms you talked about." He turned and walked away.

Brad held the light above their heads. The passageway extended yards ahead of them. Keeping one hand on each wall, LuAnn started walking.

She tried to think of a way to stop this exploration until after they'd gotten a thumbs-up from Joe and signed the offer to purchase. But Brad was onto her. Could she fake sudden-onset basement phobia? Or anaphylactic shock brought on by breathing 190-year-old dust? Or what if she screamed and said something bit her? She smiled in the dark. She could always pull the ghost card. She stopped suddenly. Brad smashed into her. A scent of spicy earthiness filled her senses. She didn't have to fake the sharp inhale. "Did you see that?"

"No. What?"

"Eyes. Four eyes. They were glowing. Green and glowing and"—she turned around, showing him her best look of abject fear—"as big around as my fist and—" She pressed her lips together to hold back the laughter triggered by his bulging eyes.

Brad took a step back. The moment the truth hit was priceless. "Seriously?" He grabbed her hand and pressed it to his chest. His heart pounded like it was hammering its way out.

"I'm s-sorry." She covered her mouth, but it did little to tone down the laughter.

After a moment of recovery, Brad grinned. "You got me."

Feeling smug, she turned around. "Yep. I did. But in all seriousness, we probably shouldn't be walking into a dark space without better lighting. Who knows what's down here."

"I'm not afraid. Are *you*?"

I'm only afraid of you pulling the rug out from under us if we find anything else. Reluctantly, she started walking again. Beneath her left hand, the thick stone was cold. The wood on the right was rough. Fearing splinters, she touched it lightly. Then suddenly, her fingers slid across something cold and smooth. Something metal. This time, she wasn't going to let on. Three more steps and she hit the end. "That's it. Better turn around."

Brad stepped out of her way. "Let's go. Wouldn't want to take a chance on discovering something even more historically momentous than you already have." His laughter rumbled in the enclosed passage. And his light glinted off a black metal door.

"It's structurally sound." Joe leaned against the old carved bar. "No cracks in the foundation, at least that I can see. You'll need a more detailed inspection before you start renovations, of course. I'm going to go up and check the roof, though I'm already sure you'll have to replace it. But I don't think you're going to run into any big surprises."

"Right," Brad whispered next to LuAnn's ear—close enough that both Tess and Janice raised eyebrows in unison.

Tess nodded. "Be honest, do you think we're crazy?"

Marv snickered. "That's a given. What they mean, Joe, is would they be making a wise business move to buy it?"

Joe rubbed the stubble on his chin. "You'll have to sink a lot into it, but with the river view and all the history in this place, I think it could pay for itself in the first two years." Over cheers and clapping, he said, "I'll itemize everything I find, but I think you could go ahead and make an offer with the contingency that no structural issues are found in my final inspec—"

A low, mournful howl filled the room and rattled the windows, growing louder by the second.

LuAnn latched on to Brad's arm, and Tess grabbed LuAnn's. Janice dug her fingers into her brother-in-law's shoulder.

"What is that?" LuAnn looked to Brad for an answer and got a shrug in return.

Janice covered her face with her hands. "I do *not* believe in ghosts. I do *not* believe in ghosts…"

"It's like someone blowing through a pipe."

Joe strode to the window. "Tornado siren?" he yelled over the din.

Brad shook his head. "It doesn't sound—" The noise stopped abruptly. "Whatever"—he swallowed audibly—"it was, it sounded like it was coming from somewhere in the building."

Joe turned from the window. His gaze shot toward the front door. "I don't mind risking my macho-ness to say this place flat-out gives me the heebie-jeebies. I'll be back later with an extension ladder. And the Ghostbusters." He shook hands with everyone and hurried out the door. Marv said his quick goodbyes and followed him.

"Well, ladies…" Brad rubbed the back of his neck. The corners of his mouth lifted in a weak smile. "I hope you aren't letting all this ghost nonsense get to you. I do *not* believe this building is haunted."

"I don't either." Janice scratched the red blotches on her neck. "But I think we shouldn't sign any papers until after the meeting tonight."

LuAnn stared up at the scarfless fan. "I agree. None of us believe this place is haunted." She looked again at the words on the mirror. "But somebody is trying hard to change our minds."

They got out of Janice's car at the mansion just as Brad drove up. Janice carried a bouquet of daisies, Tess had a bottle of sparkling grape juice, and LuAnn followed with a box of chocolate-covered strawberries from Putnam Chocolates. Brad laughed. "The aunts will want to adopt all of you. There goes my inheritance."

Inheritance? LuAnn stepped around a bronze sculpture of a wood nymph playing a flute. A riot of color surrounded the statue. Yellow sundrops lifting their faces to the sky, lavender petunias, and coral impatiens. The sloping lawn was dotted with fountains and stone benches, all engulfed in a kaleidoscope of flowers. The house rose like a majestic mountain above them, stone walls, turrets, leaded glass windows. "Will this all be yours and your brother's someday?"

"Not a bit of it. Irene's son, Prince Leo, gets it all." A hint of bitterness tinged his voice. "He should, of course, since he's the closest heir, but—"

"He hasn't done anything to deserve it, I gather."

"Very perceptive. Don't get me started, I'll just sound like a whiny, jealous shirttail relative. I don't even want the house—it scared the willies out of me when I was a kid. Too big and dark."

"I'm also guessing you do a lot for your aunts."

"I do. Leo lives here, technically, but he spends most of his time in exotic destinations."

"Working?"

"Ha. The word has never touched his lips. Anyway, on to something uplifting." He touched her elbow, slowing her steps. "I need you to know something."

"Yes?"

"I need you to know I'm rooting for you. I want you to get the inn. And after you do, I want to help you explore every inch of it—secret doors and all." His gaze searched hers. "I hope the three of you know you can trust me."

Trusting a man wasn't something that came easy to her. But this was a business kind of trust. She nodded.

Smile waves lapped at the corners of his eyes. "Let's go meet the eccentrics."

They joined Tess and Janice on the back step, and Brad opened the door. "Talk loud and compliment everything and they will love you. And, I might add, having them love you is definitely in your best interest tonight. They're old and quirky, but money talks." He winked as he pushed the door open and yelled, "I brought my girlfriends to meet you, Aunt Thelma!"

"August 2, 1923. I was born the day President Warren G. Harding died." Thelma Bickerton patted tight silver curls. "Not bad for almost ninety-five, eh?"

"You carry it well, Thelma." LuAnn smiled. "My mother passed away last month. She was ninety-one but always seemed much younger, just like you." Until the last year when congestive heart failure slowed her body and Alzheimer's stole her joy. Thelma's rouge-dusted cheek reminded her so much of her mother it hurt. "I hope I look and act as young as you and Irene when I'm your age."

"I'm sorry to hear about your mother. That loss is hard at any age." Thelma patted LuAnn's arm. "Irene and I have our struggles. For me it's Arthur Itis. Makes it easier to deal with when I can call him by name and tell him to get lost. And Irene's got her blood sugar. Always nibbling on chicken legs or cheese sticks to keep that under control and still doesn't gain an ounce. I've always hated her for that." She smiled in a way that hinted at years of entertaining sibling rivalry.

They stood, LuAnn trying hard not to gawk, in the library of the Bickerton house. Burgundy wallpaper festooned with a turquoise and gold paisley print peeked out above floor-to-ceiling bookcases that covered two walls. Thick, leather-bound books and framed black-and-white photographs crammed the shelves. The fireplace mantle and three end tables with curved legs were crowded with small statues, more framed photos, and vintage musical instruments. What looked to be a Civil

War–era bugle, a miniature accordion, and a set of three brass bells sat on a round, marble-topped table. "Your collection is astounding."

"Family keepsakes." Thelma picked up a daguerreotype picture and handed it to LuAnn. "My mother on her wedding day. She was only sixteen."

"What a beautiful dress." Sleeves, puffed at the shoulders but form-fitting below the elbow, a cinched waist, and bodice encrusted with lace and pearls.

"Irene wore it when she got married too." A hint of sadness drifted around her words. "I never married."

LuAnn put a hand on Thelma's arm. "Neither did I."

Surprise lit the pale, watery eyes. "Why? You're so pretty."

"Thank you." She wasn't sure how to answer the question Thelma had posed.

"Were you ever in love? Everyone should be in love at least once in their life."

Was that really true? Even if the love left wounds that might never completely heal? "I was. Twice." She'd known the worst, Phillip, and the best, Jesse, and vowed decades ago she would never allow that kind of pain again. "You?"

Thelma nodded. "A very long time ago." She picked up another picture, one of the few in color. A younger Thelma with a little boy. "Leo. Irene's son. Her only child." Evidently the subject of past loves was closed for now.

"Brad said Leo lives here."

Thelma looked aside and set the picture down. "Leo is a traveler. Doesn't like putting down roots unless he runs out—"

She waved her hand, as if brushing away the rest of her thought.

"How old is Leo?" The question bypassed LuAnn's filter.

"He was what they call a 'late in life' baby. Irene was forty-one when he was born. Which I guess makes him forty-seven." She picked up another picture. "Irene's husband. Dashing young man, wasn't he? Fred and I were born a day apart. We went all through school together." The wistfulness in her voice hinted at something deep and locked away. LuAnn knew that tone.

A stray thought slunk into her mind. Her father was born in 1923. In Marietta. Was it possible Thelma knew the man who'd disappeared from her life when she was six? "Were you—"

"Did you grow up in this house, Thelma?" Janice came up behind them and stood over a cherry piano, her fingers probably itching to touch the time-yellowed ivory. There were few instruments Janice couldn't play.

"Yes. It was built to my great-grandfather Howard Bickerton's specifications before he came over from England." Leaning on her cane, Thelma shuffled across the room, and LuAnn and Tess followed. "My great-grandfather started the foundation that helped build the first hospital in Marietta." She showed them a picture of a full-bearded man wearing a narrow tie and a wide, stiff-looking shirt collar. "He was—"

"Dinner is ready, Thelma." A tall and willowy dark-skinned woman, probably in her fifties, walked in, wiping her hands on a towel.

"Winnie, these are our Bradley's young ladies, Janet, Bess, and Louise." She looked at the women whose names she'd just massacred and smiled. "Ladies, Winnie is the best cook north or south of the Mason-Dixon. She'll be joining us for dinner."

"I don't need to intrude, Thelma."

"Winnie, you're not intruding, you're eating. Irene set seven places."

At the mention of her name, Irene bustled in, a jar of jam held in the jaws of what looked like a long-barrel rifle with a crab claw fastened to its end. "Sorry to be late. I was down in the cellar looking for this and I got distracted." She squinted. "Can't remember what distracted me, but what does it matter? I'm here, and I have jam." She pointed her contraption at Brad. "Strawberry rhubarb."

Brad took the jam. "Ladies, meet the Gripper Grabber. My aunt doesn't go anywhere without it."

"When you've shrunk to four-foot-nine you need a little help, you know?" Irene's elfin smile made them all laugh. "Let's eat. I'm *raaavenous.* Doctor says I'm supposed to eat every two hours, and it's been three. Wait till you taste Winnie's biscuits. To. Die. For. As the kids would say." The mite of a woman didn't look capable of eating an entire biscuit.

They sat, Thelma at one end, Irene at the other. Brad was placed on one side between LuAnn and Winnie and Janice and Tess across from them. Irene lifted her hands, palms out. "Bradley, will you bless the food?"

"Of course." He held out his right hand to LuAnn and his left to Winnie. "Father, our gratitude is such a small thing compared to all You have done for us. Thank You for provision and protection, and bless the hands that prepared this food. In the name of Jesus Christ our Lord. Amen."

"Amen." Without thinking, LuAnn squeezed his hand and he returned the pressure before slowly releasing her fingers.

"There's creamed chicken with fresh-picked peas to put on top of the biscuits." Thelma pointed at Janice. "You're the closest to the biscuits, Janet, so dig in. Louise, you follow up with the chicken. There's peach cobbler for dessert, but even if I tell you to save room, you won't, so don't bother trying."

"I forgot the watermelon pickles." Winnie winked at Brad. "They're his favorite." As she stood, her lips pressed together in a wince.

"That knee giving you trouble again?" Thelma asked.

"Just once in a while. My daughter's fixin' me up with essential oils. Who knew all those concoctions my grandma used to mix up would someday be sellin' like hotcakes for beaucoup bucks." Winnie limped to the kitchen and came back with a canning jar. She sat down and handed it to Brad to open.

LuAnn slathered butter and jam on a biscuit and took a bite. And sighed. She chewed slowly before swallowing. "I would pay large amounts of money for your recipe."

Winnie laughed. "No need. Boil three good-sized potatoes, mash 'em fine, add a tablespoon of sugar and a half pint of boiling water. Let it cook and add a cup of yeast starter. Let it rise till it's fluffy, then add a quart of water and enough flour to get the right consistency for kneading. Knead for half an hour, cut your biscuits about half an inch thick, and set them to rise again before baking." Winnie grinned at Thelma. "Just remember it's a cup of yeast *starter*."

Thelma blew through pressed-thin lips. "The recipe just said a cup of yeast. How was I to know?"

Tears of laughter sprang to Irene's eyes. "There was a movie back in the fifties called *The Blob*. You woulda thought we were trying to remake it right here in our kitchen. That stuff oozed out of the bowl and spread over the counter and down the cupboard like a lava flow."

Thelma didn't seem to be finding the humor in the recollection. Holding up half a biscuit, LuAnn turned to Winnie. "I think this must be what heaven tastes like."

"Amen, sister." Tess stared at a forkful of biscuit smothered in creamed chicken.

Irene nodded. "I surely hope so. I'd hate to be up there wishin' I was down here eating Winnie's biscuits instead. You know, she's got family recipes going back before the Civil War."

Janice glanced at Tess, then LuAnn. "Do you work here full time, Winnie?"

"Heavens!" Thelma's chin jutted back. "We wouldn't fit through the back door if she did. She just blesses us on company nights."

"I was head cook over at Butter Beans until they closed. I do some cleaning for the ladies and run errands. They're paying me more than I deserve while I look for something else."

Again, knowing looks crisscrossed the table. Tess gave an almost imperceptible nod. "Do you have any leads?"

"Nothing yet."

LuAnn swallowed a bite of golden gravy. "Do you make soup?"

"You have to taste her peanut soup," Irene said. "Talk about a taste of Glory."

"We might be"—LuAnn looked around to make sure the three were on the same page—"looking to hire a cook in a couple of months."

"Winnie lives on the other side of Second Street, right across from the inn." Brad tipped his head and shrugged one shoulder.

"Oh really..." LuAnn smiled at her best buddies. *This is destiny, right, girls?*

Thelma, who'd appeared on the brink of a nap, opened her eyes. "For the inn? You're turning it into a restaurant?"

"We think we'd like to start a bed-and-breakfast with a soup café."

"What a wonderful idea." Irene took a sip of her sweet tea. "Tell us your plans. We want to hear every little detail."

"Before we do, we'd love to hear about your family's history with the inn."

Thelma took off her glasses and cleaned them on her napkin. "We know so little, I'm afraid. And after all these years, who knows what's fact and what's fiction. But I do know that Winnie's family was brought to freedom because of the Riverfront House."

"Really?" The three spoke at the same time.

Winnie took a pinch of salt from a cut-glass cellar and stirred it into the tureen of creamed chicken. "My great-great-grandma was pregnant with her only son when she escaped from a plantation in what is now West Virginia with the help of a Melungeon woman who lived on a farm on the Muskingum."

"Melungeon?" Tess shrugged. "I guess I didn't pay attention in history class."

"Mixed race. Most of them descended from white mothers, probably indentured Gypsies, and black slave fathers. Plus, often, some Native American thrown in." Winnie passed the jam. "The woman brought her across the Ohio on a moonless night, and my great-great-grandmother gave birth right there at the Riverfront House. She wasn't fit to travel, so they kept her on as a cook. Lots of my recipes come from her."

Goose bumps scampered from the small of LuAnn's back to the nape of her neck. "If we hired you, those recipes would be coming back home."

"They would, wouldn't they?" Winnie sat back, arms crossed, index finger tapping her chin. "But before I take that job, you gotta assure me of somethin'."

"What's that?"

"I gotta know that none of the stories passed down in my family are true."

"What stories?"

"That there was a murder in that place, and there's long-dead spirits still walkin' the halls and howlin' at night."

July 14, 1857

Bare feet tucked beneath her in her rocking chair on the porch, Prudence dipped her pen and scrawled the date. Squinting in the flickering lamp light, she began to write.

It is long past dark and Jason is soundly sleeping, but God has not let me get off my knees until this moment. This day that began with heartfelt praise to our preserving Lord, is ending with supplication. We were not told of the pending delivery, but several arrived by packet boat in broad daylight shortly after noon. What tattered parcels, in such need of mending. We will do what we can to make them whole over the next few days of rain but must send them on again once it stops. I should see this as blessing—the rivers will be higher and passage swifter. No need to portage.

She set the pen down on the upended crate she used for a table and closed her eyes. "Lord, what a day it has been. I've heard said Thee never gives us more than we can handle, but today I would have crumbled like stale bread if Thee had not held me up. I have dressed wounds before but never on a child. Lord, how I rail inside against the inhumanness in this world. I know I should not question, but how can I help but ask why? Why does Thee allow such atrocities to one so innocent?"

The children were the hardest. She would steel herself for the moment she would leave them at Stockport Mill. Rial Cheadle would be waiting to usher them on to Zanesville. They would be in good hands. Mr. Cheadle would entertain the little one with his silly rhymes, all the while keeping watch. In good hands, yes, yet her heart ached at the thought of another goodbye.

Needing to lift her thoughts before they consumed her, she pulled out the letter she'd found in the twisted oak. River mail, she called it. She didn't know who'd left it there for her. Mr. Putnam? Maybe. Any one of the Quakers who attended the monthly meetings could be her contact. It was better not to know. The letter was addressed to a Reverend Roland Maurice, probably not a real name. It was from a Howard Bickerton of Manchester, England.

Prudence ran her finger across the reddish stamp with a profile of a woman wearing a crown. The Queen of England, most likely. Strange to think she held a paper that had crossed an ocean. The letter read:

My Dear Reverend,

I have just received word that my house is finished, and we are preparing to sail. Might you be able to arrange a meeting for me? Barring any unforeseen or unfortunate events, my partner and I shall arrive on October 8th. I hope to be advised of how I may be of service in the current activity you spoke of. If at all possible, please contact me before my departure date of September 18th.

Yours sincerely,
Howard H. W. Bickerton

Prudence refolded the letter. The note accompanying it was tucked inside the envelope.

Are you free to examine the contents of our shipment on October 8 at RFH12?

Riverfront House at midnight on the eighth of October. The man's help would be ever so welcome.

As long as it wasn't a trap.

Chapter Six

"Oh my." The shock in Janice's voice spoke for all of them as they stood in the doorway of the basement meeting room at Midtown Bank. A black-shirted man shouldered a massive video camera. Four banquet tables, arranged in a square, took up the center of the room. Every seat around the table was filled, and two men wheeled in a cart of at least twenty folding chairs—not nearly enough. There had to be fifty people in the room.

"Do they bus them in?" Tess whispered.

"I know a few people." Janice waved at a tall woman with spiky gray hair. Another, wearing a pink visor and seated at one of the tables, smiled in recognition. A murmur that grew like the roar of an oncoming storm swept through the room as they walked in. Insufficiently discreet finger-pointing by those in the crowd singled the three of them out. LuAnn felt her antiperspirant failing. "So much for keeping this quiet."

"We are not the enemy, people," Tess said under her breath.

They headed for the back of the room, but two couples stood up from the table and offered their seats, with a smile and quick hugs for Janice. Friends. LuAnn hadn't considered the possibility of encountering more support than just Thelma and Irene, who sat across from them at the table.

"This is just an informational meeting." Paul Townsend, CEO of the bank, opened the meeting. "There will be time for questions, but please hold them until the end."

A hand shot up. Green Girl. She stood along the wall closest to the door amid a sea of green shirts. "Are you going to address the possibility of razing the building and allowing the plot to return to its natural flora and fauna? If not, we would like it put on the agenda."

Mr. Townsend's Adam's apple bounced. "Noted." He cleared his throat. "Wayfarers Inn has been on the National Register of Historic Places for thirty years. It came into the bank's possession several weeks ago and I think we all"—he glanced toward the wall of green—"most of us can agree it's a shame for it to go unused and in need of repair. To that end, we have placed it on the market." The murmur rose again, and he attempted to quell it with a push-down hand motion. "I assure you, the bank is not in this for the money. We want to see this building returned to being a landmark we can all—"

"Not if they turn it into a soup kitchen!" A portly man with a sagging comb-over stood, hands in pockets, looking like he thought he owned the world. "I run a thriving business near the river. My dealership caters to high-end clients, and I don't want a bunch of homeless people loitering around my—"

Mr. Townsend raised his hand. "I don't know where you got that idea, Bart. No one has suggested turning it into a soup kitchen."

"Well, there are other concerns. I'm on the city council and familiar with codes most of you have never heard of. Do you know there's a no-sound-after-nine-p.m. law still in effect for riverfront businesses? Can you guarantee that any business that goes in there will be able to ensure absolute silence after nine? And then there's the no-spitting law and the no loitering within fifty feet of—"

"Yes, ma'am?" Mr. Townsend pointed to a woman who looked like she would very much benefit from a soup kitchen.

The woman lowered her hand. "I heard they's going to put a new Butter Beans in there. I came to vote yes."

"That would ruin the historicity of the building! Do any of you want their neon signs in the windows of such a grand old building?" Comb-over Man stood again. "If Butter Beans buys it, I'm staging a formal protest. We can't handle that kind of traffic down by the river. I'm starting a petition right now to—"

"Please! People!" Mr. Townsend dabbed his forehead with a handkerchief. "We have accepted no offers to purchase at this point. It is our intention to make sure the inn is acquired by someone who will respect the history of the building and repurpose it into something that can be appreciated by the commun—"

"'Repurpose' is such a...nebulous word, isn't it?" A tiny woman, with a deeply lined face and hair dyed the color of the barbeque sauce at Bar-B-Cutie, rose to her feet. "For those of you who don't know me, I am Maybelline Rector, curator of the Marietta Underground Railroad Museum. I have had several"—she cast a fierce look at Mr. Townsend—"conversations with the bank over the past few weeks. We do not see eye to eye on the concept of repurposing, so I am bringing my appeal to the good citizens of our fair history-laden city. I am proposing that city, and possibly state, funds be allocated to purchase the building and restore it, as meticulously as possible, to its 1826 splendor. The MURM is only leasing our current facility." She glanced toward Thelma and Irene. "We are prepared to move our collections and make the Riverfront House our new home." She gave a slight bow as a handful of people clapped.

"That is surely one viable option, Mrs. Rector, providing adequate funding can be acquired in a timely..."

A dry cough from the corner of the room drew LuAnn's attention away from the tension between the MURM lady and Mr. Townsend. A scruffy, bearded man, maybe in his early fifties, dressed in ragged jeans and camouflage jacket and cap. Gray-streaked hair pulled back in a ponytail. The backpack slung over one shoulder had seen better days. She tried not to be obvious as she stared at his tired face, at eyes that seemed too old for his years. What was his story? She wished the café was open so she could invite him into the kitchen for a bowl of soup and a biscuit that tasted like heaven. Was he homeless? Just passing through? Why was he here? She glanced at the table on the far wall. Coffee. And cookies. Had he come for that? A tattoo on his neck said something in Gothic script—next to a dove. And a stylized cross. Did the cross mean anything? She squinted, trying to read the words, and her gaze landed on his ear. A pierced ear. Without an earring.

LuAnn looked away. She laced icy fingers and folded them on her lap. Could the earring she'd found belong to him? The realization dawned slowly, as she scanned the crowd...whoever was trying to spook them was probably in this room. The person who wanted to scare them away from buying the inn was right here.

As Mrs. Rector droned on, LuAnn studied ears.

"Why don't we just ask the elephants in the room?"

The deep voice broke into LuAnn's ear lobe study. Tess tensed like a tiger ready to spring. LuAnn leaned toward her. "Is that the guy who called?"

"It could be," she whispered.

"Rumors are ricocheting all over this town about three women who are going to buy the building and turn it into something." The middle-aged man, dressed in unthreatening tan shorts and a purple polo shirt, stood, and pointed directly at Janice. "What are your intentions, ladies? We need to hear—"

"Sit down, Ralph." The woman in the pink visor tugged at his sleeve. She rolled her eyes at Janice and mouthed, "I'm sorry," as her husband guffawed.

Janice visibly relaxed and gave a weak laugh. "I didn't recognize him," she whispered to LuAnn. "I taught with Jody for years. Ralph's a prankster."

"That might be a good idea, Mrs. Eastman," Mr. Townsend said. "Would you mind sharing your plans?"

They'd decided before the meeting not to draw attention to themselves, but here they were, the focus of fifty pairs of eyes. And a good number of pierced ears. With an audible inhale, Janice got to her feet. "My name is Janice Eastman. I taught at the high school for many years." She looked around the room. "Taught a couple of you how to set a table and boil an egg." Her shoulders lowered a fraction as a soft ripple of laughter spread over the room. "My husband was the pastor of Christ Fellowship for many years. He baptized and married a number of people in this room."

LuAnn slid her right hand behind her left and gave Janice a discreet thumbs-up. *Way to work the crowd, girlfriend.*

"My friend LuAnn Sherrill was born here and just moved back, and I'm sure many of you know Tessa Wallace. We are retired school teachers looking for a new adventure. We looked at the inn yesterday and are interested in restoring it to much of its former glory"—Janice glanced at Mrs. Rector and received a steely glare in return—"and turning it into a bed-and-breakfast."

The rumble of voices began again. Janice stood there, looking as if she had no idea if she should sit down or keep talking. Mr. Townsend nodded. "Thank you. I believe this will put the rumors to—"

"I've looked at the spec sheet. There's so much potential in that old building. I'm not at all surprised so many people showed up today." The woman, middle-aged but stunning in a form-fitting red dress, leaned against the wall, red-nailed hand on a perfectly trim hip. She spoke with a hint of a British accent. Cockney, maybe, reminding LuAnn of the summer she'd spent in London studying dialects of the UK. Lyrical words, musical phrases...*Just going down the apples and pears for a cup o' tay. Ay, Lu, what say you give us a butcher's at your new watch?* She blinked back to the meeting. What had she missed?

"...it as a night club, all lit up in the dark, just a place to make people happy, you know? Or maybe the whole thing all full of cute little shops. Maybe even a spa on one floor. Right, ladies?" Blonde hair tumbled over one shoulder as long-lashed eyes swept the room, landing at the front. "Will the building go to the highest bidder, Meestah 'Ownsend?"

Mr. Townsend blushed like a ten-year-old boy who'd just gotten his first kiss. "Charlotte. Th-that's a good question. This isn't an auction." His smile seemed to morph from curved mouth to lopsided, the way an actor might practice a smile in front of a mirror. "But I suppose there is the possibility of a bidding war."

"Thank you much." She smiled a smile that reminded LuAnn of Kate Winslet.

"Mr. Townsend?" A well-padded woman with graying hair pulled back in a tight bun waved from the back of the crowd like she was hailing a cab. When the CEO nodded, she continued. "I don't talk about it much, but y'all know I'm Marla Still and my great-great-great granddaddy was William Still. Y'all know only Harriet Tubman ushered more slaves out of the south than Granddaddy Still. I'm just wondering if somethin' could be put in the bill o' sale sayin' those of us who are direct descendants can have a look-see and a say-so over what's bein' done with the building. Like Maybelline said, we sure would like to see the inn returned to its former glory." She fanned herself with an envelope and swept the room with a smile.

Mr. Townsend cleared his throat again. But it was Irene who rose to her full fifty-seven inches and spoke next. "I've met these three women, had them in my home this very day, and I can vouch for their good intentions. I say we all stand down and let them do what they're planning to do. I'm quite sure they'll be open to suggestions along the way, but I don't see anyone else stepping up with cash to buy the inn and fix it up. Since our grandpa once owned the inn, Thelma and I have as much interest in seeing it done up right as anyone does. And we intend to donate to the cause of preserving the 'glory' of the building that was used by people like our great-grandfather to bring many to freedom. I say we vote yes."

"Thank you, Irene. This is just an informational meeting, but I'm sure many in this room appreciate your endorsement. So now that we have shot down some rumors and you all know the bank's intentions, are there any other questions?"

"Yes!" Green Girl raised her hand. "What about the mussels?"

"Well, that went well. I think." Tess took her keys out of her purse as they walked across the parking lot. "At least now we know who's fer us and who's agin us." She clicked the remote. "Sorry. With everybody talking about their granddaddies, I had to quote mine."

LuAnn reached for the door handle on the passenger side. "At least now we have a list of suspects."

"Suspects?" Janice lowered her head and stared at her.

"Whoever is trying to psych us out was probably in that room."

Tess nodded. "I was looking at hands. We should have made a tracing of the hand on the mirror."

"I was looking at ears." LuAnn pulled a pen out of her purse and reached in for her notebook. "I counted twenty-two people with pierced ears."

Janice's mouth formed an O. "But it could be pierced anything."

"True." LuAnn got in the car. Three doors slammed. Buckles snapped. "Green Girl had a post in her eyebrow. I think she was the only one." She opened her notebook and leaned it on the dashboard. "So, counting all suspicious people, pierced and not pierced, we have Green Girl and her boyfriend, Comb-Over Man…"

Janice held up two fingers. "What about the blonde in the red dress?" She ticked off another finger. "What's her story?"

"Good question." LuAnn wrote Red Dress on the list. "Did you see the guy in the camo jacket?"

Tess and Janice shook their heads.

"I couldn't fit him in any category. He didn't look like a businessman or an environmentalist." She wrote Camo Guy.

Janice held up her other hand. "Then there's Maybelline. Who would name their kid after mascara?"

"Weird, huh? Who else?" Tess rubbed her right eyebrow. "The aunts? Irene has pierced ears."

"Right." LuAnn laughed as a picture formed in her mind. "They may be wanting to start a dance club. Maybe another foam party place like The Foam Garage."

Janice giggled. “Can’t you see Irene cuttin’ a move in a pile of soapsuds? Did you get Marla Still?”

“Oh yeah.” LuAnn added Marla while still entertaining the image of little Irene covered in suds that matched her hair. “And Server Kid at the restaurant. And these are just people we’ve met.” She tapped the list, counting. “That’s ten. Wow.”

“Who do we start with?” Tess turned onto Wooster Street.

“Who’s easiest? Who can we get the most info on without stalking?”

Janice scrolled on her phone. “The Underground Railroad Museum opens at nine a.m. I say we descend on Maybelline en masse. She won’t know what hit her.”

“Janice Eastman.” Tess feigned shock. “Are you suggesting we physically attack the poor woman?”

“Of course not, silly. But let’s start with hitting her with questions.” She pointed over the seat at LuAnn’s notebook. “Let’s make a list of interrogation questions for each suspect.”

LuAnn turned a page. “Where were you on the morning of June fifth?”

Janice leaned forward, shoulder harness straining. “Do you now or have you ever owned a gigantic ghostly lace scarf?”

“What color lipstick do you wear?” Tess snapped her fingers. “We should have used a Kleenex to gather evidence from the mirror.”

LuAnn wrote the question. “Not too late.” Four eyes turned her way. “We just slip in through the tunnel.”

"*You* just slip in through the pitch black, mouse infested, slimy, slippery, smelly tunnel." Janice sat back, wrapping her arms around her waist.

"I'll do it. Just have to change clothes."

Tess swerved to avoid a garbage can. "You're serious?"

"Why not?"

"Um, well—" Janice raised her counting hand again. "One, because it's breaking and entering. Two, because we might get caught. Three, because you might get HPS."

"What's that?"

"Hantavirus Pulmonary Syndrome. You get it from mouse droppings. First you think you have the flu, then your lungs fill up." Janice gripped her throat with both hands. "And then you die."

"I'll wear a mask."

"And gloves. And boots."

"All of the above. Goggles too."

Tess nodded, and a half smile lifted her cheeks.

LuAnn narrowed her eyes. "What?"

"I think our Lu is back."

"What do you mean?"

Janice put a hand on her shoulder. "Even with your mom sick, you were always there for us, but it's been hard on you and we've missed our wild and crazy, adventure-planning Lu."

LuAnn nodded. "I've had to play life too safe the last couple of years. Time to bring the crazy back, right? In the words of Mark Twain, 'Sanity and happiness are an impossible combination.'"

Chapter Seven

"Stop! Picture!" Tess's phone wobbled in her hands as she attempted to control convulsions of laughter.

LuAnn stepped under Tess's porch light and curtseyed—as well as she could in Tess's late husband's coveralls and hunting boots. She wore waterproof gloves, a dust mask, goggles, and a red bandana over her hair. "I may suffocate, but I won't die of cryptosporidium."

"You'll thank me." Janice opened front and back car doors and told LuAnn to sit in front. "When you're eye-to-beady-yellow-eye with a rabid mouse, you'll thank me you don't have any exposed skin for his sharp little virus-infested teeth to chomp on."

"O…kay…" LuAnn said as Janice held out her arm to help her down the steps. "On that cheery note, let's go break and enter."

On the drive to the river, LuAnn clutched a flashlight in both hands. This was a bit extreme, even for her old adventure-planning self, but it was too late to turn back now. She had a responsibility to bring joy into the lives of these dear friends. She'd taken on the job of keeping them supplied with reasons to laugh and experiences to look forward to, as well as a listening ear, hugs, and liberal doses of prayer. In the "reason to laugh" category she'd scored a ten tonight. She wouldn't tell the others, but, just to make sure they'd still be laughing at the end of the night, she'd called Brad and gotten his official blessing. Armed with their Realtor's permission, they should be able to wriggle out of a night in jail.

Tess parked a block away. With her best buddies flanking her, LuAnn slogged down the block and then down the bank to the hidden door. She looked around. No one was out on this cloudy, chance-of-rain night. A chorus of spring peepers and crickets, punctuated by an occasional bullfrog belch, created the soundtrack for their break-in. "Stand guard," she whispered, parting the brush with the clumsy gloves. A jumble of dried grass and small sticks covered the wooden door. Intentional camouflage. Which probably meant whoever had been sneaking in was probably not in at the moment. She forced a calming breath and pulled on the rusty handle. Instead of groaning and grating, the door opened on what must be well-oiled hinges. Soundless.

Two stone steps led down, and then she could stand. She painted the walls and ceiling with light, looking for unstable bricks or clues. Or beady yellow eyes. What she saw, carved into a dozen or more stones, stopped her pulse for the space of a breath. Hash marks.

She counted. Seventy-four. Goose bumps covered the backs of her arms. Had seventy-four people passed through this tunnel on their way to freedom? Men, women, children. Even babies? What would she be thinking right now if someone handed her a sharpened stone and said, "Make your mark, LuAnn

Sherrill, you are now on Ohio soil. You are a free woman." The goose bumps danced up the back of her neck. There would still be fear. Until her feet crossed the border into Canada, there would still be danger.

The floor and walls were damp. Even through the mask, the musty odor was almost overpowering. Inching forward, she imagined being Winnie Washington's great-great-grandmother, stumbling in the darkness, heavy with child, exhausted. Maybe the contractions had already started. The fear for her baby's life would outshadow all other fear. Would she meet friend or foe at the end of the tunnel?

Her eyes were damp with tears of empathy when she reached the end. She lowered to her knees and shoved the square of wood. The stool scraped against the floor as she shoved it out of the way.

She shined the light into the room.

And screamed.

A hand reached out to her.

LuAnn flattened against the wall. Her heart smacked against her sternum, threatening to explode. The flashlight clanged to the ground.

"Need a hand?"

Her knees buckled. And Brad shimmied through the opening. Laughter echoed off the damp walls. Brad doubled over. "What were you expecting to find in here? Nuclear waste?"

"Toxic mouse droppings." Her hand pressed against her chest. "You c-can't do that to an old lady."

"'To me, fair friend, you never can be old, for as you were when first your eye I eyed, such seems your beauty still.'"

"Shakespeare."

"Sonnet 104."

"You can wax eloquent since you first eyed my eye only two days ago." She glared at the mirth glistening in his eyes in the eerie light and couldn't stay mad. "What are you doing here?"

"Are you kidding? I wouldn't have missed this for the world. You know, I would have unlocked the door for you."

"I know. But I wanted to experience this." She pointed to the opening. "I have evidence to collect."

"Let's go, Sherlock."

She didn't relish the idea of squirming through the opening with Brad behind her, witnessing the most ungraceful thing she'd done since falling off a camel in Madagascar. She imagined getting wedged, more like Winnie the Pooh than Winnie Washington's foremother, but she managed to get through. When she stood in the small room, she once again became the woman heavy with child. Where would she go from here? Was she so far into labor that she collapsed on a bed in this very room? Who attended her birth? What was she feeling? Fear, gratitude, or a mixture or both? A baby born into freedom…everything she had fought for, cuddled in her arms, nursing at—

"You okay?" Brad stood beside her, head cocked to one side.

"Oh. Yes. Sorry. I do that. You've seen *The Secret Life of Walter Mitty*?"

"The movie about the guy who was always living in a day-dream? Irene loves that one."

"Well, that's me. Lost in a daydream. I should have been a writer."

He smiled. "You're a fascinating woman, Miss Sherrill."

"L-let's go gather evidence."

"Let's." He followed her through the basement and up the stairs.

And she screamed again.

The scarf, airy and ethereal and terrifying, twirled on the ceiling fan.

"V-very funny."

"I didn't do it. It wasn't there ten minutes ago."

LuAnn leaned against the back of the yellow-cushioned chair at the small corner desk in Tess's guest room. Morning light filtered through lace curtains and landed in scallops on the spread. She opened her Bible and devotional journal. Today's verse to ponder: Psalm 90:12, "Teach us to number our days, that we may gain a heart of wisdom."

Wisdom. *Lord, we need a ton of it.* Should they follow through with making an offer on the inn? Should they really consider living there? Would it be a time drain? A risk to their friend-ship? And what about the hidden costs they were likely to encounter? They were already committing to spend more of their resources than would seem logical to anyone who hadn't calculated in the fact that their Father owned the cattle on a thousand hills.

She glanced down at the desk. Neat stacks of notebooks and envelopes, layered in order of importance—bills on top, sympathy cards on the bottom. The only thing disturbing the sense of order was the small plastic bag containing a folded tissue smeared with lipstick. LuAnn felt her neck warm. Tess and Janice had teased her mercilessly about Brad being there to meet her. Why, oh why, had she told them about the corny Shakespeare quote? In spite of what her best friends said, the man was not interested in anything more than making a sale.

Or was he?

She was not going to let her thoughts go there. Life was complicated enough at the moment. She picked up the stack of bills and sorted through them. Nothing urgent. That left her staring at the sympathy cards. She'd dealt with all but these last six. Did she have the strength to tackle them this morning? Especially the one from Eleanor, her mother's only close friend?

After fifty-five years of silence on the topic of her father's disappearance, it was her illness that finally eroded the seal on her mother's secrets. But the truth, if it really was the truth, had come in jumbled bits and pieces, mixed with what sounded like dialogue from a CSI episode. "*It could only bring trouble. I told him not to tell. You don't mess with the mob. It was only supposed to be for a couple of months. Was I wrong to keep the letters from you? I told him they'd come after us too. I couldn't bear to see you hurt, baby. It's not his fault. It's not his fault."*

LuAnn had told Tess that one of the reasons she was moving back to Marietta was to face her past, to take the clues she'd written in her notebook—every disjointed fragment her mother had uttered—and finally uncover the reason her father had left. But now that she was here, she wasn't so sure. She'd had a good life in spite of the missing puzzle piece. At sixty-three, did it even make sense to unearth the past?

Tess tapped on the half-open door.

"Come on in." LuAnn closed her journal.

A tray laden with steaming coffee, an apple fritter smothered in white glaze, and a vase of lilacs floated into the room in the hands of a woman with her hair in a towel and brown clay mask on her face.

"You know, when I think of ministering angels, I never quite picture them like this." LuAnn took the tray.

"D-nt m-k mi l-ff."

"Oh, but it's so tempting. Will your face crack along with the clay? Hey, did you hear about the man who lost his job at the orange juice factory?"

As Tess covered her face and ran, LuAnn yelled, "He couldn't concentrate!" Over the gurgle of running water, she added, "Thank you!"

She picked up the phone and looked up the MURM number. They'd decided on a more direct approach with Maybelline. She dialed.

"Good morning. Thank you for calling the Marietta Underground Railroad Museum. Our hours are noon to four today. How may I help you?"

"May I speak to Maybelline, please?"

"I'm sorry, ma'am, she won't be in until two today. May I take a message?"

"No thank you. I'll just stop by this afternoon."

So they had time to fill after their ten o'clock appointment at Grimes Realty. Only one option seemed viable. Shopping. She said the magical word to Tess when she reentered, face clean and glowing.

"Shoes? Bags? Jewelry?" Tess sat on the corner of the bed.

"Door handles. Sink knobs. Crown molding."

"Huh? Oh. *Oh.* Yes!"

"No reason we can't buy stuff now, right? We can always have a didn't-get-the-estate sale if this falls through."

"Yeah, I guess we could." Tess's gaze was aimed at the window, but LuAnn had a feeling her thoughts were far from the blue and yellow room.

"Talk."

Her friend's shoulders rose, then slowly lowered. "This was one of those mornings."

LuAnn picked up the fritter. "I figured so." Tess and Jeffrey had enjoyed a Saturday ritual of donuts and coffee at a place that opened at five a.m. When she was missing him, she'd often take a drive, sit at their favorite picnic table behind McHappy's, and remember.

"It probably makes me sound like a crazy lady, but sometimes I just need to think through things the way Jeffrey would. Imagining his calm answers to my fears helps me see straight. Anyway, this morning I just needed a little McHappy's time, but first I drove over to the inn. I was just going to park by the river and watch the sunrise and pray."

"And?"

"I saw something—a light, flickering like a candle—in one of the upstairs windows."

"You're sure it wasn't just a reflection of the sun coming up?"

"I'm sure." Tess reached out for a gingham pillow and hugged it to her chest. "The light was moving."

"The purchase price shall be paid in its entirety in cash at the time of closing the sale." Tess tapped her foot as she read under her breath.

Seller shall provide purchaser prior to the closing and promptly after the acceptance of this offer, at Seller's expense and at... LuAnn skimmed to the end. Having just gone through closing on her condo, she was familiar with the lingo. It all seemed straightforward. She looked up, caught Brad staring at her, and quickly shifted her gaze to the picture on the wall behind his surprisingly modest desk. If she'd thought about it before entering Grimes Realty, she would have imagined an expansive mahogany desk and walls covered with framed sales awards. Instead,

Brad sat behind what appeared to be an Ikea DIY desk—simple and white. On the taupe walls, black-and-white photographs on canvas. She pointed to the one behind him—a white clapboard church with tall, narrow windows. No trees. In the misty background, several weathered gravestones. Hauntingly beautiful. "Did you take that?" she whispered.

He nodded. "Berg Church. Have you seen it?"

She shook her head.

"I'll take you sometime."

Tess looked up, rolled her eyes, and turned back to the document in front of her. Janice merely smiled—like it was killing her not to laugh out loud. LuAnn focused every ounce of concentration she could summon on the boring legalese. *Seller's option an abstract of title to the property brought down to date or an owner's policy of title insurance in an amount equal to the purchase price, said abstract—*

A tentative knock on the door startled them all.

"What is it, Saffron?"

Saffron? What an incredible name. Brad had mentioned his receptionist would be in before noon. The woman on the other side of the door would surely be wearing a sari, gold and turquoise and flowing. Or maybe she was the matured hippie type in a gauzy Bohemian skirt.

"Aunt—I mean *your* aunt is on the phone, Mr. Graves. She says it's urgent."

The voice was oddly familiar. Strange, since ninety percent of the people she knew in this town occupied chairs in this room.

Brad sighed. "It's always urgent with them," he muttered. "Come on in. I'll take the call. Which one?"

"Irene."

"Well, that makes it more fun, whatever the crisis." His eyes shimmered as he reached for the phone. The door opened. Cautiously, LuAnn thought. "Introduce yourself," he told the woman still hidden by the door.

"Hi." She stepped into the room. Stunned surprise registered on three faces. "Saffron Navratilova. We've kind of met."

Yes we have. LuAnn stood and offered her hand to the girl she'd met twice before—at Bar-B-Cutie when she confronted them about endangered mussels, and again at the meeting. The transformation was stunning. Instead of the bright-green shirt and skinny jeans, the girl now wore a conservative white blouse and black pants. "LuAnn Sherrill." She introduced Tess and Janice, who shook Saffron's hand while maintaining the dumbfounded looks.

"You work here?" *Isn't that a conflict of interest? Do the Grimes Brothers know you're probably sabotaging the sale of every house within half a mile of the river?*

"Yes." A thin laugh accompanied a fingertip rubbing her eyebrow where the post had been removed. "I suppose it seems funny, considering my environmental stance, but Dad and Uncle Brad hired me anyway."

Dad? Uncle Brad? What were they getting themselves into? One of the suspects on their list was very likely the one who typed up their Offer to Purchase.

"Yes, my dear, I'll be there. Right away. Just breathe. Tell Thelma to take a heart pill. And tell Winnie I'm not upset. No, I don't think you can die of heat prostration in ten minutes. I'll be there in three. Bye." He hung up the phone, gave a shrug of resignation, and looked at Saffron. "Can I borrow your car?"

The girl without the stud shrugged. "I walked this morning."

"We can take you." Tess jumped in, almost cutting off Saffron's last word.

"Could you? I rode my bike today. Winnie drove the eccentrics over to play bingo, and the car broke down out on Wagner Road. Winnie thinks I'll get her fired, and the aunts are convinced they're going to expire before I get there."

"Why in the world did you take the Benz instead of the Porsche?" Brad stood with the sleeves of his white shirt rolled to the elbows and hands covered with grease. "You know the transmission fluid leaks."

Winnie was on the verge of tears, but Brad had his back to her as he volleyed questions at Irene. Winnie blew her nose. "I'm so sorry, Mr. Grimes. I didn't know."

"It's not your fault, Winnie. Not at all. My aunts know they shouldn't be using this car. If it were up to me, Hilltop Auto Wrecking would have smashed this thing into a coffee table years ago."

Irene daintily mopped her forehead. They'd transferred Thelma to Tess's air-conditioned car where Janice was, at the moment, trying to convince her she didn't have heat stroke. "We sold the Porsche."

"*What*?" A vein bulged on the side of his neck. "Why would you do that? And why didn't you say something? Did Leo help you?"

An indelicate sputter came from the mite of a woman. "We don't need help. Bart took care of everything."

The sound that came from Brad could have been emitted by a panther preparing to pounce on his prey. LuAnn stepped closer and put her arm around Irene's shoulder. "Why don't you and Winnie come sit in our car where it's nice and cool?" As she tucked Irene in the back seat next to Winnie and Thelma, she wasn't sure if she'd done it to help them or Brad.

"Thank you." Brad tossed an empty bottle of transmission fluid on the ground and opened another one. "This is a thirty-two-year-old car. Leo abused it for years, then very generously traded it back to his mother a couple of years ago in exchange for her five-year-old Cadillac. Told her this one got better gas mileage. Like she needs that for going to the beauty parlor and church."

"They owned a Porsche too?"

He nodded. "I helped Irene pick it out in 2010, and it's only got 18,000 miles on it. It's in mint condition and without a doubt Bart Sandman swindled them out of a gob of money. The guy may have been a hero back in the day, but everybody but my aunts know he's a shyster when it comes to selling cars."

"Why did they sell the good car and keep this one?"

Brad laughed and wiped his hands on a rag. "I've long since given up trying to figure them—"

The back window rolled down and Irene's wrinkled face peered out. "Tess is going to take us home. You two follow as soon as you get it going. Winnie and I will whip us up a nice meat pie."

Before they could answer, the car sped off as if the eccentrics really were in need of a trip to the ER.

Chapter Eight

"Saffron? A suspect? No. What makes you think that?" Brad looked across the front seat with genuine perplexity.

"Didn't you hear her at the meeting? And she said pretty much the same thing to us the day we looked at the inn."

"She's harmless. Kind of messed up, but harmless. Her mom took her and left my brother when Saffron was ten. Mom remarried a guy who's never home, so replacement dad is absentee dad. Not good for a girl's self-esteem. Saffron needs this job too much to do anything stupid. Besides, this save-the-earth stuff is all new. Probably all fake too. Did you see the guy with his arm around her at the meeting?"

"Yes."

"She's way more interested in *his* muscles than the endangered kind."

"But he's the serious kind?"

"Militant."

Hmm. "What's his name?"

"Vinnie, or something like that."

LuAnn slid her hand into her purse and pulled out her notebook. Vinnie or Something was now officially on The List.

Brad eased to a stop sign. "How are you liking Marietta so far?"

"I like it. I was born here. Lived here until I was six. This place has a lot of memories." They passed a two-story house with a purple bicycle in the front yard. What would her life have been like if she'd been able to grow up here? If the man who was supposed to help her grow into a confident woman hadn't deserted his wife and child?

"Not all good?"

Was he fishing again? "Not all." She took a quick breath and lunged into a question. "Have you always been in real estate?"

"Since right after college. Before that I was a tour guide for Marietta Trolley Tours."

"No wonder you've got the history spiel down pat."

"Want to hear the rest? Let's see how much I can remember." He took a deep breath. "Marietta, originally known as Adelphia, meaning 'brotherhood,' was the first permanent settlement in what would become the Northwest Territory. Investors of the Ohio Company of Associates renamed the community after Marie Antoinette, in honor of France's contributions to the American Revolution victory.

"The town was laid out much as communities were organized in New England. Settlers received both a lot in town and a lot outside of town for agricultural purposes. There were four common areas throughout the community, and the wide streets were planted with mulberry trees."

He pointed toward a sign for Mound Cemetery. "The people of Marietta left some of the local Indian mounds intact, including one that stood in the center of what is now Mound Cemetery. Something-something-blah-blah-blah, and the early settlers also built a fortification known as Campus Martius to protect themselves from American Indian attacks.

"Because of its location along the Ohio River, Marietta grew quickly. It became a major trading center and was also known for its shipbuilding industry. Ships, barges, and flatboats moved from Marietta down the Ohio River to the Mississippi River and then to New Orleans and to ports in the East. Something-something-blah-blah-blah."

LuAnn clapped. "I taught from the same American History textbook for so many years the spine broke, but I never had anything memorized quite like that."

"What can I say? It's a gift."

"Do you know anything about more current history? Was there any organized crime here back in the sixties?"

His head drew back. The question had clearly caught him off guard. "Not in Marietta, that I know of, but the Cleveland mob was active back then. Still is. Why?"

"I'm a history buff, remember? Inquiring minds want to know."

"John Scalish took over as mob boss in the forties and stayed in control until he died in the seventies. The family had ties to the Chicago Outfit and even had their fingers in shady dealings in Las Vegas. They were part of taking over the Desert Inn from Bugsy Siegel. Here in Ohio, it was pretty much gambling, loan sharking, and a lot of union corruption. His guys were heavies in the Teamsters Union."

LuAnn wrapped her arms across her chest. She had so few clear memories of her father, but she remembered the union.

"Got a union meeting tonight, sugarplum." He'd kiss her on the top of her head and tell her to sleep tight.

"Any specific questions I can try to answer?"

Yes. How could such a tenderhearted man be part of the mob? "No. Thanks."

Brad turned into the Bickerton House driveway and once again, LuAnn drank in the riot of color. Daisies, purple phlox, daylilies.

She walked next to him on the stone path. They passed the statue of the piper and one of an angel, wings spread, holding a candle. "Oh! That reminds me. Tess went down by the river to watch the sunrise this morning, and she saw a light in the top floor of the inn."

Brad stopped and turned. "Sure it wasn't just a reflection?"

"That's what I said. She's positive it was inside. She said it flickered like candlelight. And moved."

"Moved?"

"Like someone walking around. Do you think the bank could set up security cameras?"

"I doubt they'd put out the money. But something to consider when you take ownership."

"Which we will never do unless things and people stop interfer…ing." She pivoted slowly and looked at the Mercedes Benz. "Who did you say swindled your aunts?"

"Bart Sandman. He owns a snobby Porsche dealership down by the river. You heard him—" His lips parted and stayed that way.

"At the meeting? Bart Sandman is Comb-Over Man?"

"Yeah." Brad touched the tip of the concrete angel's candle, then turned his gaze to the run-down car. "That would describe him. And he's been busy since the meeting. Did you see this morning's editorial in the *Times*?"

"No."

"It seems there's a law against piano playing in public establishments if children are present. And a law against serving coffee on Sundays."

"Are those actual laws?"

"Apparently, but someone left a comment on the paper's online site saying he was digging up statutes that hadn't been enforced since the 1800s."

"Well, as long as he doesn't find a law against making soup on the Sabbath, I think we'll keep going. Do you think he's our suspect?"

"I have no idea."

The clock struck twelve just as Winnie pulled the potpie out of the oven. Thelma dozed in a wing-back chair. Brad was on his phone somewhere in the house. LuAnn had tried to find a way to convey her news about Comb-Over Bart to Tess and Janice, but, unlike Thelma, Irene had excellent hearing. And the little woman did love to talk.

"What are your plans for the rest of the day, ladies?" Irene used the thumb of her oven mitt to shove her glasses back in place. The thick lenses gave her a googly-eyed look that only enhanced her adorableness.

Sure won't be shopping, thank you. LuAnn unwrapped a stick of butter and placed it on a cut-glass dish. "We thought we'd visit the Underground Railroad Museum. Since the inn was used as a station, we want to learn as much as we can."

"Bradley says you were a history teacher. Didn't you study the Railroad?"

"In general, yes, but I can't wait to learn more about the part Marietta played." She made a mental note to ask Brad the tour guide for more information. She looked at Winnie. "Do you have anything—keepsakes or diaries—from your great-great-grandmother?"

"I don't have it, but there's a cookbook with my great-great-grandma's name on it. Mrs. Rector from the Underground Railroad museum got it at an auction a few years back. She said it was rightfully mine, but I'd rather have it on display for others to see. I copied some of the recipes though. My peanut soup and those biscuits come outa that." She filled a teapot with boiling water as she talked. "And there was a letter in it, a love letter from—"

"Winnie, could you go pick some mint for the tea?" Irene smiled at LuAnn. "Nothing like an ice-cold glass of sweet tea with a sprig of mint. My daddy used to love that after a long day at work." Her magnified eyes blinked fast as if the thought had brought her to the edge of tears.

Winnie slipped out the back door, so LuAnn turned her attention back to Irene's question. "Maybe you'd like to go with us to the museum."

The lined skin around Irene's mouth blanched. "Not if Maybelline is there."

Tess, taking real silver silverware out of a velvet-lined chest, raised an eyebrow. "You're not fond of Maybelline?"

"More like she's not fond of me. Us. Our entire family." Irene pointed a spatula at Tess, then at Janice and LuAnn. "And she clearly isn't fond of you three now that she knows you're trying to buy the inn."

Winnie entered the kitchen, glass pitcher in hand. "I'd steer clear of Mrs. Rector. No telling what she might try just to get her way."

Janice looked up from folding cloth napkins. "You think she's... dangerous?"

"Oh, I don't know as I'd say that. Manipulative, yes. Like I said, she's got a way of gettin' her way."

"We were hoping we could work with her—maybe invite her to have a rotating display of artifacts that would draw interest to the museum."

A *humph* came from the woman who apparently wasn't as sweet an old lady as she appeared. "Maybelline just wants to cause trouble, it's her MO, as they say. Anyway"—she held the meat pie out like an offering to their growling stomachs—"if one of you can find Bradley, we can eat."

As if they'd rehearsed the move ahead of time, Tess and Janice nodded toward LuAnn.

She made a second mental note—to have a talk with those two. The last thing she needed was a couple of matchmaking friends trying to set her up with a guy who spoke charm as a second language. She left the kitchen in search of the charmer.

She heard him, still engaged in a phone conversation, before she saw him.

"...signed the offer yet. Great show, by the way. You deserve an Oscar."

LuAnn turned the corner into the parlor and stopped in the doorway, not wanting to intrude. His back was turned to her.

"Are you kidding? It's a done deal. You had Townsend eating out of your hand." His laugh was low and husky. "Trust me, Charlie, I'll keep playing dumb. You too. Bye." He tapped his phone and turned. "Oh! Hi! Didn't see you there," he stammered.

Charlie. Who's Charlie? None of my business. Unless it is my business. Unless he's trying to steal my business. "Lunch is ready." She kept her tone even, her expression neutral.

"Great. I'm starving."

Playing dumb will do that to a person. The snarkiness rose like bile in her throat. *Lord, I'm sorry. I don't want to be that person anymore.*

She'd seen a mug in a gift shop once that said, "Sarcasm is my spiritual gift." She'd laughed and shown it to Tess. But it wasn't really funny. Spending her days with teens hadn't helped in her goal of overcoming the cynicism in her sense of humor. For some, it was the only language that got through to them. She had no need for her Sarcasm as a Second Language in this retirement world. No more SASL. "The pie looks amazing."

"Winnie helped, I hope. Irene's measurements are sometimes a bit off these days."

She laughed, leaving all thought of Charlie and Mr. Townsend and Realtors who played dumb—*Was he really double-crossing them?*—behind. "Irene only did the mixing. Winnie did all the measuring." She smiled sweetly and walked ahead of him to the dining room, then took four quick steps to get to the chair Tess had occupied the night before—a vantage point from which to watch his every expression.

If Bradley Grimes was playing them—knowing full well Charlie Somebody's offer on the inn would be considered over theirs—she was going to find out.

The first room in the Marietta Underground Railroad Museum, crammed with artifacts, reminded LuAnn of the Bickerton sisters' library. A framed photograph of Frederick Douglass, one of David Putnam, Jr., a Marietta abolitionist, along with an old painting of his Maple Street house. Tacked to the wall, a map of Underground Railroad stations in Washington County—Marietta, Rainbow, Waterford, Stockport Mill, Malta Station, Putnam, Zanesville. Shackles once used on a slave ship. A shadowbox displaying a coin depicting a woman kneeling in chains. A placard explained that the token, minted in 1838 and inscribed with "Am I Not a Woman and a Sister?" was sold at antislavery fairs by abolitionist women to raise money for their cause. Every step around the room only increased LuAnn's despondency.

"You okay?" Janice aimed her counselor look at her.

"I'm fine." Not a line she expected Janice to believe, but it would buy her time until she could explain. "This is all just... so sad."

Janice nodded. "What's our first question?"

Tess picked up a book titled *Bound for Canaan.* "Let's just be flat-out honest. 'We know you have an interest in the inn and we don't want to have bad feelings between us, so why don't we work together? We'll do everything we can to promote the museum if you'll do the same for us.'" She turned the book over. "It's business, girls, not personal."

"I hate conflict." Janice stood in front of a shadowbox containing a leather whip. She shuddered. "People can be so cruel."

LuAnn sighed her agreement. "'Do everything without grumbling or arguing, so that you may become blameless and pure, "children of God without fault in a warped and crooked generation." Then you will shine among them like stars in the sky as you hold firmly to the word of life.'"

The door labeled Office opened and the twig-like woman with burnt orange hair walked out.

"Okay, peeps, let's go shine." Tess smiled through stiff lips and held her hand out to Maybelline.

Tess's smile may have been stiff, but Maybelline's expression was something that didn't involve any upward bend of the lips at all. "Were you expecting a tour, or is this a private meeting?" The look she shot was nothing short of adversarial.

"Shine, shine, shine," LuAnn whispered without moving her mouth.

"We just wanted to chat for a bit, Mrs. Rector, but we'd love a tour." Tess put her hand on the edge of the door, as if expecting it to slam in their faces.

"The displays are self-explanatory. What did you want to talk about? I know you signed papers today."

"Actually—" Janice bit off the next word when Tess's hand glommed onto her bicep.

LuAnn jumped in. "Could we sit and talk for a minute?"

Maybelline stepped back, then strode to her desk. Massive, dark, intricately carved and heavily adorned with inlay, it was the kind of piece LuAnn had expected to see in Brad's office. Effectively barricaded by the desk, Maybelline crossed her arms across her chest, adding another layer of defense. "Yes?"

Tess dragged a chair from a corner to join the two facing Maybelline. "We are proceeding with an offer on the inn and, knowing your hopes for it, we want to invite your input and—"

"I gave my input at the meeting."

"Yes"—LuAnn chanted *shine shine shine* in her head as she spoke—"and we know it must be a disappointment, but it would be wonderful if we could work together. We would love to set aside some wall space if you'd be interested in showcasing some of your displays. That would give the museum some wonderful exposure."

"And be a cheap way to decorate." Gray eyes bored into LuAnn.

"I...we...aren't the enemy, Mrs. Rector. We share your love of history and your desire to preserve the past."

Maybelline squared her shoulders, and took a long, slow breath. "I will consider your invitation, since it seems my vision for the inn is not to be." She lifted a business card from its holder and slid it across the table with her fingertip. "Please consider the repercussions of making too many modern changes to a house that is surveilled by a host of witnesses"—she stood and pressed her palms together—"witnesses past and present."

Chapter Nine

That went well, I thought." A warm breeze fluffed Janice's curls and buffeted her fake smile as they walked out of the MURM. "Next?"

LuAnn let out a breath she didn't know she'd been holding. "Next, we suggest a bizarre meeting place to sign that offer."

"Bizarre?" Janice's eyebrows converged above her nose.

Tess rubbed her hands together. "Clandestine. So we won't be 'surveilled' by witnesses, dead or alive. What about that abandoned gas station just east of town?"

LuAnn mirrored Janice's baffled expression. "'Bizarre' as in unexpected, not horror movie stuff."

Tess waved away their protests. "When we decide where we're meeting, we have to call Brad and tell him not to tell anyone our plan and to make sure he's not being followed."

LuAnn rolled her eyes. "Tell him to wear a baseball cap and sunglasses and a fake nose."

Tess lifted the collar of her teal blouse until the points jutted toward her ears and looked shiftily from side to side.

"I was kidding!"

"It's not a dumb idea." Tess, usually the most grounded-in-reality of the three, shrugged. "We need disguises too. Ooh! I know where we should meet him! There's an oldies band at Muskingum Park tonight. People are dressing up." She pointed at LuAnn's purse. "Call him."

"You call him." LuAnn retrieved her phone and jabbed it toward Tess, who jabbed back with a questioning look but found Brad in the Contacts list and called him. To LuAnn's mortification, she told him to come incognito. After a smug look that lasted longer than necessary, Tess looked to the right. "There. Follow me."

Like obedient ducklings, they followed, single file, and turned the corner onto Front Street. "Resale extravaganza!" Tess flung open the front door of Antoinette's Closet. "If we're going incognito, we might as well have some fun with it." She swiped her phone and tapped on her timer. "We've got fifteen minutes to find the most outrageous disguise, as judged by . . . " She scanned the front of the store. " . . . her." She pointed at the woman behind the front counter. Early twenties, wearing a red and white polka-dot blouse with cap sleeves. A giant red Minnie Mouse bow was held in place by a headband on waist-length black hair. Earrings that looked like mini marshmallows dotted her ears. "Losers treat for Whitsers."

Janice nodded and took off in the direction of a sequin-slathered mannequin.

"Whatsers?" LuAnn eyed an orange angora stocking cap.

"Frozen custard with mix-ins at Whit's Custard. You'll love it." Tess walked away, her strides long and determined.

LuAnn stood alone just inside the door.

"May I help you?" Polka Dot walked around the end of the counter. "Can I point you to something?"

"Happiness. Joy. Purpose." The latch on her voice box wasn't working. But she stopped before adding, "Men you can trust."

The girl blinked, then laughed. "It is my experience that happiness always begins with the perfect outfit. Is there an occasion?"

"A costume party of sorts. I need to look as retro-outrageous as possible."

Polka Dot squealed. "Delicious! Right over here." She led the way past a circular rack labeled Vintage and straight to a wall of outdated, but not old enough to be truly cool, clothes.

"Thank you."

"Have a blast."

"I will." She pulled out a purple satin blouse with a rhinestone collar and padded shoulders. "I *will*." Wasn't that why she was moving here? To have a blast? To not be bored or boring and not act her age on a daily basis? She tucked her hair behind her ears and put the strap of her purse over her head, telling her brain she meant business. Shopping business. She could do "outrageous" better than the best of them.

When Tess's timer chimed out the first rings, LuAnn had an armful of things she hadn't had time to try on. She scurried into the dressing room and came out in pink-and-white-striped bell-bottoms, a gold velour shirt, platform shoes, a turquoise boa, white sunglasses that would do Elvis proud, and the orange angora hat.

Tess let out a whoop. "Definitely got our old Lu back!" She struck a pose in a wildly flowered muumuu roomy enough to cover all three of them. A tiny straw hat with a checkered blue-and-white ribbon teetered on her head. On her feet, purple rain boots.

"Love it!" LuAnn laughed. The old Lu was definitely back. "Where's Janice?"

"Over here!" The voice was part whisper, part giggle.

Janice stepped from behind a rack of jeans. She wore a floor-length cobalt-blue gown made of solid sequins. A neon-green curly wig sprouted from her head and a red lace parasol twirled over her shoulder.

Their laughter brought Polka Dot on the run. "Ooh! You guys are so fun. I hope I can be half this silly when I get to be your age." Her hand flew to her mouth. "I didn't mean..."

"No worries." LuAnn wiped her eyes. "We know we're old. The trick is to embrace every minute."

"I'm going to—" The bell over the door chimed and Polka Dot turned.

"Irene!" LuAnn rushed to hold the door open for the little woman who was almost hidden behind the pile of clothes in her arms.

Tess grabbed the stack of dresses, all on hangers, and Irene sighed. "Thank you. I was about to suffocate."

Polka Dot motioned for Tess to hang the dresses on a rack next to the counter. "Ooh. More dresses. I wish I was your size."

"You should try them on. Some of those might fit you, my dear. I was a couple of inches taller before my disks started dehydrating and a little more...curvy once upon a time."

LuAnn ran her fingers along a brown velvet dress with padded shoulders and matching belt. "Forties?"

Irene nodded. Polka Dot brought her a chair, and she smiled gratefully as she eased onto it. "I wore that little frock the night I met my sweet Fred."

"How can you bear to part with these?"

"Well, you know what they say—you can't take it with you." She opened the zipper on her purse. "I brought these too." She handed a small satin bag to Polka Dot, who opened it and poured the contents onto the counter, and gasped.

"Mrs. Martin, as much as I would love, love, love to sell these, or buy them, you really need to take them to a jeweler and have them appraised." She slid a silver ring with a large blue stone onto her finger. "I'd venture to guess you're talking five digits, maybe more, for all of these." Polka Dot scooped them up. The gems and rings click-clacked as they fell back into the bag.

"Should be." Irene straightened her shoulders. "I thought you could sell them."

"I wish we could." Polka Dot gave a wistful sigh. "But you really need to get them appraised so you get what they're worth. Would you like the money you made from the other things you brought in? Your retro gowns are a huge hit."

"Yes. Please. They're selling well, huh?" She picked up the satin bag and glanced at her watch. "Guess I have time to get over to the jeweler right now. You really think they'll fetch that much?"

Polka Dot nodded as she counted bills into Irene's hand.

Irene turned to LuAnn and Tess. "So nice to see you three. We will have to do lunch again soon. How are things going with your offer on the inn?"

"Actually, we haven't submitted an offer yet."

"Oh? Second thoughts?"

"No. Just a lot of... interferences."

"Human or otherwise?" Pale eyes twinkled.

"Both."

Irene laughed. "I recall the last buyers having some difficulties."

"Like what?"

"Strange things. Can't recall right now. Unexplainable." She picked up her purse. "Just be careful." She waved with her fingertips and walked out the door Janice held open for her.

LuAnn walked back to the rack and grabbed the purple blouse. Polka Dot came up beside her. "That's a beautiful—"

The bell above the door jangled again. The door thudded shut and a blur of drab green darted toward the back of the store.

Camo Guy.

"Do you know him?" LuAnn asked.

Polka Dot stretched her neck to one side. "He's a... neighbor." She refastened her smile. "Ready to check out?" Her attention was clearly on the door at the back of the store.

"What's his name?"

"He goes by Thorn." She spoke over her shoulder as she walked ahead of them back to the counter.

"Is that a first or last name?"

"It's just what he likes to be called." Her hands seemed to be trembling as she reached for the tag that dangled from LuAnn's arm. "Just tell me the prices and I'll ring them up." A door opened and closed in the distance, and the girl instantly regained her poise.

"Sorry to be so nosy, but where does the guy live?"

The poise disintegrated. She opened the cash register and took the bill LuAnn handed her before answering. "No one knows."

Polka Dot had refused to pick the most outrageous costume, so LuAnn had offered to treat her friends. Whitsers in hand, they got out of the car at Muskingum Park. LuAnn looked at her watch. They had half an hour before Brad would arrive. She sighed. "Can't wait to get this over with."

"This…what? Ice cream? Concert? Submitting our offer?" Tess was doing her amateur psychologist stare.

"The last one. Don't you think all the weirdness will stop and everyone will leave us alone once the bank accepts our offer?" It wasn't just the zany costumes that made this feel like a charade. Should she tell them about Charlie? It seemed cruel to dash their hopes with something that might not come to pass.

Tess lifted her sunglasses, squinting at her. "By 'everyone,' are we talking about people like Saffron and Maybelline, or someone else?"

Another sigh, this one more forceful than the first. "We're talking about every single person or non-person who's trying to interfere with us."

"And I'm guessing we're including people who are not interfering with our buying the inn but might be interfering with our desire to never be attracted to a nice, kind, utterly handsome man?"

"What?" LuAnn felt her blood pressure shoot to a dangerous level. "What are you talking—No! Well, yes, but no, it's not what you're thinking." The cords on the back of her neck knotted. She sighed. "I think Brad is stringing us along. I think he's keeping us in his pocket in case another deal falls through."

Janice's lips parted. Tess's forehead pleated. "What aren't you telling us?"

"I heard him on the phone with someone named Charlie. He was talking about some Oscar-worthy performance and Mr. Townsend eating out of the guy's hand."

Tess dropped onto the bench of a picnic table. Janice and LuAnn joined her.

They sat in silence until Janice stuck her index finger in the air. "I knew a girl in high school everyone called Charlie. Her real name was Charlotte. What if he was talking to Charlotte?" Janice leaned forward. "The woman in the red dress."

Why did the possibility he'd been colluding against them with a woman seem so much more devious? "How do you know her name?"

"Mr. Townsend said her name. And I have a bulletproof memory."

LuAnn gave a half smile. "With all the weird stuff going on, I'm not so sure we want to use 'bulletproof' in any context right now."

Sugared up on Buckeye Madness Whitsers, they linked arms in front of the gazebo and belted "Yoooou light up my life..." The first few lines of the song had always been a heart-stab to LuAnn. It was all too easy to picture herself the girl in the lyrics, sitting by the window waiting for someone to sing his song to her. She understood sitting alone with only the "dreams kept deep inside" for company.

This time, when the chorus began, she turned the words into a prayer. *Lord,* You *light up my life.* By the second round of the chorus, she was laughing as she sang, leaving thoughts of untrustworthy men behind and swaying back and forth to the music with her two best friends.

And then Bradley Grimes appeared. In horn-rimmed glasses, a clown nose, and a baseball cap, looking boyishly disheveled. And deceptively trustworthy.

"Ladies, you are ravishing tonight. I mean...groovy." He shifted the leather strap on his shoulder. "And you sound amazing. You could seriously sing professionally."

Janice giggled. "We tried that once."

"We were the In Crowd." Tess blew on an imaginary pitch pipe. Janice hummed. LuAnn had a split second to realize she'd look more foolish not joining in, so she leaned in and began to sing her alto part. "I'm in with the in crowd..."

The song took over, transporting her back to a stage in a crowded college auditorium. Bright lights, thundering applause.

They'd won the talent contest and gone on to State where they'd finished second and been approached by a talent scout. For two days, tension over the decision had almost destroyed their friendship. What would have happened if they'd said yes?

"...at the B&B." Lost in reverie, she'd missed the first part of Brad's statement.

"We should!" Janice clasped her hands in front of her as if to keep them from clapping on their own.

"Soup and song." Tess's eyes lit with a sparkle LuAnn hadn't seen since before Jeffrey died.

She wanted to hate the idea. Who wanted to hear three old ladies singing songs from the olden days? But she couldn't fight the warmth rising in her chest or the goose bumps rising on her arms. "Remember the coffee house?"

Tess inhaled, sharp and loud. "Ooh..." She rubbed her arms. "This is a God thing."

In their last two years of school they'd performed at Cool Water Coffee House every Friday night. And every night, God had opened doors for them to talk and pray with students who wandered in, some looking for answers, some who came for nothing more than iced Thai coffee but found Jesus. What would an updated version of Cool Water look like?

"...every Friday night." She caught the end of Janice's explanation to Brad.

Brad nodded. "That would be incredible. I know people in my small group who would jump at a chance to serve at something like that."

Small Group? Serve? Was Christianese a mandatory language for Realtors in the Bible Belt? Or was he for real?

LuAnn stared at him, trying to read him. "Do you really think it would be a draw? Would people actually—"

Brad held up one finger, his gaze fixed on something over her right shoulder. LuAnn turned.

Charlotte, wearing peach today, leaned, slim and cat-like, against the hood of Brad's car.

Brad stacked the papers and tapped them on the picnic table, evening out the edges, then stopped to straighten his red clown nose and laugh for the eight hundredth time. "In spite of all the unexplainable things going on"—he looked at LuAnn and she looked at the gazebo behind him—"I'm confident the bank will accept your offer and we'll be able to schedule a closing date before the end of the month." The smile that spread across his tanned face seemed genuine, sincere. No dollar signs. "I'm so excited for you three. I hope you won't mind if I snoop around to check your progress. And if you're looking for volunteer labor, I'd be more than happy to lend a hand with the renovations."

LuAnn stifled a groan. Was this all part of the charade? Part of playing dumb?

His smile broadened. "Since you're all dolled up, you need somewhere to go. May I take the three of you out for a piece of pie to celebrate?"

What are you planning on doing with Charlotte? Are you bringing our competition along—

Janice's perky smile cut off her mental monologue. "That sounds—"

"Like something we don't have time for today." LuAnn ignored the irritation on Janice's face and headed to the car.

"Lu, that was just plain rude." Janice leaned in the open driver's side window, hands on hips. "Did you see the look on his face? The man was absolutely crestfallen."

LuAnn uttered a sound that could have come from a snarling street cat. "*The man* is an actor."

"We don't know that for sure," Tess butted in. "You heard one side of a conversation. We can't be sure what he meant unless we ask him."

"You're right." LuAnn was no more convinced of that than she was that the moon was made of Limburger cheese, but she needed to stop the downward spiral. She flashed a smile she didn't feel. "Let's stop and pick up a pizza, then go back to Tess's and start planning our future as if no one was trying to steal it from us."

"I want to swing by the inn first and get a couple of pictures for the website we need up and running two seconds after closing." Tess gestured toward the lowering sun. "The light is perfect."

She was right. Trees along the river cast long, spindly shadows in the late afternoon sunlight. The surface of the river was glasslike, reflecting the few lazy clouds floating above it. Variegated colors of stone seemed more vibrant than the other times they'd been here. Tess shot the front of the building from several angles while LuAnn and Janice picked their way down the grassy slope to the water. LuAnn lifted her face to the sun. "Are you ready to wake up to this view every morning?"

"A little scared, but ready." Janice looked at her, concern on her face again. "You?"

"I guess I've been the slow one. Everything's changing so fast. I'm only now realizing I need to quit trying to catch up and just hang on and enjoy the ride." LuAnn bent and picked a dandelion and held it to her nose as she turned back to the inn. "As your hubby was so fond of saying, 'When God says jump, jump—'"

"'And trust Him to pull the ripcord.' I love—Lu? Look." She pointed at the brush camouflaging the door to the tunnel.

A pair of work gloves, new-looking and stacked one on top of the other, lay in the grass. LuAnn stepped over them and parted the brush. The door was halfway open.

September 27, 1857

Patience walked in front of them in the dark, the arrogant goose pretending she knew the way. Prudence held Jason's hand, and they scrambled down the bank toward the river. Three-quarters of a moon lit their steps. The river was quiet and the air still. They spoke in whispers.

"I still do not understand why they need to involve thee in this." Jason's frustration tensed his arm.

This was not the first, nor the tenth, time they had discussed this. She looked down at her pet, waddling ahead without a care in the world. Oh, for a little of Patience's patience. She uttered a silent prayer before she spoke. "They have invited me because I have asked to be involved. Jason, thee has said thyself that this is my calling. Until the scourge of slavery is routed from this land, I cannot rest. I lost my mother, my father, my little brother, everything that was dear to me when I fled. And since we lost Hope, there is a hole in my heart I cannot seem to fill any other way. Is it not possible God allowed this sadness in our lives for this very reason, so that we would desire to spend our days giving and helping others who hurt rather than in tears?"

He dropped her hand and halted. Her breath stopped with him until his arms encircled her. "Oh, Pru, doesn't thee understand? The calling God has put on *my* heart is to protect *thee*. Does thee know how hard it is to do that when thee are slipping away in the skiff in the middle of the night to meet people thee doesn't know? Every night I fear thee are rowing directly into a trap. Every night I want to take thy place." He groaned as he slapped his bad leg. "There is nothing a man hates more than feeling powerless to protect the people he loves."

She leaned into him. "Thee is anything but powerless, my dear. I know no one who is a fiercer contender in prayer than thee. How else does thee think I arrive home safe every—"

"Shh." Jason's finger touched her lips. Two shadows emerged from a thicket.

Prudence held her breath until she heard the loon's cry. Their signal. Jason answered, echoing the sound.

The two men approached. She did not recognize them, and it wasn't likely she would learn their names in this conversation. *Please, God, let them be true*. It was a fear she faced constantly. She had once been enslaved and did not have freedom papers. Any meeting could be a trap.

"Good Sabbath." The taller man tipped his hat. "Come with us."

They walked toward the Riverfront House but stopped at a small building. The stockier man opened the door and beckoned them in. A toolshed. With a window facing the dirt road between the hotel and the river. The man unrolled a large paper. "Plans for the changes Mr. Bickerton has commissioned." He turned to Prudence. "This, ma'am, is why we desire your input." He pointed at a spot on the drawing and then out the window. "This is where the tunnel comes out. It will be your drop-off point."

The tall one cleared his throat. "We have something else to ask of you."

"Yes?" Her voice wobbled. Jason's hand tightened over hers.

"We'd like you to find a way to get yourself hired at the inn before Mr. Bickerton arrives." He looked out the window and sighed. "I don't have to tell either of you how dangerous this is, do I?"

Chapter Ten

Tess's dining room looked like a CIA operations room. Three laptops, two tablets, and a collage of loose pages and three-by-five cards covered the table. LuAnn had acquired four new notebooks for the project: Layout and Design, Menu, Finances, and Permits and Licensing.

"Read off the room themes." Tess stretched her neck from one side to the other.

Janice picked up the Layout and Design book and turned to the Decor section. "Woodbine and Roses, Lilac and Sage, Sunshine and Daisies, Woodsmoke and Pine, Apples and Cinnamon, Maple and Mum, Moonlight and Snowflakes, and Lily and Lace. We need one more."

Tess yawned. "Later. My brain hurts."

LuAnn stood and touched her toes, walked her hands out away from her feet, and moved into a forward lunge to clear her tired mind. Her original notebook lay open to the page marked Suspects.

Janice tugged on it. "Are we all in agreement we made the right call not to tell anyone about the gloves?" She smashed scone crumbs with her fingertips.

"I am." LuAnn answered a bit quicker than she needed to.

"So am I." Tess stirred coffee she hadn't touched in over an hour. "The tunnel door isn't on the inn property. And we don't need any more publicity. We did the right thing."

Janice closed her laptop. "I'm giving in to you guys, but I'm not convinced. What if someone broke in?"

"You can't technically break in to something that's not locked, can you?" LuAnn circled *gloves* on her list labeled Clues. "They were Youngstown gloves. One hundred percent leather and lined with Kevlar. And I might have happened to take a picture of them. And compared them to my hand. The fingers are a half inch longer than mine."

Her two best friends gaped at her.

"What? We need to pay attention to details." LuAnn tapped to a page on her iPad. "As far as I can tell, only two hardware stores within a one-mile radius sell these."

The gleam returned to Tess's eyes. "Then what are we waiting for? We need to make a visit to"—she leaned over LuAnn's shoulder—"Vance Hardware."

"As long as we're going out, we need measurements." Janice reached for her purse. "I think we need to get into the inn with tape measures."

Tess got up and dumped cold coffee in the sink. "We need to see what's behind that door you and Brad found, and we need pictures of every corner before we go to the salvage store. We'll want to match trim and tile and I just want to get a better feel for the whole thing, don't you guys?"

Yes. But not if it meant calling their shifty Realtor and asking him to go with them. LuAnn picked up her Menu book. "I think we need muffins. Wouldn't cranberry walnut muffins be perfect with all of our harvest soups?"

"I think someone is being evasive." Tess picked up her phone. "What's his number? I'll call him. Maybe he'll just give us the key."

"I've got his number." Janice tapped on her phone, then slid it across the table to Tess.

A strand of hair blew over LuAnn's face with the force of her exhale. Had she ever crammed this many exasperated sighs into a week before? A classroom of twenty-five hormonal teenagers hadn't evoked this much frustration. She rolled her shoulders and gave in. "Fine. Call him."

Bradley Grimes surrendered the keys. Apparently, Mr. Townsend had promoted him to manager of the property.

"This is so cool. And *so* creepy." Janice clutched her arms to her belly as Tess slid the key into the inn door. "What if whoever—"

"No what-ifs." LuAnn tapped a yardstick on the crumbling concrete. "We have to get this done."

"Maybe we should visit the hardware stores first. We might learn something about the person who could be in there *right now.*" Janice tightened her grip on the metal tape measure poised in her hand like a grenade.

Tess shoved the door open. Stale air wafted out. Stale air with a hint of… "What is that? Smells like a spa."

"Eucalyptus." Tess stepped inside, nose in the air, sniffing. "I don't remember smelling that before."

"So our suspect has a cold or sinus problems. Have we met anyone who *sou'ds like dis*?" Janice walked to the mirror. "Guys? Look."

The old words had been erased. The new ones read, "If my walls you don't tear down, you'll soon see I'm not around."

"The *house* is leaving us messages?" LuAnn laughed and locked eyes with Tess. If they didn't make light of this, Janice would run. Out of the inn and out of the deal. "This just gets more intriguing all the time."

Janice exhaled through red cheeks. "Do you know the real meaning of the word *intrigue*?"

She did. In French, *intriguer*, one of the root words, meant to tangle, to plot, deceive, or cheat. "I mean it gets more exciting all the time. This is an adventure." LuAnn looked to Tess for backup. "Right?"

"Right. Absolutely. We're going to find the person who's doing this, and we're going to have fun doing it." She opened her tape measure. "Get out your notebook, Lu. No house is going to outsmart us."

Janice hadn't moved. "This is different lipstick."

"What?" LuAnn dug in her purse as she walked closer. She pulled out their first evidence bag. The first lipstick was red. This was a deep coral. "Did you pay attention to what Charlotte was wearing at the park?"

Both of her friends arrowed an eyebrow at her.

LuAnn stared down at the tissue in her hand. "What if Charlotte wrote it, but not for us?" It sounded dumb in her head. It would sound stranger when she said it. "You know that line from the book, *The Princess Bride*? 'Her heart was a secret garden and the walls were very high.' What if she wrote it for Brad?"

They looked at her, clueless, until Tess's eyes widened in a light bulb moment expression. "You think she and Brad are a couple? Makes sense, I guess. She was waiting for him at the park, he has a cutesy nickname for her…"

"Wow." Janice touched the mirror's frame. "'If my walls you don't tear down…'" she read it in a soft, intimate tone. "That's so romantic."

"What if all the other stuff was her doing?" Tess looked up at the ceiling fan. "What if the scarf was a sign, a secret message?"

"Telling Brad to meet her somewhere." LuAnn felt herself getting swept into the fantasy. "Maybe she has to sneak out to see him. Maybe she works for a competitor, and they can't be seen together. Maybe she has a rich, controlling father who will cut her out of the will if she doesn't marry the man he's picked out for her. But she's hopelessly in love with Brad so they meet in secret, in the inn."

"Except she was sitting on his car at the park." Janice lifted her hands, palms up.

"Maybe that was Daddy's golf day." LuAnn pressed her hands together. "'I pray you tell my lord and father, madam, I will not marry yet; and when I do, I swear it shall be Romeo.'"

"Okay…" Tess snapped her fingers. "Back to the real world, Walter Mitty. It's an interesting, romantic theory, but it's ignoring a very important piece of evidence." She grinned.

"What's that?" LuAnn wasn't sure she wanted to hear the answer.

"We are forgetting the way his eyes sparkle when he looks at Lu."

"And Shakespeare," Janice chimed in, mirroring Tess's grin. "We cannot forget '...for as you were when first your eye I eyed, such seems your beauty still.'"

LuAnn was about to sputter an answer when Janice's phone rang. Her brow furrowed as she began to talk to the person on the other end. "Yes, she did. No, she doesn't know much of anything." Janice glanced at her watch. "Sure. We'll meet you at the church in fifteen minutes. Bye, Ben."

"Let me get this straight." LuAnn walked under the cream-colored brick arch behind Janice. She couldn't walk into this building without thinking of the line of people that stretched around the block at Lawrence's funeral. "Pastor Ben knows someone who knows someone whose father knew my father?"

"Something like that. The man saw you at the meeting at the bank and, because you were with me and he knew Lawrence, he asked Ben about you."

LuAnn rubbed her temple. What if the man knew things she didn't want to hear?

"Another mystery." Janice opened the church door wearing an expression of delightful anticipation.

Janice's smile did not match the feeling in LuAnn's gut. Tess stepped in behind her. "You sure you want to do this?"

"Not at all."

Tess rested her hand on LuAnn's back. "Do you want us with you or do you want to talk to Pastor Ben alone?"

"I need you guys there."

Janice chatted with the church secretary as they waited. Pastor Ben walked out of his office, arms open wide in a welcoming gesture. They walked in. A circle of five chairs surrounded a low table. Pastor Ben hugged Janet and shook hands with Tess and LuAnn. "Wilbur will be here any—"

The partially open door opened all the way, and a bent man wearing a plaid short-sleeved shirt under clean but worn bib overalls entered. "Howdy, Pastor. Ladies." He removed a frayed billed cap and ran knobby fingers through silk-soft snowy-white hair in need of a trim.

Pastor Ben made introductions as Wilbur VanDuson lowered his lanky frame into a chair. He turned still-vibrant eyes on LuAnn. "I remember you."

Her pulse tripped. "You do?"

"You stood up on a table at the Union picnic and sang 'The Star Spangled Banner.' Brought tears to my eyes."

A dim memory surfaced, then faded like morning mist "You knew my father."

"Sure did. We worked side by side at the shipyard. Missed him sorely when he disa—when he left." His eyes closed for a moment, then opened, somehow dimmer than moments earlier. "Did he—is he still alive?"

LuAnn's shoulders lowered. "I have no idea."

"Oh, I'm so sorry. You saw him, after, didn't you? I mean, he came back, didn't he?"

"After what? I haven't seen or heard from my father since he left us when I was six."

The man's lined face seemed to harden. His bent posture straightened. "I'm so sorry. And here I go digging up old hurts. I'm just…so sorry."

"Tell me what you know, Wilbur. Why did my father leave?"

Wilbur glanced toward the door. "I don't know, ma'am. I was hoping you could tell me what happened to him." His hands trembled as he placed the cap back on his head. "I just, well, I'm sorry is all. Didn't mean to raise more questions than I can answer. I was sure hoping…" Using the chair arms for support, he raised himself to a stand. "And your mama?"

"She passed away three weeks ago."

"My sympathies. Fine lady. So sorry she had to go through all that. Wasn't fair to her at all."

"All what, Mr. VanDuson?"

"Just, the loss, is all I meant." He nodded to Pastor Ben. "Sorry to take up your time, folks." He walked unsteadily toward the door. "Just so very sorry."

The boy behind the counter at Vance Hardware didn't look a day over fourteen. "May I help you?"

Probably not. The way this week was going, it was better to err on the side of pessimism. A dull ache at the base of LuAnn's skull was ramping into something that would require two extra-strength aspirin and a dark room. "I hope so." LuAnn faked a smile and showed him a picture of the gloves. "We're conducting an investigation and wonder if you remember selling these recently."

He stared at the picture, and his face reddened. "Yeah. I remember."

"Do you know his or her name? Or can you describe the person?"

"He has a po—" The boy suddenly looked genuinely scared. "Are you cops?"

"No. This is a private investigation. You're not in any trouble, son."

"Kip!" the boy yelled over his shoulder.

Footsteps sounded from the back of the store. A boy appeared. Their server from Bar-B-Cutie. The one who questioned when they would start working on the inn. The one with the gold stud in his ear. He did a double take. "You're the people who are buying the inn."

"Yes, we are. Are you working here now?"

"Part-time. What can we help you with?"

LuAnn went back through the explanation, showing him the picture.

"Nope. Don't think we've sold any of those. Sorry we can't help you." He turned to the other boy. "Go finish stocking those wrenches."

The first boy opened his mouth, then nodded and left.

"You're sure?" LuAnn pointed to a rack of Youngstown gloves.

"Yep. I'm sure. Y'all have a nice day." He turned and walked away.

Tess pointed to a security camera aimed at the front door. "We could always talk to the manager and figure out a way to look at their security footage."

"I think we have enough information to go on for now," Janice whispered as she headed for the door.

"What information?" LuAnn followed her out.

"It's a he and he has something starting with 'po.'"

"Portly belly?" Tess chimed in.

"Potato nose?" Janice continued.

"Poor self-esteem?"

"Pogo stick?"

"Pole barn?"

"Got it!" LuAnn skidded to a stop. "Porsche."

"Comb-Over Man!" Tess and Janice said in unison.

"His name is Bart Sandman. Brad said he's a shyster."

Tess grinned. "Ladies, I think the In Crowd needs a new touring car. A very, very nice touring car."

In the five minutes it took them to walk to Metro Porsche, they'd devised a plan—the first step being to walk to the dealership rather than drive up in Tess's five-year-old Honda. They wouldn't utter a single untruth: now that they were resurrecting their formerly successful singing trio, which would soon be showcased at Wayfarers Inn, they needed a new image and thought they'd start with shopping for new wheels. While Tess peppered the man with questions, LuAnn and Janice would search—and smell—for clues. Did he have the sniffles? Any piercings? Were his hands the right size for the gloves? Wedding ring? A wife would give him easy access to lipstick. And lace scarves.

Bart Sandman hovered, hands in pockets again, over a young, well-dressed couple admiring a sleek silver car. When he looked up and spotted the women, his expression morphed from surprise to something LuAnn could only compare to a wolf salivating over roadkill. They were fresh meat.

LuAnn stood downwind of the man. No eucalyptus. She squinted through her sunglasses. Something sparkled in the sunlight. A diamond chip in his left ear. If the guy would just take his hands out of his pockets she could check for a ring.

When the young couple walked away, Bart turned his full, greedy attention on the women. "Well, well, if it isn't my new neighbors."

They were suddenly best buds now that they were potential customers? Tess stepped closer. "Mr. Sandman. How nice to see you again. You are quite close to the inn, aren't you?"

"Now you see why I'm concerned about the type of patrons you would attract. Are you here to talk about your business or"—a sleazy grin narrowed his beady eyes—"mine?" He nodded toward the silver car.

As Tess asked Bart about the merits of the Boxster versus the Cayman—one could do 0 to 60 in 4.4 while the other took almost a full 5 seconds—LuAnn walked into the dealership lobby, looking for someone to interrogate. A sweet-looking young woman smiled from behind a chicly industrial metal and glass desk. LuAnn approached her with an even bigger smile. "Hi. I'm just killing time, waiting for my friends."

"Would you like some coffee?" The woman motioned to two hot pots and a tower of Styrofoam cups.

"Love some." LuAnn squirted steaming coffee into a cup. "How long have you worked here?"

"Two years."

"Is Mr. Sandman easy to work for?"

"Well, he's...a fair boss."

"I was thinking I might know his wife."

"Must be a different Mrs. Sandman. He's not married."

Hmm. Well, a guy could still buy lipstick. Or...She stepped closer. Peach. Or he could borrow it from his secretary.

A wall of photos caught her eye. "Mr. Sandman was in the military?"

"Yep. Afghanistan. Purple heart."

Brad's words came back to her. *Maybe he was a hero back in the day, but...* "He was wound—" She leaned in to a picture of a not-so-portly Mr. Sandman in full dress uniform, a white glove on his left hand and...

She turned just as Tess thrust her hand out to Mr. Sandman, who shrugged and pulled his hands from his pockets. *Hand.* Only one.

"Yeah," the girl said, "in an IED explosion. He rescued three of his men after he lost his hand."

LuAnn scribbled Comb-Over Man off her list with bold strokes, then hugged her mug and read, once again, the words on the chalkboard at Jeremiah's Coffee House. *"For I know the plans I have for you," declares the* LORD, *"plans to prosper you and not to harm you, plans to give you hope and a future."*

"Well, I guess we should call this progress." Tess stirred her latte. "Who's next? Should we give up on the glove thing and go back to Charlotte?"

Janice shook her head. "I'm still stuck on 'He has a po.' Po what? Po*ny*?"

LuAnn inhaled, almost choking on her coffee. "Pony*tail*."

In ten minutes they were back at Antoinette's Closet. Polka-Dot was nowhere in sight. Tess walked up to a clerk who was straightening sweaters on a shelf. "Excuse me. We were in the other day and talked to a young woman with long black hair."

"Emma. She's the manager. Unfortunately, she's off today. Is there something I can help you with?"

"There was a man who came in while we were talking to her. Camouflage jacket, ponytail..."

The woman nodded. "Thorn. He comes in to use the restroom and wash up. Emma leaves food out for him every day."

"Is he homeless?"

"We're not sure. He's just in and out, doesn't say much. Sad-looking man."

"Does he come in here at the same time every day?"

"No. It's random." Her face sagged. "He's not in trouble is he? Are you social workers or something?"

"No. Just wanted to know if there was any way we could help him."

"That's really nice. I'm sure Emma would welcome food donations."

Janice nodded. "Consider it done. We'll be back tomorrow with food."

"Thank you so much. Who should I tell her to expect?"

LuAnn laughed. "Just tell her the retro-outrageous ladies."

Chapter Eleven

LuAnn stood in front of Tess's open fridge. How long had she been there, her mind on Wilbur VanDuson and Maybelline Rector and Charlotte Red Dress and a kid named Kip? Two weeks ago she was so alone her soul ached. How had it happened that in just a matter of days her brain was overloaded with names and faces and secrets, and questions without answers? She pulled out thin-sliced ham, a tomato, lettuce, and mayo. "Lettuce wraps?"

"Perfect." Janice offered to make iced tea and a fruit salad, and Tess pulled plates and glasses from her cupboards.

LuAnn had just set three ham wraps on plates when her phone rang. Brad. Was it too early to hope for an answer from the bank? "Tess, can you answer?" She held up fingers smeared with mayonnaise.

"LuAnn's phone. This is Tess." She pressed a button on the phone. "We're all here. I'm putting you on speaker."

"Good morning, ladies!" Brad's voice seemed slightly huskier on the phone than in person. "I have news. Unfortunately, it's not the news I'd hoped to be giving you."

Janice plopped onto a stool. "They rejected our offer?"

"No. No, not yet. It seems we have a bidding war."

"Oh..." The sigh was collective.

LuAnn sneered and mouthed "Charlotte."

"All is not lost. If you're willing to raise your offer." When only silence answered him, Brad added, "I'd like to meet you for dinner tomorrow night to talk about it if you're free."

"We're free." Janice answered before LuAnn could open her mouth.

"Um." Tess grabbed Janice's arm and mouthed something LuAnn couldn't decipher. "Not all of us. We were planning on…getting massages tomorrow night. LuAnn can go. We'll talk it over, and she can represent us."

Janice nodded. "The ahi tuna with wasabi aioli at Austyn's is divine."

"Maybe you could give her a tour of downtown," Tess added. "It's been a while since she's been here, and we just haven't had time for sightseeing. She—"

"I'm. Right. Here." LuAnn bit off each hushed word as if tackling too-tough tuna.

"That would be…great. Text me your address, LuAnn, and I'll pick you up. Six thirty work?"

Face burning like she'd been attacked by fire ants, she nodded. "Six thirty is fine," she answered through locked jaws. Gripping the back of a chair, she turned on her best friends after they'd hung up from the call. "That house may not be haunted, but I will haunt both of you until the day you—"

"You could have said no." Tess popped a blueberry in her mouth, shoulders jiggling with laughter that was echoed by the blonde traitor beside her.

"What?"

"You heard me." Tess winked as she pulled napkins from a holder. "If you hadn't wanted to go, you would have just said no."

LuAnn slunk into the chair. And covered her face with splayed fingers.

"Nothing but fun today." Tess set a coffee carafe on her kitchen table and took three mugs out of the cupboard. "We'll drop the box off at Antoinette's Closet and then it's all easy-peasy for the rest of the day."

Janice's eyes brightened. "Fun, as in getting Lu dolled up for her date tonight?"

Teeth gritting, LuAnn opened the oven and touched the top of a poppy seed muffin. She hadn't been in a morning mood like this since her teens. Janice had spent yesterday afternoon and evening watching grandkids and Tess had gone to her book club, leaving her alone to make lists and ponder life. And friends. And Bradley Grimes. She'd taken a hot bath and crawled into bed at eight, falling asleep in seconds after winning a wrestling match with doubt—at least on one topic. She was not ready for, interested in, nor willing to consider the possibility of a relationship at her age. And if she'd correctly read Brad's stuttering response to Tess's suggestion, he wasn't either.

She glared at the cheery blonde. "Fun as in retail therapy." She needed something to overshadow the other questions hurting her brain.

Tess opened the Layout and Design notebook. "Salvage, furniture, antiques, bedding, dishes?"

Janice answered "Antiques" at the same time LuAnn said, "Salvage."

"Done. We can do both in one stop."

Good. Hours of distraction. LuAnn slipped on an oven mitt and pulled the pan out of the oven.

"And then we can get you ready." Janice singsonged the proclamation.

LuAnn smacked the pan onto the top of the stove a bit harder than necessary. Three muffins popped out.

"She's chickening out," Tess whispered.

"She needs to be open to possibilities. Have you noticed how they match? Blue eyes, silver hair."

"So true, but she—"

"*She's* right here!" A steaming muffin dropped from her fingers and bounced off the plate. "*She* doesn't want to go because *she* doesn't need a man in her life." She cringed. Not the thing to say to two women who had recently lost their husbands. She lifted the rest of the muffins from the tin, then arranged them on a plate and carried it to the table. "In the first place, I don't think the guy is a straight shooter and in the second place, why would I complicate my life after all these years of being perfectly content?"

Tess handed out napkins, then sat at the table. "It's just a date. Not a proposal."

"It's not a date. It's dinner. And if it were a date, dates can lead to proposals and proposals lead to misery." Again, not a thoughtful thing to say. She took a seat and massaged her temples. "Shouldn't we be focusing on who is out to get us? And how did we get from not trusting the guy two days ago to thinking it's okay for me to go out with him?"

Janice shrugged. "We just want you to be happy."

"I know. I get that, and I love you guys for it, but God showed me loud and clear years ago that I can be just fine without a man in my life." She split the top of a steaming muffin. "You two were blessed with amazing men and I ache for you both that something so wonderful ended too soon, but I don't want that for myself."

"The love? Or the grief?" Tess's grandfather clock struck seven, as if emphasizing her words.

"I don't want either." She shoved a bite in her mouth, chewed, and managed to swallow through a too-tight throat. "I thought this was going to be a fun day."

"It will be." Janice filled their cups with coffee. "Just as soon as we figure out what you're going to wear tonight."

"That was odd." LuAnn walked out of Antoinette's Closet ten minutes after she'd walked in carrying the box filled with granola bars, foil packets of chicken, pull-tab cans of beef stew, cheesy peanut butter crackers, juice boxes, a note written by each one of them, and a Bible. She got in the back seat of Tess's car. "Emma thanked me for the contribution, took the box to the back room, and never came out again."

"That's it?" Tess pulled away from the curb. "No other conversation?"

"Well, I might have grilled her just a bit. I asked how long she'd known Thorn and what she knew about his story. That's all."

Janice nodded. "You spooked her."

"Some people spook too easily." She wasn't in the mood for Janice's astute observations.

They rode to the Antique and Salvage Mall in rare silence. Just inside the front door, Janice picked up a small blue and gray crock. "We need this."

"And these." Tess stuck three handmade wooden spoons in their basket.

LuAnn wandered off toward a wall of framed cross-stitch samplers. The first one that caught her eye made her almost laugh. "It is to a man's glory to overlook an offense."

Ouch.

Her friends meant well. And tonight wasn't a date. In fact, she might get more information out of Brad one on one. She'd ask him about the Underground Railroad and more about Marietta history, and somehow weave in Charlotte Red Dress and her intentions for the inn.

"Hello." The plump woman who approached her looked familiar.

"Hi."

"You probably remember me. I'm Marla Still. My great-great-great-granddaddy was William Still."

"Yes. I remember. He worked with Harriet Tubman, right?"

"Well, they knew each other, for sure." Marla picked up a tatted pillowcase. "I suppose you thought I was just an awful, controllin' woman at that meetin'."

"No. Of course not." *Not that I would admit to your face, anyway.* "You struck me as someone who is very passionate about preserving history. We have that in common."

"I'm so glad to hear that. I know I can't demand anything, but, if you get the inn, and I hear someone's biddin' against you, I sure would like to help." She set the pillowcase back on the shelf. "It's Maybelline Rector biddin' against you, isn't it?"

"We don't know."

"Uh-huh, well, just watch your back."

The woman walked away and LuAnn took two long, slow breaths and joined her scheming but well-meaning friends at the front of the store where they were talking to a man with "Harry" on his name badge.

He ushered them to a room overflowing with cornices, arches, window frames, newel posts, and fireplace mantels. They stood in hushed reverence, none of them knowing where to start. "I'll leave you to it. Name's Harry. Come find me if you have any questions. And if there's anything you'd like me to hold for you, I'm happy to do it for five percent down."

LuAnn laughed. This time for real. "That man does not know what he just offered." She picked up a semicircular window frame with glass still in one of the wedge-shaped spaces. "I want this in my apartment."

"And I want this." Janice pointed to a wall shelf with curled supports and peeling paint.

"That's gorgeous."

For two hours they walked from room to room, making notes and taking pictures and filling a basket with door handles, switch plates, and light pulls. They bought the things they wanted for themselves and filled a third of an almost empty back room with things they hoped to come back and get. As they were leaving the room, Harry approached. "I've been hunting since you got here. Got something to show you."

He led them back to the front where a large brass lantern sat on the counter. Square sides, looped handle. The old, wavy glass was still intact. The price tag read $225.

"This could so easily be electrified, couldn't it?" Janice clasped her hands in a pleading pose. "We *need* this for next to the front door."

"You do need this, actually." Harry opened a spiral-bound record book and showed them an entry dated June 4, 1997. *Brass oil lantern. c. 1850. From Wayfarers Inn.* "A buddy of mine managed the place when it was a warehouse. He brought a few things to me. Couldn't stand to see it all just get trashed. There was something else." His finger skimmed the entries. "There."

Metal box. Unknown contents. No key.

LuAnn pressed her hand against the spot at the base of her neck where her pulse had begun wildly beating. "Where is it?"

The man's face squinched as he looked around at a thousand square feet of overcrowded mess. "I have no idea."

Chapter Twelve

Can I ask you something?" Brad fastened his seat belt and started the car.

"I suppose."

"The questions you asked me about organized crime. Something personal was there, wasn't it?"

She sighed. Why not tell him? "My father left when I was six years old. Left us with no money and I don't know why."

"No clue? But you think the mob has something to do with it?"

"Maybe. I don't know. I've tried searching for his name so many times. There is a record of his birth and marriage. Nothing else."

"You don't even know if he's still alive?"

"No." She didn't want to talk about that part. "My mother had never worked a day in her life other than keeping house and taking care of me, and there we were, alone in the world and penniless. She knew a lady who owned a diner in Charleston, West Virginia, so we moved there, into a one-bedroom apartment, and she started waitressing."

"Wow. That must have been tough."

"It was. But there were good parts." She stared out the window and imagined herself back in the diner, sitting at the table with yellow Formica top. "The woman who owned it was, in her own words, 'a Bible-thumpin', Jesus-lovin', loudmouth.' Funny lady. Her kitchen was clean but so disorganized. I would spend hours lining up her canned goods and sorting her spices only to have her mess up my system the next day. But she loved on hurting people better than anyone I've ever met.

"I remember listening in to her kitchen counseling sessions while I sat at the table making lists. She'd be praying and I'd be scribbling down what I would wear the next day, what I wanted to be when I grew up. I planned my wedding and my future house and named my future children."

"It made you feel in control of an out-of-control life."

"Exactly. But none of those things on my wish lists ever came true. You'd think I would have learned."

"Old habits die hard."

She nodded. "Teaching was the perfect profession for a list maker. Literally half my job was making lesson plans. And in my spare time I planned my summer vacations."

"I hope some of those wish lists came true."

"They did. I've had a good life so far, lots of planned adventures, but I want this new phase to be different. I just want to wake up every morning and ask Jesus where we're going and who He wants me to talk to. I want to be a little messy and a little bolder."

"A Bible thumpin', Jesus lovin', loudmouth?"

"A little bit of that. I want the inn to be a place where we can love on hurting people."

"I don't think the three of you could do anything less." He winked at her. "Hey, you want to do something unplanned before dinner?"

"I . . . don't know. Do I?"

"I'm going to say yes." He flipped on his left blinker, reached behind the seat, and handed her the largest flashlight she had ever seen in her life. "How about we take a look at what's behind door number three?"

She clicked the flashlight on with a perfectly manicured nail. The fussing over her hair, nails, and makeup by her two best friends had transformed her into a woman actually looking forward to the evening. "Sounds like the perfect way to work up an appetite."

He parked in front of the inn and pulled the key out of his pocket. LuAnn pointed the massive yellow flashlight at the door, and he opened it. She stuffed the guilt twinge that said she should wait to do this with the girls. They were, after all, the ones who'd forced her on this date. Not date. This dinner. With their Realtor.

Brad turned on the lights. They both looked up at the fan, then to the mirror, and breathed a collective sigh. Nothing new. "How about if we take the basement stairs instead of the ladder?"

"Good idea." LuAnn kicked a high-heeled foot out in front of her. "I didn't dress for ladder climbing."

"I see that." He eyed the short-sleeved navy and white flowered dress Tess had forced her to borrow. "You look very nice tonight."

"Thank you."

She set her clutch purse on the bar and pressed both hands on the wall to open the hidden door to the basement. The sound of their footsteps bounced off stone walls, and then a loud *crunch.* She looked down. An open bag of peanuts in the shells. She picked it up and showed it to Brad. "There are other Realtors showing the place, right?"

"Not that I know of. We haven't put a lockbox out, so they'd have to get the key from us or the bank. Townsend said the other party had already seen the place. Makes me think it must be Maybelline or someone with the Historical Society."

Or your secretary. Or Camo Guy. Or Charlotte.

When they reached the bottom of the stairs, LuAnn walked over to the cistern. Definite hot tub possibilities.

"The door Joe found would be...where?"

She walked to a wall lined with cupboards and built-in shelves. "The passageway has to be behind here, right?" She opened a cupboard door, knelt down, and pushed against the back of the cupboard. Solid wood.

Brad opened the next door, and they tag-teamed down the wall of built-ins. When they reached the end, LuAnn pressed on the wall next to it. The wall gave way, swinging out. "Door number four," she whispered.

They walked through, past the ladder, and LuAnn aimed the light at the metal door. The light glinted off a small brass plate on the upper right corner. *Cooper Safe Company 1924.*

"Not as old as I thought." Brad touched the door handle. "What are the chances it'll open?"

"Wait!" The word escaped her lips before it had fully formed in her head. "I can't do this."

"You'd like Tess and Janice to be here."

The man got points for being intuitive. "I'm sorry. I just hate to—"

"I understand. Fully. In fact, why don't we eat in? All four of us. If you're okay with that idea."

I'm so much more than okay with it. And, clearly, he was too. It hadn't taken him more than an eighth of a second to suggest canceling their date. *Dinner.* "That would be fun."

"Great. What's your fancy?"

LuAnn played with the pearl on the silver chain she wore around her neck. "How does Thai sound?"

"I'm already wearing one, but thanks."

"Ha ha. Let's call it in and ask the girls to pick it up."

"Works for me." He loosened his tie. "Maybe a rain check on the dinner?"

"Maybe."

It had taken a bit of cajoling to convince Tess and Janice she wasn't just "chickening out." Now the four of them hovered around the metal door.

Brad cranked the silver handle and pulled. The door swung out. They looked in. And down.

LuAnn sucked in a quick breath. "Another basement."

Stone steps led down into a stone-walled room with a dirt floor. The ceiling was just high enough for Brad to stand up straight between thick, rough-hewn wood beams. "I'm guessing this room is way older than the door." Ducking beams, he paced off the length and width. "Eight by ten."

Janice stood at the door, making no attempt to enter. LuAnn arced the light from floor to ceiling and around all four walls. "Do you think this could have been—" She stopped, took two steps, and concentrated the light on something wedged between the stones along the ceiling.

Tess gasped. "Papers."

Brad reached up, and tugged. A rolled, soft-cover book slid out. Something clattered to the floor. She pointed the light at it. A quill pen, thin spines where feathers would have been. Tess picked it up in her fingertips.

Brad held the book, its thin leather still bent around curved pages, as if he held a bird about to take flight. A reverent silence filled the room until Tess whispered, "It looks really, really old."

Janice leaned in as far as her phobias would let her. "This room would have been under water in the 2004 flood and a couple before that one. Paper would have been ruined. Either it's not as old as it looks, or someone put it here in the last decade."

"Let's take it upstairs." Brad cradled it in his palms. "I'm scared it's just going to disintegrate."

LuAnn led the way back through the narrow door, across the basement, and up the stairs. Janice and Tess shoved away empty carry-out cartons porcupined with chopsticks and wiped the bar with a stack of napkins. Brad rested the book on it. The pages were yellowed and crumbling on the edges. One corner looked like it had been chewed by a mouse.

Tess touched the smooth, dust-caked spine. "Do we dare open it?"

"Open the cover," Janice said, voice still hushed. "If we hear it cracking, stop."

With one fingertip, LuAnn lifted the edge and opened it halfway. Enough to read the scripture verse penned in fluid brown letters on the stained and spotted page. "It is better to trust in the LORD than to put confidence in man. Psalm 118:8."

"Amen to that," Tess said.

LuAnn turned another page. "It's a record book. A ledger of some kind." Names and dates filled the page in neatly scribed rows.

"What's the first date?" Janice leaned in next to LuAnn.

"May 23, 1854."

"These are Underground Railroad records." Tess sounded like she was barely breathing as she voiced the words.

LuAnn felt every sense surge. "Do you guys have any idea how incredibly rare this is? People didn't keep written records—they were too scared of getting caught."

Janice took a picture. "This is history." She pointed at the book. "*This* is history, and we're making history by reading it." She turned a page the way she'd touch butterfly wings. "'June 14, 1858 Mason Johnson 34.' There's a question mark after his age. 'Gerald Davis 52 Louisiana 3 weeks. Good health. Night crossing.'" She moved her finger to the next row. "'June 30, 1858 Marion Hill 18 Georgia 12 days. Hungry. Blisters on feet. Frightened. Read scripture over her. RFH.'"

"Riverfront House?" Tess asked.

"Sounds likely." Janice turned several pages at a time. "Looks like a different kind of list. Only names on this page."

"I recognize some of these." Tess held the giant flashlight high over the ledger. "'Palmer, Putnam, Williamson, Rankin, Frederick. *Bickerton*!' But..."

"But what?" Brad took a pair of reading glasses out of his pocket and slipped them on. "I thought it was a list of runaways." He bent over the ledger. "Howard Bickerton. My great-great-grandfather. What's the question mark for? And what does it say next to it?"

LuAnn shook her head. "It's so faded. I can only make out two words. *Truth* and *free*."

"'The truth shall set you free?'"

"Maybe. But why would someone write it next to his name?"

"Good question."

"This is more than just a ledger. It's a journal too. Listen to this." Tess's finger hovered over a line. "'From the lips of the woman who died in my arms last night just moments after touching shore on the Ohio side—"I never lost hope that I would see the goodness of the Lord in the land of the living. Because of you, my last breath is free air." Oh Lord, that I might never fail to hope in your goodness.'"

The skin on LuAnn's arms tightened as goose bumps prickled her flesh. "Who wrote this?"

Tess turned to the back of the book. "We need pictures of every page, and then we need to give it to... Who? We need to give it to someone we can trust."

"Margaret Ashworth?" Janice suggested.

"I guess."

"It belongs to the bank." Brad spoke with disappointment edging his tone. "I'll tell Paul Townsend about it and strongly, strongly urge he give it to Margaret Ashworth for safekeeping and preservation. I'll also strongly urge him to let it remain with the inn. That is, if they accept your offer. Which we need to talk about, by the way."

Janice rested her fists on the bar. "How much do we have to up our offer to secure it? I'll throw in my husband's pension if that's what it takes."

LuAnn nodded. "I can dip deeper into my savings than I'd planned."

"Me too." Tess rested her fists next to Janice's.

LuAnn looked around at the room, willing the walls to speak to her about the hidden ladder and the tunnel and the woman who kept this record. God was going to do something with this place. With *them* in this place. She was sure of it. Her mother had some investments and told her to further invest the money, but that wasn't living on faith. Her mother would have loved this dream. She took a deep breath and a leap into the future. "We can use my inheritance."

Tess snapped pictures of each page as Janice held the book open and LuAnn held the flashlight above them for adequate light.

"Wait." The brighter light enabled LuAnn to decipher more of the journal entries. "She mentions Howard Bickerton again. This one is in October of 1857." She bent close and began to read. "'Howard Bickerton is not who he says he is. Is it possible I am the only one who knows this truth? Oh Lord, my God, what shall I do with this heavy weight? If I tell anyone, including my husband, our work will end. Yet if I do not, my conscience shall taunt me. What will I say when I stand before Thee? What will Thee say to me? Shall I, like Rahab, be commended for my deceit because it saved the lives of others, or will I be condemned for allowing a lie to continue, and an evil man to prosper with his lies?'" She stopped and looked up.

Brad's brow was lined with deep grooves. "Lies? Is she saying my great-great-grandfather is the evil man who was lying?"

"It sounds like it." Janice cringed as she answered, as if hating to deliver bad news. "Do you know anything about it?"

"No clue. There's a statue in his honor over in East Park. He was a philanthropist. He helped found the hospital, and I think he and his wife started an orphanage." He shook his head, dazed. "Don't mention this to the aunts until we can figure out more. I don't think Irene remembers her great-grandfather, but Thelma idealized him. This might, quite literally, kill her."

Tess continued taking pictures. "My printer is out of ink, but I'll buy more tomorrow and print copies for all of us. There must be more clues here. The diary goes until 1863."

When Tess finished, Janice carefully wrapped the journal in her sweater and ceremoniously handed it to Brad.

"I hope you guys will still let me hang out here with you if it turns out I'm the great-great-grandson of a horse thief or a pirate."

Janice's eyes gleamed. "I, for one, would love to hang out with a pirate. Wouldn't you, LuAnn?"

Ignoring the question, LuAnn picked up a pair of unwrapped chopsticks and stuck them in her purse. "*If* we get it."

Brad clasped the journal to his chest. "I just have a sense in my spirit that you three are going to be living here. I don't know who the other bidder is, but I just can't imagine anyone else doing justice to the inn. I can already see myself sitting at a table right over there"—he pointed to a spot in the corner near the bar—"enjoying a cup of coffee and something delectable whipped up in that kitchen."

Janice sighed. "I can see book clubs and Bible studies meeting here."

LuAnn envisioned the room the way it could look by Christmas. A fire in the hearth. A Christmas tree in one corner, covered with clip-on electric candles and handmade wood ornaments and looped with strings of popcorn and cranberries. Soft music, maybe by a harpist or a violin trio playing Christmas carols. The coffee bar side would be filled with small round tables—antiques finished with high-gloss polyurethane tops for easy cleaning. Fresh flowers in small crocks on each one. On the fireplace side, plush, comfy love seats and chairs. An old trunk for a coffee table. Boston ferns spilling from brightly painted pots on wrought iron stands. The entire first floor would smell of roasting coffee beans, homemade oatmeal spice muffins, and cranberry pumpkin soup. And there in the corner, a couple, gazes locked as if they're alone in the room as they drink hot chocolate or peppermint mocha from red and white Christmas mugs. Then slowly, without her noticing, he pulls a small velvet box from his pocket and slides it across the table. She opens it and gasps, tears springing to her eyes. He takes her hand, sliding the ring onto her finger. "All I want for Christmas this year, and every year, is you."

She wipes her cheek, nods, and—

"Lu?" Tess smiled her. "We're going back down to the room to look for more treasure. Are you coming?"

"Me? Sure." She blinked, trying to erase the vision of the couple. What was happening to her? Was all this romanticism a result of time on her hands? A reaction to stress or grief? Or something else?

When they reached the sub-basement room, Janice ducked her head in but still couldn't force herself to set foot in what she labeled a "dirt-floored subterranean tomb that smells like dead fish." Tess looked very Sherlock Holmes, going over every inch with a magnifying lens on her camera as Brad meticulously moved the light from top to bottom, left to right.

"It's so cold in here. If this was used to hide escaped slaves, it must have been miserable." Tess ran her hand along the stones and suddenly yelped. "This one's loose!"

Brad aimed the light at the brick as Tess wriggled it free. The brick came out, and LuAnn crowded in close to Brad.

In the rectangular cavity sat a single brass skeleton key.

October 8, 1857

Prudence stumbled, foot caught on a limb she hadn't seen in the dark. On her knees, she paused a moment before rising. *Heavenly Father, I need Thee. Grant me wisdom. May I discern Thy will with sure confidence. If this man is not to be trusted, let me know.* Rising to her feet, she brushed dead leaves and dry grass from her skirt. In the silence, her pulse drummed in her ears. A rustle behind her caused it to stop altogether.

Patience. A laugh shook from her. "Thee can't follow me, goose. Go back," she whispered. Then again, a protective goose might be a help. Patience had once attacked Jason. They'd been laughing one moment, his large hands about her waist, lifting her off the ground and twirling her in a dizzying circle. The next moment, he was yelping in pain, his ankle bleeding, and a fierce, hissing white goose flapping around him. Prudence had laughed. A very wrong response. But the thought still made her smile. "Come, my little protector." She dipped into her pocket for kernels of dried corn.

She should have told Jason she was going out tonight. If he woke and found her gone, he would be alarmed. A trip to the privy only took so long. What would she say if he was awake when she returned? *Lord, I hate deceiving.* Yet wasn't that the very nature of what they did? She, a Melungeon woman, her grandfather stolen from his home in Africa, her grandmother from Portugal, had passed herself off as a good little Quaker—a white woman—just a simple farm wife who spent much time in the sun—when the mission called for it. When the delivery required her to look like a house servant bringing produce to market in Virginia, she could play that role too. Deception was what God had called her to.

She reached the water just as the boat docked and a man stepped out. Of solid build, with a full bushy beard. If he did not respond correctly to the password, she would pretend to be inebriated, a Riverfront House guest who'd imbibed a bit too much, and she would stumble on her way. Though she'd never tasted spirits, she could play that role too.

Stepping out of the shadows, she cleared her throat, making her presence known. "Good evening, sir. A fine moonlit night."

"Indeed, ma'am. A sky full of stars."

Rising from her curtsy, Prudence waited as the man doffed his cap, then tied the small boat to a tree limb.

Pulling a handkerchief from the pocket of a well-cut suit, he sighed and wiped his face. The night was cool. Fear had dampened his brow. "Very glad to meet you. I have heard so much good."

"And I, of thee and thy father, sir." There would be no names spoken aloud. "Have you been to the Riverfront?"

"Not yet. My partner and his family and my son and I are staying onboard the steamboat we came in on tonight. I will meet the current owner in the morning. I felt it important to connect with you first. I'm told you have procured employment there?"

"Yes. I am a housemaid. It gives me access to the whole house. I understand thee plan some additions?"

"Thanks to your recommendations. We hope to start within the week." He glanced over his shoulder. "I fear I may need to hire someone else who shares the vision. My partner and I…shall I say…on the journey here we discovered a difference in our life philosophies."

"I'm sorry to hear that."

"Thank you. I'm just glad I discovered it before we actually started work. We will begin with what we have. The tunnel is functional?"

"I believe it can be used immediately."

"Praise be to God. I want to be of service as soon as possible."

"Sooner than thee may be ready, I fear. A shipment is due tomorrow night."

The man stroked his moustache. "You will be there?"

"I will bring them across the river."

"Then I shall see you on the morrow."

"Godspeed, sir."

CHAPTER THIRTEEN

LuAnn woke just after three a.m. She'd been restless all night. No sense continuing to tussle with her pillow. And her thoughts. She pulled out her laptop and read a message from one of her former students. Caleb had just graduated from Ohio State with a degree in journalism. "All because you encouraged me to keep writing, Ms. Sherrill. I'll dedicate my first book to you."

She blinked away the mist that gathered in her eyes. Would she always miss teaching? Would there be other opportunities to mold young minds? God had gifted her with a passion for teaching and a love of teenagers. He wouldn't take the gift away just because she was no longer getting a paycheck, would He? She answered Caleb, telling him she was proud of him. This was her legacy. Though she'd never physically given birth, she had ushered more than two thousand young men and women into adulthood.

Picking up the unused notebook she'd found in a box in her closet, she said a quick prayer. "This one is more important than all the others, Lord. Guide these possibilities." This book was just for her, though the contents would overlap with the ongoing mission of the inn. Janice and Tess had children and grandchildren to fill their nurturing needs. She needed something to move into the empty hole in her life once filled by her students and caring for her mother. These were the pages she would fill with ideas of how she could touch the people around her. She opened it and began her first list. *Teach ESL classes. Volunteer at a food bank. Form a poetry-writing group for teen girls. Start a blog.* After filling a page, she closed the book and fell asleep. And dreamed.

Ivory lace draped over her shoulders, she walked toward the hazy light at the end of a dark, narrow tunnel. Someone was there, waiting for her. A mournful howl echoed off the brick walls. "Just keep walking," he said. "Walk to me." Something crunched under her foot. She looked down to find the floor littered with peanuts. "I have the key, LuAnn. Come and get it." She tried to yell but couldn't form the words. Like floodwater, the peanuts rose, to her ankles and then her knees. *Please wait. I'm coming. I'm—* His hand gripped hers, pulled her to his chest. "I'm here. It's all okay. You're safe with me. You can rest now."

Her eyes popped open. The sense of peace remained, until the questions started. Who was that? Jesse? Jesus? Brad? No. The answer left her more confused than ever.

Her father.

Throwing off the covers, she got up and dressed, and headed out for a bike ride. A sheer veil of pink covered the eastern sky. A cacophony of birds—robins, finches, sparrows—warbled and twittered, encouraging the sun to rise. She rode toward the river, a destination in mind. This was the time of day Tess had seen a light in the window of the inn. If she saw it, she was calling the police.

Grass, wet with dew, sparkling under streetlights. The first sleepy residents ambling about, walking dogs or stretching for a morning run. She loved the sounds of a city awakening to a new day.

The smell of the river, mingled with the heady scent of roses, gladiolas, and daylilies, reminded her of being a little girl. Back when things were happy. Before her father left, and fear became a daily companion.

Shaking off the memories that dampened her morning joy, she sped up, slowing when she reached the cobblestones on Second Street. The shaking made her laugh, but she resisted the urge to hum with her mouth open like she'd done as a child on these bumpy streets, giggling as her voice jiggled. She leaned her bike against the side of the building she hoped she'd be calling home. Ramping up all five senses, she took a deep breath. No eucalyptus this morning. She listened. Nothing but the cry of a loon and the lap of the river against the hulls of the boats tied at the dock. She padded across the street and stood in the brush surrounding the entrance to the tunnel and looked up at the windows, phone in hand.

Nothing.

And then footsteps. Distant, across the road. A spike of sunlight flashed on a rustling bush next to the inn—on the side of the building blocked from the wind.

On shaking legs, she strode across the street, toward the bush. *Lord, keep me safe. Stop me if this is stupid.*

The branches stilled. Not a leaf moved. Something white dangled from a twig. She grabbed it. A receipt, from the 24-hour convenience store on the next block, for a two-liter bottle of soda. And a bag of peanuts.

"You got him, Lu! Or her. Or it." Tess set her phone on the counter next to the sink. "The girl who answered says we can come over any time and look at their surveillance videos. I don't know if she's supposed to do that or not. I wasn't going to ask."

Janice sighed and laced her fingers around her coffee cup. "The exact minute our suspect checked out is on the receipt, so all we have to do is take pictures of the person."

LuAnn looked again at the date and time. "We were at the inn at that very moment."

"You're right. That's when we were there with Marv and Joe. Our suspect was at the inn at the same time." Janice gave a faux shiver. "Ick."

"Let's pray he or she or it isn't wearing a hoodie." Tess picked up her keys. "Or a ski mask."

"What if we don't recognize him?" LuAnn pulled her hair back with a headband. She was still sweaty and out of breath from the ride home. She'd called Janice from the inn, waking her up to tell her to hightail it over to Tess's. "'Him' because it's easier to say, though if I were a betting person I'd put money on it being Saffron or Maybelline. Or Charlotte."

"Then we're back to square one." Tess sighed. "Can't exactly report someone to the police for buying peanuts. Unless we have actual hard evidence of a crime being committed, we need to keep it quiet. If the authorities get involved, there may be reporters and that could lead to the whole world finding out about the journal."

Janice downed the last of her coffee. "Well, let's go do this thing."

"The In Crowd is in the house and ready to find the culprit."

"Hey." LuAnn laughed. "If we close this deal, we're going to be the double *n* Inn Crowd."

"Oh!" Janice giggled. "Why didn't we think of that before?"

"It's a sign." Tess raised both hands, high-fiving Janice and LuAnn. "We are absolutely going to get it."

LuAnn jumped out of the chair she'd just eased into. "Let's go catch Peanut Person."

The girl, probably no more than eighteen, showed them how to reverse and fast forward then, stepped out of their way. "This is from the camera pointed at the front of the store. You'll be able to see the front counter and the door. The peanuts are right here." She pointed at the small screen. "I set it at ten minutes before the check-out time on the receipt."

"Thank you." Tess leaned over and pressed the arrow.

The picture wasn't good. Black and white and grainy. An elderly woman walked in, leaning on a cane. LuAnn settled between Tess and Janice. "Could that be Margaret Ashworth?"

"Too tall. Maybelline?"

"Too round."

The door opened again and a young woman walked in, head down.

"Saffron?"

"Maybe." Tess bent to within six inches of the screen. "No. Not unless she's wearing a wig."

"Which she would if she were smart." Janice nibbled on her fingernail.

They waited. Six minutes passed. The old lady walked out. "What's the girl doing? How long does it take to buy a bag—?"

The three exhaled at the same time, a sigh of sheer frustration.

"That's Joe!"

Tess pounded the steering wheel with the heel of her hand. "I was so sure we were going to figure this out today."

LuAnn shrugged. "We're sure Joe's not guilty?" She sent Janice an apologetic glance. "No stone unturned, you know."

Janice scowled. "I know. But Joe bought the peanuts just minutes before he joined us at the inn, and the peanuts were already there, scattered all over. I suppose he could have been there earlier with a different bag of peanuts, but...I've known Joe since high school. He's a good guy. I can't think of a single motive he'd have for buying the inn or stopping us. Can we not put him on the list, please?"

"We have much more obvious suspects. No lineup or mug shot for Joe yet." LuAnn felt the heaviness in the car and once again felt a responsibility to lighten the mood. "Can we do something totally self-serving? I want to look at bedding and curtain fabric for our apartments. Or for my future house. Anyone want to join me?"

Tess put the car in gear, and they headed for Linen Lines.

"Thirty percent off on quilts." LuAnn scanned the window-size posters. "And half off flannel sheets. Might be nice to have those for winter." She took out the Design and Decor notebook. "Especially in our Northwoods room."

"Do you guys know what you want for your own themes?" Janice held the front door open. "I'm thinking nautical."

LuAnn shrugged. "Whatever jumps out and says, 'Pick me!'"

"Now that's the adventurous spirit." Tess pointed to a swath of pale-gold fabric covered in deep-red flowers and trailing green vines. "Those colors."

"Nice." LuAnn fingered the fabric. "Makes me think 1930s. Curtains out of this with a plaid spread in the same color—" Her phone buzzed, and she pulled it out of her pocket. Brad. "Hello."

"LuAnn, I found something. Can the three of you meet me at the inn?"

Shopping vs. clues? No contest. "We'll be right there."

Brad was waiting in front, pacing from the road to the door.

"What did you find? Must be something big to have you—"

"Did you write this?" Excitement, not accusation, riddled his words. He thrust a piece of paper at Tess—the note she'd written Camo Guy. It said, "No matter what you have done or what has been done to you, God loves you and longs for you to turn to him." She'd signed it, *Tess, a friend who cares.*

"Yes. Where did you get this?"

"Up on the fourth floor. Townsend wanted to see the ladder. This was just outside the closet. Maybe I should have, but I didn't show it to him. Did you leave it there?" It was clear he was hoping she hadn't and that this was another piece of evidence leading to answers.

"No, but I wrote it."

Talking over each other, they told him about Thorn and the box. LuAnn shook her head. "He's been living here? Going in through the tunnel every night?"

Brad nodded. "Apparently."

"That explains the light. And it makes sense why he'd try to stop us. Poor guy."

A grin split Brad's face. "Well done. An act of generosity solves the puzzle. I've heard people mention Thorn."

"What do we do now?"

"I say we surround the building tonight." Brad's eager expression reminded LuAnn of a kid playing cowboy. *I'll be the sheriff, guys. Gimme the white hat.*

Tess shook her head. "Pretty sure the guy would run if we set a trap for him."

LuAnn had a gentler approach in mind. "Why don't we write another letter and leave it where this one was?"

"We could leave a pen and paper and see if he answers." The most beautiful smile touched Janice's eyes. Something LuAnn hadn't seen on her in a long time. Hope. Strange, yet not, that offering it to someone else sometimes increased your own.

"I love the idea." LuAnn gave her a quick hug.

Brad raised both hands, palms up. "Well, it's not quite as exciting as mine, but it's nice. Very Jesus-like."

Janice nodded. "It is, isn't it?"

Sunday morning dawned hot and humid, promising the warmest day they'd had yet. LuAnn woke with more joy than she'd felt in months. They knew who'd been trying to stop them and why. And God had given them their first opportunity to use the inn for ministry. Without knowing it, they'd fed their first guest. She stuffed an extra pillow behind her, opened her Bible to Matthew 25 and read:

For I was hungry and you gave me something to eat, I was thirsty and you gave me something to drink, I was a stranger and you invited me in, I needed clothes and you clothed me, I was sick and you looked after me, I was in prison and you came to visit me.'

"Then the righteous will answer him, 'Lord, when did we see you hungry and feed you, or thirsty and give you something to

drink? When did we see you a stranger and invite you in, or needing clothes and clothe you? When did we see you sick or in prison and go to visit you?'

"The King will reply, 'Truly I tell you, whatever you did for one of the least of these brothers and sisters of mine, you did for me.'

She dressed for church in a teal sundress and tan sandals, grabbed a sweater, then went out to join Tess on her deck.

"There's something very strange here." Tess was poring over copies of the pictures they'd taken of the old journal. "I had enough ink to print the ledger part. Look." She handed LuAnn a page with names, question marks, and equal signs.

Howard Bickerton and ? Bickerton = Zephaniah Bickerton
Stuart and Charisse Dawson = Romulus Dawson
"Howard" and Charisse "Bickerton" = Zephaniah and Romulus "Bickerton"

"What do the equal signs mean?"

"I don't know. At first I thought it meant the names on the right were the children of the names on the left."

LuAnn stepped out of the shade to get a better look in direct sunlight. "This is the triangle!"

"What? Oh! Howard stole Charisse from Stuart?"

"I bet that's it. But who are Zephaniah and Romulus?"

"The twins, right? Then why are they listed separately like that?"

"The real question is, who would name a kid Romulus?"

"No kidding. Should we show this to Brad?"

"Absolutely. Bring it to show Janice after church, and we can call Brad later when you guys are free."

"You know you're invited." Tess's expression held a hint of pity. "My kids love you."

"I know. Thanks. I need coffee." She walked into the house and stood by the coffeepot, staring out the window. Sundays were going to be awkward until she made some other friends. Or lived at a busy B&B. She'd take them up on their offers once in a while, but she wasn't going to barge in on their time with kids and grandkids every week. She poured coffee and pulled a packaged protein bar from the cupboard. By the time she walked back out, she had a plan for the afternoon. "I want to check out the River Trail. I haven't been on a long ride since I got here." She patted her thighs. "And it shows."

Chapter Fourteen

The thermometer hovered just over ninety when LuAnn set out on the trail that had once been a railroad. The gravel path started a block from the inn and ran along the Ohio River, then turned north when it reached the Muskingum. She passed stately homes set on the hillside with a perfect view of the river. She'd always thought a home along the water would be peaceful. Would she still think that when all nine guest rooms were filled and the café was buzzing with conversation and orders for soup and muffins, lattes and cappuccinos? But there would be those times, in the off season, when things slowed down, mornings when she could sit at one of the small round tables-for-two she pictured near the front door. Time to gather her thoughts in notebooks, fill calendar spaces, and pray over the patrons who would fill their rooms and, sometimes, their hearts.

Would there be people who returned often, and those who came back every year to celebrate an anniversary or attend a convention? This wasn't an aspect she'd really considered—lifelong friends. *Lord, make us ready for whatever You have planned. Prepare us for busyness or disappointment. Help me to trust You with setbacks, delays, and difficult people. Please don't let the stress of running a business strain our friendship.*

The trail ended after a little over three miles so she turned around. The still river reflected the homes along its banks. What would have been visible back in the 1800s to the woman who'd kept the ledger and wrote the journal? Very few houses. Did a road run along the banks the way it did now? Did she live at the inn? How far did she venture away from it?

She would have loved to go home and spend the rest of the day devouring the journal, but it wouldn't be fair to the rest of them. She'd wait. Until then, to not look like a pitiful single woman, she'd keep busy. Maybe pick up a decorating magazine and check out McHappy's. She'd earned a doughnut.

On a whim, she rode toward Fifth Street. She'd been in her thirties before she'd wanted to return to Marietta to visit Janice, and in her forties before she had the courage to search out the house she'd lived in as a child. The two-story house with its white pillars and curved porch spindles was just as she remembered it. Tess had pushed her to knock on the door and ask for a tour. She couldn't, so Tess did it for her. The woman who answered was surprised but gracious, taking them upstairs and giving LuAnn a minute alone in her sewing room, the room that had once been LuAnn's bedroom—a place that had meant security, a symbol of a carefree childhood.

Until the morning her mother woke her before dawn to say Daddy had left and they were moving. Now.

What had her father done? Her memories were dim, but she couldn't meld the pictures in her head with the suspicions her mother's words, and Wilbur's, conjured. Her father, involved in loan sharking, gambling, or union corruption? It didn't fit with her image of him or the few pictures she had. But then, didn't the men who did those things have to live lives of deception?

Her life had so many parallels to the woman who'd penned the journal.

She slowed as she passed the house, now painted gray instead of blue, but didn't stop.

Shaking off the dark mood, she changed her mind about the doughnut and rode to the inn. She needed a future vision to dispel the one from the past.

She jumped off her bike when she reached the cobblestones and leaned it against the side of the building. Rounding the corner, she studied the tangled mess of overgrown woodbine and lilac bushes surrounding the inn. Janice loved gardening, but this was beyond anything the three of them could handle. They'd need to hire a landscaper to make sense of it.

Flowers. They needed baskets of blossoms and trailing vines. Fuchsia, lobelia, alyssum, and every shade of petunia known to God. And then they'd line the walkway with mums that would surround the place with yellow, orange, and rust just as the leaves were starting to turn. They'd need giant pots of—

"Hi."

LuAnn's foot slid off the sidewalk and she almost stumbled into Brad. "Oh!" She righted herself and stepped away. "You scared me."

"You were deep in thought." He laughed. "I know, you warned me that happens."

"I was landscaping in my head."

"Sounds painful. All that hoeing and raking." He grinned and crossed his arms over a neatly pressed striped shirt.

"Funny. What are you up to?"

He pointed at the top floor. "Thought I'd see if Thorn left you an answer. Very serendipitous that you're here."

"Very." She stood behind him as he unlocked the door. "Any word from the bank?"

He stopped, hand on the door handle. "No."

"What aren't you saying?"

"That I'm getting strange vibes from Townsend. He's being all mysterious about it. Won't tell me anything about the other offer. I doubt it came from our Mr. Thorn, unless he's a rich recluse who prefers to live in abandoned buildings rather than on his yacht."

Was it possible it was Charlotte, and he didn't know? Or was he just pretending? "Stranger things have happened."

"True." He opened the door. "Stranger things—"

The scarf flapped from the fan. And a new message covered the mirror.

Abandon all hope, ye who enter here.

Brad stood, hands on hips, elbows jutting out, in front of the mirror. "Rather ominous."

"It's a quote from Dante's *Inferno.*" LuAnn's sigh encompassed frustration and a touch of fear. "So much for reaching out in love and compassion."

"Maybe he hasn't read your note yet. Maybe he softened after that and just didn't erase it."

"Let's go see." She marched up the stairs.

"Woman on a mission." His footfalls trailed hers on the wood stairs.

"What was that snarky remark?"

"Not snarky at all. I like your focus."

"I'm a git 'er done kind o' gal."

"Like I said, I like that."

She reached the second landing and stopped. "Will we have to put in an elevator?"

"I don't know. I should have thought of that. I'll check on it for you. Unfortunately, I think if you have more than five guest rooms, you might need one. But there are loopholes for historical buildings. And I'm a loophole kind o' guy."

Her gaze swooped toward the ceiling and circled back to Brad.

He reminded her not to put any pressure on the railing leading to the fourth floor. For a moment, she bristled. She'd never welcomed the helpless female in need of protection role. Having lived most of her life without the care of a protective male in her life, she struggled to discern between genuine concern and condescension—something Tess and Janice had gently pointed out more than once over the years.

"What's that smell?" Brad banged on a warped window frame until it gave way.

"Eucalyptus." *And body odor.* "We smelled it the other day out by the tunnel opening."

"Cough drops?"

"Could be. It's used for a lot of things. Muscle aches, colds, sinus congestion."

"So we have a sick suspect."

"Or a health-conscious one." She scanned the floor, looking for clues. A skittering sound behind her made her jump. A mouse, scampering toward the stairs with a whole peanut in his mouth.

Brad laughed. "Maybe they're the culprits. They'd have good reason to keep you out."

"I'd love to see how they write on mirrors."

"Teamwork."

"Cute. Where did you leave the note?"

He pointed toward the first room on the south side. "Next to the ladder. That's where I found the one Tess wrote."

LuAnn held her breath as they walked in. The smell of sweat was stronger here. And something else.

"Dinty Moore."

"What?" She wrinkled her nose at him.

"It smells like canned stew. I lived on the stuff in college."

Good. Thorn was eating what they'd put in the box. She'd wondered if pride would make him refuse. But maybe the man didn't have the luxury of pride.

Brad bent and picked up a folded paper. Without looking at it, he handed it to her. Thorn's words covered the page in strong, bold cursive.

> Thank you for your kindness. May God bless you for caring. The world is filled with much goodness, but sometimes our hearts are too bruised to absorb it. There is no greater sorrow than to recall happiness in times of misery. I have tried to carry on, but I am tired of trying.

"Brad?" Her voice came out as a mere breath.

"What? What does it say?"

Her hand shook as she held it out. "I think it's a suicide note."

LuAnn sat on the dusty floor, knees pulled to chest. Brad sat two feet away, re-reading the note. "'... no greater sorrow than to recall happiness in times of misery.' Wow."

"It's another *Inferno* line."

"We need to talk to somebody who knows about this stuff." He pulled out his phone. "I have a buddy on the police force."

"Good idea." Hand still trembling, she took out her pocket notebook and pen. "While you do that, I need to answer this. What can I say?"

Brad looked at her for a moment, then held out his hand. "Would it be okay if we prayed?"

Would it be okay? Who was this man? She could only nod.

"Heavenly Father, You already have the answer to the question we are about to ask. You know the person who wrote this. You know him intimately, and You know what LuAnn's response needs to be. Please keep Your hand on this person. Use the words LuAnn writes to show him his life is of value and You have a plan for him, a plan for good and not evil, a plan to give him a future and a hope. Thank You in advance for what You are about to do in the name of Jesus. Amen."

"Amen." She whispered it, not wanting to disturb the holy hush that had descended on the room. A verse from the book of Matthew came to mind. *"For where two or three gather in my name, there am I with them."*

She picked up her pen and started to write words that came from the part of her she'd tried to build a wall around. *Dear friend, when I was betrayed and again when I lost the love of my life, I wanted to leave this world. In fact, I asked God to change His plans for me. Death seemed the only way to end the pain. But then a friend said, "What if you are not here on this earth to be pain-free? What if you are here to walk alongside others in their grief, to show them that life is given to us for so much more than happiness?" So I kept going, asking God to give me a purpose, a reason to get out of bed each day. And He did.*

She looked up, wiped the tears from her lashes, remembering the students and friends God had put in her path. *He brought a young pregnant girl, a boy whose father deserted him, and two widowed friends. We wept together, and prayed together, and learned to live again, together.*

My friend, we will not fully understand, this side of heaven, why God allows suffering, but we can know that we are here to do all we can to help ease it. And, by doing so, we find our own suffering diminished, and we find joy in the midst of it.

Brad sat, hands folded, eyes closed, as she wrote. He didn't ask to see it when she finished, but she held it out to him.

"I don't have to read it."

"I know. I'd like you to."

She watched his face as he read. Lips pressed together, he slowly nodded, then handed it back. "Thank you. You have no idea how much I needed to hear those words." His eyes clouded over. "It's only been a few months since I've been able to open my eyes in the morning and not almost double over when it hits me that I'm alone. I've been so self-absorbed for so long, but I think maybe I'm finally ready to do what you did, to start asking God to show me His purpose for my life. Thank you."

"I needed to be reminded of those words all over again." She reached out and set the folded note on the floor by the closet and stood. "Any chance I could interest you in a McHappy doughnut?"

A slow smile spread across his face like butter melting on one of Winnie's biscuits. "Make it a cherry Danish and I'm in."

"Deal."

Chapter Fifteen

Janice stared down at the note in her hand. "I know this handwriting." They'd convened at Muskingum Park, where Tess had spent the afternoon with her family.

"You do?" Tess froze, tea glass inches from her lips. "You know who wrote it?"

"It can't be." Janice shook her head. "It's just similar." She dipped a tortilla chip into salsa and rested her elbows on the picnic table as she ate. "What did the police say?"

"They need more information. We don't know for sure he's staying there every night. We don't even know for sure who it is." LuAnn looked down at the notes she'd taken from Brad's conversation with his buddy and hers with the hotline counselor she'd called after writing the letter. "They can't just send someone to sit there and wait for him to maybe show up."

Tess closed a bag of potato chips, then clutched her soda can with a look of resolve. "We have to do it."

"Do what?" Janice's voice held the now-familiar tremulous tone.

"Talk to him."

"How?"

"We camp outside the tunnel and wait."

"Or..." LuAnn took a quick breath. Did she have the courage to follow through with what she was about to suggest? "We camp out *in* the inn."

Janice dropped a chip, salsa splashing onto her pink blouse. "At night?"

"That's the only time he's there."

Tess nodded. "Plus, it would give us a chance to really explore the place."

"At night?" Janice dabbed at her shirt with a napkin, smearing the spot into a streak.

"Yes." LuAnn, emboldened by Tess's enthusiasm, leaned into the idea. "It'll be just like camping, only indoors and no campfire."

"Or mosquitoes," Tess added.

"Just a homeless man who eats peanuts and writes things on mirrors with lipstick." Janice gave a smile as weak as the tea she drank. "Fun."

LuAnn flipped a page in her notebook. "What do we need?"

"Sleeping bags."

"Flashlights." Janice folded her arms across the stain on her shirt. "Lots and lots of flashlights."

"Pillows."

"I've got two backpacking sleeping pads," Tess said. "Do you still have yours, Janice?"

"Somewhere."

"We need cookies."

Suggestions volleyed in rapid-fire from all of them.

"Water."

"Books."

"Porta-potty." Janice held up her hands when they stared at her. "Hey, just stating the obvious."

"We're only a block from the convenience store."

"Where I will not go alone in the middle of the night."

"We'll do the buddy system."

"Which means one of us stays alone in the inn."

Tess sighed, clearly exasperated. "Then we'll use the bushes out back."

"*Eeeeww.*"

"Pretend you're backpacking in the Tetons."

"But we're not, and there are laws against...you know, in town."

"Fine. I'll bring a coffee can."

"*Eeeeww!*"

"What else do we need?"

"Popcorn. We need enough snacks to share with Thorn."

"A gun." Janice shrugged when the other two stared at her. "I don't have one, but if I did, this would be the time to conceal carry."

"Chocolate."

"A thermos of coffee so we can stay awake."

"Permission."

Again, LuAnn and Tess stared at the wet blanket in the group. LuAnn smiled, then slowly reached in her back pocket. Brad had talked to Mr. Townsend about the notes and made sure the women had access to the inn. "Done." She dangled the key in front of them.

Tess clapped.

Janice covered her face.

"Let's go pack, girls."

“Mi pantry es su pantry,” Janice called from her bedroom. “This may take me a while. I have to find something,” They’d decided to stop at her place first, then head to Tess’s house. “Anything that sounds good, stuff it in the backpack.”

LuAnn grabbed Oreos, individual bags of Cool Ranch Doritos, and four cans of sparkling water and Tess made room for them in the pack. “Who knew sleuthing could be so fattening?”

A soft thud came from the back of the house. “Hey guys? Come here.” Janice sounded like she’d just encountered a ghost.

“What happened?” LuAnn threw a bag of trail mix onto the table and followed Tess to the bedroom. “Are you okay?”

Three open boxes, each filled with file folders, sat on the carpeted floor. “I’m fine. But look.” She held out a paper with *Syllabus* written at the top—in large, bold cursive. Writing that was all too familiar. Janice sank to the floor.

“It’s him, isn’t it?”

“Where did you get this?”

“It was from a workshop I took, probably fifteen years ago, when I was teaching up in Macksburg. The handwriting on the note kept bugging me. It’s so distinctive. I had to find this to prove I was wrong. Turns out I’m not.” She picked up the paper, hands trembling. “The shop teacher at our school wrote it. He quit teaching and left Maysville, maybe eight years ago, after his wife and daughter were killed in a head-on collision with a drunk driver. It was awful. There was always something about him, long before that, that made me think he was one of those kind but tortured souls, you know? I never heard where he went." She looked up at them, face pale. "His name is Tory Thornton."

They got to the inn just after eight and decided on the room across the hall from the one with the ladder. And the note. As they settled in, Janice told them more about the man they now thought of as Tory.

"I thought of him so often after Lawrence died. On those days when I felt like I couldn't breathe because of the grief, I thought of him. Losing a spouse is horrible, but in the back of your mind you always know it's a possibility. I just couldn't imagine losing a child at the same time. They only had the one little girl, and he was always showing pictures of her in the break room. She was only six."

Janice mopped tears with the sleeve of her shirt. "Tory was the kind of guy who should have had ten kids. They flocked around him. He'd always have a group of boys hanging out in the shop room after school. He never talked about his faith, but once I saw him sitting with a kid with his arm over his shoulders, and I could hear him praying. It was such a beautiful prayer. He could have lost his job for that, but he wasn't the kind to let that stop him." She sat on her sleeping bag and closed her eyes.

Their mood subdued, they sat and read until the light filtering in through dirty windows was too thin to see. Though they'd brought flashlights, they didn't want to take a chance on scaring Tory away. LuAnn stretched and yawned. "Why don't you guys try to get some sleep?" She opened a Thermos and poured herself a cup of coffee. "I'll keep watch."

"Okay." Tess plumped her pillow. "I'll set my alarm for two hours." She slid into her sleeping bag. "What if we hear him but we're all too stiff to move?"

LuAnn rubbed her hip. She was already feeling her joints tightening from sitting on the floor. She moved to her knees and arched her back, then stood to touch her toes.

"You make that look so easy." Janice nestled into her sleeping bag. "I wish I had your body."

"Stop that." LuAnn knelt, sitting back on her feet. "You are beautiful and there will be no more of—"

The low, keening wail they'd heard before seemed to fill the building and rattle the windows.

Janice clutched her sleeping bag to her chest. Tess scrambled to her feet, and LuAnn did the same. The noise swelled, then faded, rose again, and finally died away. "What *is* that?" Tess whispered.

"I don't know, but I'm not staying here." Janice fought her sleeping bag like a butterfly beating against the walls of its chrysalis. When she was finally free, and breathless, she picked up her pillow and draped her sleeping bag over her shoulders. "I'm leaving."

"But you're the one he knows. You have to stay." Tess tugged at Janice's pillow. "Come on." She bent and pulled something out of the backpack. "We have Dove chocolate. Sea salt and caramel. Your favorite." Her sing song voice was toned to mesmerize. "You know you want it. You know you can't resist." She opened a tiny square, foil crinkling in the silence, and waved it under Janice's nose.

The bag and pillow plopped to the floor. "Okay. I'll stay." She shoved the chocolate into her mouth. "But only because it's not safe to leave alone. And because Tory might need a familiar face." She grabbed two more pale-blue foil-wrapped squares. "Not because you bribed me with chocolate."

"Whatever you say."

They sat back down. And waited.

LuAnn, sitting up straight, woke with a start from a sound sleep. She'd heard something. What? She stood, rubbing the small of her back to quell the spasms. There it was again. Something scraping on the floor across the hall. She poked Tess's shoulder and tapped her foot against Janice's leg. Tess popped up like a jack-in-the-box. Janice didn't move.

In the dim light of the streetlamp, LuAnn pointed to her ear and mouthed, "I heard something."

Again, the muffled scraping sound. Tess nodded and shook Janice's shoulder. Finally, she opened her eyes. "What? Where?"

Moving like a woman half her age, Tess laid her fingers over Janice's mouth and whispered, in a barely audible voice, "He's here."

Janice sat up, brushed the hair out of her face, and closed her eyes again. Silently, LuAnn joined her in praying for strength and the right words. When Janice's eyes opened again, she straightened her shoulders, took a deep breath, and stood. Barefoot, in leggings and an oversized T-shirt, blond curls in comical disarray, she somehow appeared a force to be reckoned with. As she padded toward the door, she signaled LuAnn and Tess to follow.

Blue-white light illuminated the door opening on the other side of the hall. Janice stopped, shoulders rising in another bracing breath, and peeked around the corner. Without a sound, she stepped aside and motioned for LuAnn to take her place.

LuAnn clamped her hand to her mouth, muzzling the sound that wanted to escape.

Tory sat on the floor, cross-legged, holding a small LED lantern close to the letter she had left him.

Tears streamed down his face.

Janice took a hesitant step. "Tory?"

The man startled, rose to his knees. Fear widened his eyes. The letter fluttered to the floor.

"It's okay, Tory. Remember me?"

"Janice?" He squinted, as if trying to be sure it was her, then sat back on his heels. "What are you doing here?" And then he laughed. "I suppose you're wondering the same thing about me."

"I think I have some idea." She walked into the room. "You probably saw my friends LuAnn and Tess at the meeting. Can we come in?"

"S-sure." He brushed his hands across his cheeks and leaned against the wall. "You left the food with Emma."

Janice nodded as the three sat on the floor, giving him plenty of space and not blocking the door. "Is Emma a relative?"

"Almost." His eyes reddened. "My only connection to my oldest—*only* daughter."

Janice tipped her head, clearly confused by the statement.

"Anyway, thanks for the food."

"We couldn't have you living on peanuts."

"Peanuts?"

"LuAnn found a bag in the basement, and there were peanuts all over the kitchen floor."

"I saw that. I think the mice had a peanut party. But they didn't get them from me. Consumed way too many packets of runny peanut butter on hard crackers in the service. Not a fan."

Janice looked at Tess and LuAnn, a question in her eyes.

"You wrote the notes." Tory pointed at the paper next to him.

"Yes." Janice picked up the letter. "LuAnn wrote this one."

Tired, sad eyes turned to LuAnn. "Thank you. I... thank you." He looked back at Janice. "I'm so sorry about your husband. I wanted to contact you, but, sometimes it's just..."

"Too hard to get close to someone else's grief when yours is still so raw." Janice's gentle voice brought more tears.

Tess glanced down at the letter. "Everyone handles loss differently. I threw myself into my job and volunteering after my husband died. I thought if I could stay busy enough I wouldn't have time to think and the pain would just lessen with time." She folded her hands, rubbing one thumb against the other. "Eight months later, I collapsed in the classroom. I was physically and emotionally exhausted. I had to take a semester off to let myself grieve." She tipped her head toward LuAnn and Janice. "These two walked through it with me, letting me cry or scream or shake my fists at God. They literally prayed me out of the darkness." She blinked and tears lost their hold on her lashes. "All that to say, it's too hard to go it alone."

Tory nodded. "I was always the one helping someone else. Even now, the only thing that's kept me going is meeting with one of my former students once a week. Kip and I play music or build things in his dad's basement."

Kip. The boy who worked at Bar-B-Cutie and the hardware store. The boy who'd protected Tory.

"I suppose it sounds dumb, but I didn't even know how to ask for help."

"I get that." Janice's compassionate smile seemed to heighten the glow in the room. "I thought I had wisdom to offer LuAnn when her fiancé died, and I wonder now about all of the supposedly great advice I gave Tess when she lost her husband. But when Lawrence died there wasn't anything anyone could say for weeks that I could even listen to. It all sounded like noise, and all I wanted was to curl in a ball and shut everyone out." She pulled at a loose thread on the bottom of her shirt. "What you said in your note about our hearts being too bruised to absorb the goodness around us…that really resonated with me. So many people extended kindness, but it all felt like an invasion. I wanted to stay in my cocoon and pretend nothing existed beyond it."

"How long has it been?" Tory looked at Janice with the tiniest glimmer of hope.

"Fourteen months." She fingered the wedding rings she still wore. "An April snowstorm. We'd had such beautiful spring weather and then woke up to a white world. I can still see Lawrence standing at the door, Bible in hand. He was heading out to lead a worship service at the nursing home. I told him to be careful, and he laughed and quoted from Proverbs 31. 'When it snows, she has no fear for her household; for all of them are clothed in scarlet.' And then he grabbed my red knit scarf and threw it around his neck like he was the Red Baron, and kissed me and walked out. Twenty minutes later, I got the call."

"I'm so sorry. Did you know Lawrence came to see me after Margie and Jen died?"

"No. But it doesn't surprise me."

"I think I was rude to him. He was so gracious, and I just . . ."

He didn't need to finish. Everyone in the room knew the ending to that sentence.

"You're serious?"

"Absolutely." LuAnn shook Tory's large, rough hand as Janice and Tess picked up his things. "We can't guarantee anything until we know for sure it's ours, but as soon as we close, we want to start landscaping and we'll be tearing down wallpaper and sanding woodwork while the renovations are being done. We can use a pair of strong hands around here."

Though still ragged and unkempt, the man who stood before them carried himself with a confidence that hadn't been there an hour ago. He turned to Janice. "You're sure your daughter won't mind, about the apartment?"

"She's been fretting about what to do with that garage apartment after I move out."

"But are you sure you're ready to move out now, before you know if you get the building?"

"I'm sure. It's time. I've been living above Stacy's garage for a year. She and I will be much better friends if we aren't living side by side."

Tess put her arm around Janice's shoulders. "And we gain someone to do a third of the housework."

Tory offered his first wide smile. "Hate to spoil all your spooking fun, though."

Janice cocked her head to one side. "Spooking fun?"

"The notes on the mirror and that weird howling sound. Very effective, but—"

"That wasn't you?" They answered in one voice.

"Me? Huh? No. I thought you were trying to scare me out."

LuAnn rubbed her forearms. "But you put a Dante's *Inferno* quote in your letter."

"Only because you—I mean someone—had used one on the mirror." His jaw slackened. "So who…"

Another sentence he didn't need to finish.

Chapter Sixteen

"Back to square one." LuAnn crossed Camo Guy off the suspects list.

"But, hey, we have ourselves a handyman and groundskeeper." Tess stretched out on a chaise on her patio. They'd spent the morning turning her home office into Janice's bedroom. And introducing a showered and clean-shaven Tory to the man who had taken over the pulpit after Janice's husband. Pastor Ben led a men's support group that would welcome Tory with open arms. After not getting to bed until well after two the night before, they were all tired.

"Assuming we have grounds to keep."

LuAnn suddenly realized it was the first thing Janice had said since they'd settled on the patio at least fifteen minutes ago. "You okay?"

"It's just…dredging."

LuAnn nodded. "Like you said, it's still so raw for you. But while you were talking to Tory this morning I kept thinking about that tongue-twister comfort verse."

"That fits perfectly." Tess trailed a finger down the side of her iced tea glass. "'Praise be to the God and Father of our Lord Jesus Christ, the Father of compassion and the God of all comfort, who comforts us in all our troubles, so that we can comfort those in any trouble with the comfort we ourselves receive from God.' You were walking that out, sister."

"I hope so." Janice stared down at an ant crawling across the cement. "Last night, when he said he keeps asking why, I wanted something profound to say, but I didn't have it because I keep asking myself the same thing."

"You had a beautiful answer." LuAnn reached out and slid her hand over Janice's. "You told him you couldn't start living until you started saying 'What now?' more often than 'Why?' That was exactly what he needed to hear."

Tess raised the back of her chair and sat up. "If any of us had sounded all church-lady-preachy, it probably would have scared him away. Do you realize what God did with all of our messy brokenness last night?"

"This is what we're here for, isn't it?" Janice pulled a tissue from her pocket and blew her nose. "Not just life in general, but us in particular, right here, right now. God has a plan for all this hurt, doesn't He?"

Tess squeezed Janice's hand. "It was you who spoke those words to LuAnn that she passed on to Tory."

LuAnn smiled. "'What if we are not here on this earth to be pain-free? What if we are here to walk alongside others in their grief, to show them that life is given to us for so much more than happiness?'"

Pulling a damp curl off her cheek, Janice said, "Now all we need is a place with hot soup and warm beds where we can walk alongside somebody."

"It'll happen."

"Yeah. I think so. It'll—"

LuAnn's phone rang. Brad. This was getting to be a habit she didn't really mind. She answered it.

"Hey, listen, are you and Tess and Janice free? They just put Thelma in an ambulance. Can you meet me at Selby General?"

"Sure. Of course. But..." *Why?*

"She's asking for you. All three of you."

"They're pretty sure it was a TIA, a ministroke. Her speech is a little slurred, but no other paralysis." Brad leaned against the wall as if it was the only thing keeping him up. "I stop over every morning on my way to work just to check on them. They always want to know the details of my day." His gaze fixed on the door to the ICU. "Thelma was on her bedroom floor, and Irene was trying to lift her."

LuAnn rested her hand on his arm. "Thank God you were there."

He nodded. "Irene was so disoriented and scared. I don't think it had even occurred to her to call 911."

"But they think Thelma will be all right?"

Again, he nodded. "I'll go ask if it's okay for you to see her."

"She was asking for us?"

A crooked smile tipped one side of his mouth. "She asked for Bradley's women."

"Wow, what an...honor." Tess's eyebrow rose as she grinned at him.

"As they were taking her out on the gurney, she kept repeating, 'Tell Bradley's women. We have to tell them now.' I think she meant it for Irene, but just before they lifted her into the ambulance, she grabbed my arm. Her speech was so garbled, but I'm sure she said, 'Before it's too late.'" He lifted the phone next to the door. "This is Thelma Bickerton's nephew, I'm wondering if the three—" He laughed. "We'll be right in." He hung up the phone, still laughing to himself. "She said I should bring you in ASAP so she'll stop harassing the lab tech."

The doors opened and they walked past the front desk where a woman in blue scrubs clapped. "Finally, you're here."

"What in the world?" LuAnn whispered as they headed to the curtained area in the corner.

Thelma lay, pale as the sheet she was trying to kick off, waving one arm and making it almost impossible for the poor man in Scooby-Doo scrubs to draw blood from the other. Picking up his plastic bin of vials, he stepped aside. "They just gave her morphine. Not sure how long she'll be coherent."

Irene sat in a chair, visibly shaken. Brad took the chair next to her and began talking to her in a low voice. Tess and LuAnn touched Thelma's left hand and Janice her right. "We're here, Thelma. We're here."

"Finally." Thin shoulders sank back into the pillow. "You need to know... not his... fault. She made him. He didn't want to. Everything... always... about Char... loved her... not his... fault." Translucent eyelids fluttered closed.

"Thelma?" Janice gave her hand a gentle squeeze. Nothing but steady, even breathing.

A nurse walked in. "We need to let her sleep. I hope she told you whatever was so vitally important."

LuAnn stared at Brad, who was still talking in hushed tones to Irene. Had he not heard Thelma's words? Or was he pretending he hadn't? "We'll leave then." She nudged Tess and shot a look at Janice that yelled, *NOW.*

"Wait." Brad stood. "I'll walk—"

"No. Stay. They need you." *And we, most certainly, do not.*

LuAnn walked out of the hospital and kept walking. Across the parking lot and onto Meadow Lane.

"Lu, slow down." Tess's flip-flops clicked behind her.

"There's no sidewalk, Lu. This isn't safe." Janice's voice amplified as LuAnn quickened her steps.

Half running, Tess caught up with her. "What do you think she meant?"

LuAnn skidded to a stop and turned. "Isn't it obvious? Brad's been playing us. All this time he's been going along, acting all shocked at the weird things happening at the inn and all the while he was the one making it happen. So Charlotte could get her way."

"What does Charlotte want? The inn?"

"Maybe. Who knows what her agenda is? But his is certainly clear." She started walking again, this time toward the car. "He's in love with her. And his whole goal in life is to be her puppet. Whatever Charlotte wants, Charlotte gets."

It wasn't until she reached the car that she realized she was crying.

"Lu, I'm sorry." Tess put her hand out but LuAnn moved away. "I didn't think your feelings for him went that deep."

LuAnn swiped at her face. *Neither did I.* And then it hit her. She felt betrayed by Brad, but not because of some romantic longing she'd had. She felt betrayed because of what it stirred up inside her. Those words... *Not his fault.*

They were the same words her mother had said about her father.

LuAnn woke from a two-hour nap feeling heavy-eyed and groggy. She hadn't cried herself to sleep. Though every fiber in her angry body wanted to, she wouldn't let herself waste tears on a double-crossing man. Been there, done that. No more. Ever. She stumbled out of the bedroom to find her two best friends doing just what she'd told them to do without her. When Tess had suggested they look at the old journal to get their minds off Brad and Charlotte, LuAnn had stomped away, telling them to have at it.

"Look at this." Janice leaned over the papers spread across Tess's dining room table. She held a page out to LuAnn.

LuAnn held the paper under the chandelier and looked at the paragraph Janice pointed to. Though the copy was clear, the writing was faded and hard to decipher.

> I told him about the hole in my heart only this seems to fill, and I asked him to consider that maybe God allowed this sadness in our lives for this very reason, so that we would desire to spend our days giving and helping others who hurt rather than in tears.

"Wow." LuAnn fought back the tears she'd refused to shed. "That's so close to what you told me and I told Tory." She looked up. "I wish we'd known her."

Janice nodded. "It's almost like she's one of us. I think we would have been good friends."

Tess held out another paper. "This is from a couple of weeks after the one where she said Howard Bickerton isn't who he said he is."

October 28, 1857.

For the sake of the cause and the children, especially that precious orphan boy, I have found a modicum of peace in my silence. In my years as a captive, I learned never to complain, never to repeat what I overheard. In my years in the company of Friends, I learned to be silent when I wanted to shout—in joy or in sorrow. This is a secret I will carry to my grave, and generations to come will live in the shadow of a lie.

A thread of kinship tugged at LuAnn's heart. Hadn't she lived much of her childhood in that very place? "In the shadow of a lie." She read the words out loud.

"Lu"—Tess spoke gently, as if testing the waters—"we want to figure this out. We may have no chance at getting the inn and we all have questions about Brad right now, but we can't just walk away from this mystery."

LuAnn set the paper down and picked up the Suspects list. Grabbing a red felt pen, she circled Charlotte's name. Twice. Red. Scarlett. A scene from *Gone with the Wind* came to mind.

"Earth to Ms. Sherrill." Tess waved at her.

"Was I doing it again?" LuAnn pulled out a chair.

Janice's curls wagged her answer. "Let us in on your mental movie, Walter."

"I was just thinking about Scarlett O'Hara calling Melanie a pale-faced, mealymouthed ninny."

Janice cringed. "I think maybe we should give Charlotte Red Dress the benefit of the doubt. We really know nothing yet."

Reluctantly, LuAnn agreed. "Then maybe that's what we need to be focusing on instead of the journal."

Tess took three Dove chocolates out of the bag on the table. "Who is she? Where does she work? What does she want?"

LuAnn caught the foil-wrapped square Tess threw at her. "Saffron would know." She picked up her phone and typed in Grimes Realty and put it on speaker.

"Grimes Realty. This is Saffron. How may I help you?"

"Hi, Saffron, this is LuAnn Sherrill. I was wondering if you could give me some information. I wanted to invite Charlotte, Brad's friend, to a gathering we're having. Do you have her number, or can you tell me where she works?"

"I can give you her work number." She rattled off the digits. "She's head of the sales department at the Porsche dealership."

"Working for Bart Sandman?"

"Yep. Anything else I can help you with?"

"No. Thank you very much."

"Hey, we're holding a symposium on endangered species tonight on the riverfront by the bridge. Seven o'clock. Want to come? It might help you understand why some people don't want you to buy that building."

An evening with the Green Shirts. Why not? "Sure. We'll be there."

"Cool. Have fun with Charlotte Bickerton."

Bickerton?

Huddled together, they peered around the corner of the convenience store, waiting for a glimpse of Charlotte. "It's twelve thirty." Tess sighed. "She has to take a lunch break sometime."

Janice yawned. "Maybe she's off today or maybe she brings her lunch."

"Maybe she doesn't eat. How else can you be fifty-something and a size two?" LuAnn massaged the back of her neck. Her entire spine was still stiff from so many hours on a hardwood floor. "Spying is hard on a body."

"No kidding." Tess arched her back, and the popping sound made them all laugh. "Know what you're going to say?"

"Sure. Something unthreatening like, 'What's your deal, Scarlett?'"

"That'll work." Janice giggled.

The side door opened, and Charlotte stepped out. Wearing a sparkly, sapphire-blue tunic and black Capri leggings. The soles of her strappy platform sandals had to be at least two inches high. LuAnn felt her resolve fading. Charlotte carried herself like the confident person LuAnn had always dreamed lurked somewhere deep beneath her daydreaming OCD external self.

"Go!" Tess shoved her from behind.

LuAnn stepped out, blinking in the unforgiving light. The kind of light that announced to the world her decision to turn down every invite for the Botox parties popular with her co-workers. Charlotte, on the other hand, would call midday light her friend.

"Charlotte! Hi!" She scampered across the street in clapping flip-flops, feeling frumpy in the white skirt and turquoise top she'd napped in.

Hand on the door handle of a bullion-gold Porsche, Charlotte raised jeweled sunglasses. "Yes?"

Breathless, LuAnn slowed as she reached her. "I'm LuAnn Sherrill. Not sure if you know who I am."

"One of the women interested in that old building down by the river, right?"

Old building? Was the disinterested tone just a ruse? "Right."

"How can I help you?"

"This may sound a bit impertinent, but, do you have lunch plans?"

"N-no. Just grabbing a salad at the Galley." She ran her fingers through flaxen tresses. "You're a friend of Brad's, aren't you?"

I don't know, am I? "Yes."

"Hop in."

Chapter Seventeen

LuAnn swallowed hard and glanced across the street. With a wave and a thumbs-up, she walked around to the passenger seat and slid into the butter-soft, already-cooled interior of the 911 Turbo S. New car smell mingled with Charlotte's light and spicy fragrance.

Flipping her hair over her shoulder, Charlotte turned down the music—something by the Piano Guys—and backed out. The car swiveled as if on greased ball bearings rather than rubber tires. "What can I do for you, LuAnn?"

Why is Brad in love with somebody with the same last name as his great-aunt? "Well, as you know, there are people who aren't happy with what we hope to do with the inn. If we end up with it, we want to be sure we have good relations with all of our neighbors. Since you were at the meeting, I just thought we could talk." *Lame.*

"That was quite a little show you three put on at the park. You have beautiful voices."

"Thank you." *But let's stick to the subject.* And speaking of voices, the Cockney lilt seemed much more subdued than at the meeting. "We hope to do some singing at the inn when we open."

"Nice."

Nice? Such a bland word. They chatted about the weather and the Porsche and got out of the car at the Hackett Hotel. Easy walking distance. Probably not in those shoes.

Her inner jealousy was showing.

They took their seats at the Galley and Charlotte ordered "the usual," which turned out to be a berry and crispy goat cheese salad. LuAnn ordered the *caprese panzanella*, otherwise known as bread salad. She'd first tasted it twenty-five years ago in a little Tuscan bistro. Her first trip to Italy. She'd said yes to dinner with Marcos, the dark-eyed chef whose face belonged on the cover of a regency novel, long before he brought her his signature *torta co' bischeri*—a pastry-lined cake with a filling mixture of rice, chocolate, pine nuts, and raisins. Addicting. As were those dark—

"LuAnn?"

"Oh. Sorry. So, you're a Bickerton."

"Yes. Again." Her nose wrinkled—the only ripples in flawless skin.

Divorced? Widowed? Somehow single again. "You must be related to Thelma and Irene."

"Yes. Distantly. My part of the family emigrated from England in the 1950s. I guess the original Bickerton here in Marietta was my great-great-grandfather's cousin or some such thing."

"What brought your family to Marietta?"

"Some inheritance we were supposed to get. Never did pan out. Not even sure what it was all about. It all happened before I was born. My folks are back in England now. They never talk about it."

And you're not insanely curious? LuAnn sipped her coffee and smiled like there wasn't a ravenous pack of starving history wolves yapping in her head. "Fascinating."

"If you get into that kind of stuff."

"I was a history teacher."

"Oh. Guess you would then. I do like old furniture. I'm hoping to start my own interior design business. And I'm kind of partial to old jewelry." She flashed a silver ring with a giant blue stone. "My grandmother's."

"I just assumed you had an interest since you were at the meeting."

"Yes. I was. I was just—"

"Lu!" Janice appeared at her side, breathing hard, vein standing out at her temple. "Hey. Hi." She nodded and almost smiled at Charlotte, then turned back to LuAnn, eyes doing some kind of wild dance. "I hate to interrupt your lunch, but we have an emergency." The eyes continued their gymnastics. "We need you. Now."

This was weird, even for Janice. LuAnn looked around but didn't see Tess. When she turned back, Janice was pinching her lips with her thumb and forefinger. The international spy signal for "Shut up"?

"I'm sorry, Charlotte. This is so rude." She stood, opened her purse, and pulled out a twenty. "Could you ask them to box my food and keep it for me? I'll be back to pick it up."

"No problem." Charlotte pouted—more sad little girl than flirty Kate Winslet. "I hope everything's all right."

"Oh, I'm sure"—she glared at Janice—"it's nothing serious."

"She was just about to tell me why she was at the meeting." LuAnn shook off Janice's hand on her shoulder as they flew out of the hotel like they were headed for a getaway car. "And there are some major secrets hanging out with the skeletons in her family's closet. She's not a descendent of Howard Bickerton. She's from a whole different branch of the—"

"So she's not Brad's cousin. That means they could—"

"That's not the point. Where are we going? Where's Tess?"

"Hostage."

"*What?*"

"At the inn. Green Shirts."

"I know. They're giving a symposium on endangered species. What does that have to do with Tess?"

Janice didn't answer. Not surprising since they were trekking at a speed fast enough to qualify for the Flying Pig Marathon.

Janice led across Second Street and then Greene, until they stood diagonally across from the inn.

"What's that noise?" LuAnn bent, hands on knees.

"Chanting."

Straightening up, she gaped at the ring of green circling the inn. Green shirts, sandwich boards, and picket signs that read: Copperbelly Snakes Have Rights! Bring Back the Fringed Orchid! You Are Not More Important than the American Burying Beetle!

And the angry chant "Make room for mussels! Make room for mussels!"

LuAnn fought for breath, then did the only thing a person could do under the circumstances. She laughed. And laughed. Until tears streamed onto her rumpled blouse.

Janice joined her. "I guess... it is... kind of funny."

And it was. Until she saw Tess, standing on the steps of the inn, arms jutted out like Wonder Woman. "What's she doing there?"

"They won't let her leave. She went to talk to Saffron. The Green Shirts were just hanging out on the road and all of a sudden they organized. I ran. I thought she was right behind me, but they got her. If she tries to walk away from the door, they swarm together like hornets."

"Did you call the—"

Saffron's long-haired, pale-skinned boyfriend pointed at them. "There they are!"

A wall of green surged toward them, led by a cameraman hoisting a massive-lensed camera that might as well have been a rocket-propelled grenade launcher. Janice latched on to LuAnn's arm, and they ran.

Until they just missed smashing into Brad.

Janice tightened her grip on LuAnn and gave a sheepish shrug. "I called him. Hope it's okay."

It was anything but okay. LuAnn glared at him. "Go stop your niece. Threaten to fire her or—"

He grabbed their hands and pulled them into the alley and across a parking lot. The Green Shirts were on their heels. Without knocking, he stepped inside the back door of Much Kneaded Massage and Back2Back Chiropractic. "Shh." He held a finger to his lips.

They padded lightly past closed doors to the front of the building. A petite forty-something woman in a pink yoga outfit sat at the front desk, all but drooling as she gazed up at Brad. "Hey, stranger."

"Okay if we hide out here for a few minutes, Brandy Sue?"

Brandy Sue? Who names their kid Brandy Sue? LuAnn wondered.

"You can stay as long as you want, sugar."

Ew.

Janice stood watch at the picture window. "Can we call the cops?"

Brad shook his head. "They're peacefully protesting. Sort of."

"Nothing about that is peaceful!" Janice wailed, then shrugged an apology at the girl behind the front desk. "Tess is going to end up on the endangered species list!" she whispered.

LuAnn took her first full breath since leaving the hotel. "We have to move with them." The thought turned to words before she'd really had time to analyze its wisdom.

"Huh?" Janice and Brad stared at her.

"I took a self-defense class. If you move with your opponent, you catch him off guard. Instead of resisting, you go along, using the other person's momentum against him."

"So..." Janice's mouth twisted to one side. "We march with them?"

"No. But we show them we're on their side. Maybe we donate money to their cause."

Janice nodded her head in agreement, her blonde curls, tightened by perspiration, bouncing. "What if we do what we offered Maybelline? We give them a corner of the basement for a display about endangered species and how we can all help to protect the environment."

"That could work." Brad put his hand on the doorknob. "Why don't we start by giving them a tour of the inn? You can offer to meet them halfway—you'll support their cause if they agree to be open-minded about the importance of preserving historic landmarks because of what they stand for."

"I like it." LuAnn shot a wary look at the front door. "How do we get them to listen?"

Brad held up one finger, then turned to Brandy Sue. "Mind if I use your restroom?"

Really? At a time like this? They were about to rescue Tess and sign a peace treaty with the people who had been wreaking havoc on their lives, and he had to answer a call of nature?

He was back in ten seconds, waving a white paper towel. "Surrender flag."

Hiding behind Brad, they walked out the front door.

"Stop! Hear them out! Be quiet!" Saffron waved her arms as she marched through the crowd. The ocean of green shirts parted like the Red Sea. Minutes passed before a semblance of quiet reigned. Saffron swept her hand out to LuAnn.

Me? She hadn't thought of what she wanted to say. She cleared her throat and summoned her teacher voice. She'd spoken to an entire assembly of squirrely ninth through twelfth graders. This was nothing. "We come in peace."

The Green Shirts were not impressed. Only Janice laughed.

"Seriously, we are not the enemy. We support your concern for the environment. We want to work with you. If we buy the inn, we need people like you to advise us on how to leave as small a footprint as possible"—where was all this coming from?—"to be a leader in this community when it comes to recycling and only using earth-friendly products. We want to buy only sustainably sourced and locally grown produce. It is our goal to landscape in a way that honors nature, planting flowers that are native to this land along the river."

The crowd stilled, and in the calm, she saw Tess step away from the door, unnoticed by the swarm.

"We applaud your desire to reclaim and preserve. We share that passion. This building, built in 1826, represents the indomitable spirit of Marietta. Within these walls, possibly hundreds of people escaping bondage and brutality on southern plantations, found safety. Right here, on the ground we now occupy, Ohioans, some freed slaves, some abolitionists willing to risk their lives and the lives of their families, fought, under the cover of darkness, to give men, women, and children the right to choose their own destinies, to not live and die under the yoke of oppression and discrimination. We owe it to those brave forefathers and mothers of this town to preserve their legacy. To remind successive generations of why we must defend the rights of all men, women, and children, no matter their skin color or ethnic origin, to live in a country where they are guaranteed life, liberty, and the pursuit of happiness!"

A slight girl with long black hair began to clap. Others joined in, slowly at first, until the applause expanded, exploding into a crescendo of cheers and high-fives.

LuAnn, suddenly drained and shaking, stepped back, making room for Brad to deliver his invitation. He slid in beside her. "Quite a proclamation, Abe."

"... originally called the Riverfront House, but around the time of the First World War, a new owner renamed it after a poem called 'The Wayfarer.'" Brad, who could still hold his own as a tour guide, unlocked the front door and led the troops into the main room. LuAnn's foot landed on something just inside. More peanuts? But it didn't crush under her foot. She bent quickly to avoid being stampeded by Green Shirts, picked it up, and stepped out of the way before opening her hand.

A button. An unusual button. Wood, about an inch and a half across, four holes, with an anchor carved in the middle.

Another clue?

Was it hand-carved? Had it been here for decades? More than a century? She could see the riverboat captain staggering in on his wooden leg, sidling up to the bar to spin tall tales of defending his cargo against pirates to anyone who would listen. And then, across the room, there she was, descending the stairs in her pale-blue gown, petticoats swishing, banana curls bouncing as she ran to him. His girl. Sure, he had one in every port, but this one was special. He reached out to her, picked her up, and a button popped off his coat. The coat she had made for— A woman with a leafless tree tattooed on her arm bumped into LuAnn, and her handsome captain and his one true love faded back into the walls.

"...building has served as—"

The now-familiar blaring, bleating, wail filled the room, vibrating window panes and eardrums. And it didn't stop. Saffron and the dark-haired girl screamed. A bald, tattooed man lurched for the door. Several brave protesters ran out with him. The others huddled together, hands over ears.

"What is that?"

"I heard this place was haunted."

"See, it should be torn down."

"Saffron, we need to do a séance and talk to the lost spirits." This from Saffron's boyfriend.

Finally, the mournful cow-in-labor sound tapered and stopped. Brad raised his hand. "If any of you know who is doing that, please ask them to just come and talk to one of us. This game is getting old. The place is not haunted. There are no lost spirits—"

"How do you know? There's only one way to find out." Boyfriend sat on the floor, closed his eyes, and began to hum.

"Moving right along." Brad grimaced at LuAnn and, in spite of the fact that she currently didn't care for the man, she laughed. "Let's take a look at the kitchen, and these ladies can tell you their vision. You may have heard"—he sidled around the end of the bar without missing a beat—"that these incredible ladies have already begun to reach out to the homeless in our community. Just yesterday they..."

Oh brother. One small act of kindness and he was using it as a bargaining tool. And how did he know about Tory anyway?

To LuAnn's surprise, Saffron left her boyfriend humming on the floor with the long-haired girl and two others and walked next to her into the kitchen. "I don't...I'm not...into all that." She scratched her neck.

LuAnn put a hand on Saffron's back. "Relationships can be hard, can't they?"

Saffron nodded. And clutched her throat. "I...can't..."

"Peanuts!" Brad dove at his niece. "I totally forgot!" He tackled her, throwing her over his shoulder. "LuAnn! Grab her purse! Find her EpiPen. Janice, call 911."

She had to run with him to untangle the purse from Saffron's shoulder without slowing him down. She found the plastic tube and flipped it open, dropping the case on the floor as she fumbled with the injector.

Brad laid Saffron on the sidewalk and LuAnn slammed the pen into her skinny-jean-clad outer thigh, counted to three, then pulled it out, dropping it to the ground. "Try to relax, honey." She rubbed the injection site. Brad cradled Saffron's head on his knee. Tess took her pulse.

LuAnn counted seconds until Saffron stopped struggling. The bluish tint of her lips began to pink, and then she breathed with her.

“I’m so sorry, baby.” Brad’s voice was rough, raw. “I never even thought about the peanuts.”

Saffron gave a weak smile. “It’s okay.”

A siren wailed in the distance.

Tess patted Saffron’s hand. “Guess you’re not our suspect.”

“Your what?” the girl whispered.

“Somebody left peanuts here. At least twice. We figure that person is the one trying to stop us from buying.”

Saffron’s eyebrows arched. “I would never do that.”

“Any idea who would?” Janice nodded toward the inn. A gray-ponytailed woman held the door open. Inside, Boyfriend still sat on the floor, completely oblivious to the fact that his girlfriend had almost become extinct.

“I think I’ll just rent a room here.” Brad collapsed into a chair in the ER waiting area. “I was in the ICU most of the night. If my family is going to keep scheduling reunions at the hospital, I might as well have my own bed.”

“Not a dumb idea.” LuAnn sat on the opposite side of the room. She had a list of his dumb ideas she’d like to ask him about, but the past hour had jumbled those thoughts into a mishmash of doubt.

She pulled a notebook out and began writing. Tess yawned and asked what she was doing. “Making a new suspects list.” Saffron had assured them Vincent, the boy in the trance, would never do any of the things they’d told her. In her words—"He's just not that creative." A doomed relationship if ever there was one.

"Who's left?" Janice poured four coffee cups and passed them around.

"Maybelline." *And Charlotte Red Dress.*

"We should have just stuck with her in the beginning. She has the best motive."

Brad blew on the steam coming from his Styrofoam cup. "She just might—" His phone, sitting on the end table beside him, rang. "Townsend." He held the phone to his ear. "Tell me you have good news for me, Paul."

"Seriously?" The smile left his face. Grooves carved into his forehead. "No. Of course you can't. I understand." He set the phone down, looked across the room at LuAnn, and shook his head. "I'm so sorry. The bank got an offer that's twenty thousand over the asking price. They accepted it."

October 9, 1857

"Don't forget the chandeliers." Prudence called across the kitchen to one of the two women working under her. If the Riverfront did not meet Mr. Bickerton's standards, they could be in danger of losing their positions. Though he didn't seem like a hard taskmaster, she could not be sure after only meeting him once, and then in a coded conversation in the dark.

She tipped the bread pans on their sides. Dark brown loaves rolled onto the table. The smell of warm, sweet yeast bread filled the room and she breathed a sigh. In less than an hour the true mission would begin.

She'd used the past few weeks to learn every inch of the Riverfront. Rumor had it that the previous owner had built the tunnel for smugglers, or pirates needing a place to hide out and store their plunder. She couldn't help but reflect on Joseph's story in the last chapter of Genesis and his words to the brothers who had sold him into slavery. *Ye thought evil against me; but God meant it unto good, to bring to pass, as it is this day, to save much people alive.* The tunnel may have been built for evil purposes, but God was about to use it to save many people.

"They're here!" Annie ran in, red-faced and perspiring.

Prudence wiped her hands on her apron and tucked stray wisps of damp hair under her cap. "Still thy soul, Annie.

We have done all we can. Mr. Bickerton is a kind man with a generous heart." She walked out of the kitchen ahead of Annie and around the end of the great carved bar. She glanced quickly at the mirror behind it. Spotless.

The front door opened and a bearded man walked in, followed by a plump woman covered in frills. Behind her, two little boys, maybe three or four years old, cowered. Prudence extended her hand. "Welcome to Riverfront House, Mr. . . . ?"

"Bickerton. Howard Bickerton. And this is my wife Charisse and my sons, Zephaniah and Romulus."

Blood rushed from her head. The room swayed. Prudence curtsied, bowing for as long as she could to regain her equilibrium. *Father God, what should I do?*

The man touched his lips to her hand. The contents of her stomach rose into her throat but she fought it down.

Another Bible story came to mind. Rahab, lying to save the lives of Caleb and Joshua.

Were there times when a lie was sanctioned by God? Was this one of those times? She needed to decide now, with her hand in the larger, gloved hand, and the scared, red-rimmed eyes of one of the little boys looking up at her in terror.

She needed to decide now.

Because the man who hovered over her hand was not Howard Bickerton.

Chapter Eighteen

Outbid. LuAnn stacked the notebooks, shoved them into a box, then marched into her room and kicked the box under the bed.

When she came out, Janice and Tess were on the patio, looking as wilted as she felt. Tess pointed with one unenthusiastic finger at the glass of lemonade she'd set next to LuAnn's chair. "This makes no sense. How could we all be so sure this was our destiny?"

Janice kicked off her sandals. "Maybe it's just a right turn. Maybe God had to dangle this in front of us to get us to look at the possibility of a B&B. Let's get back on the horse, start looking for another building. We have a business plan and menus and decor. We just need to transfer all that to another location. It might end up being something we'll like even better and we might just walk in, fall in love, make an offer, and that'll be it. No ghosts, no green shirts. I think the Lord was just giving us a challenge to make us ready, don't you?" Pearly white teeth flashed.

LuAnn closed her eyes against the bubbliness. "I don't have the energy to do this all over again." She held the cold wet glass against her forehead.

"Me neither." Tess sprawled in her chaise lounge, arms and legs hanging like they belonged to a limp and lifeless Raggedy Ann doll.

"Come on, guys." Janice hunched over her phone. "There has to be something in the area." After a minute, she said, "Here. This warehouse is only about a block from the inn. I remember it. It used to be an appliance store when I was a kid. Look at these cool old windows. We could totally go with an industrial look. You know, all steel and concrete."

Tess picked up the novel she'd set on the ground beside her chair. "Sounds cozy."

"No, you know what I mean. A modern look. Very minimalist. White walls, white bed linens. Then we bring in just a pop of color with a bouquet of flowers."

LuAnn growled. "Minimalism is just another word for stark and cold. If we were ever going to attempt this again—which we aren't—we'd want warm and welcoming."

"But we also want unique. How about this. A geodesic dome north of town. Oh, this is so cute. All the rooms are pie-shaped. Listen: 'For those searching for a back-to-nature getaway. Close to town and off the grid.'"

"Which means no electricity or running water."

"Fine. Okay, this one is more us. Cozy Victorian overlooking the river."

Tess's tinny laugh echoed off the side of the house. "When we say cozy, we mean adorable and inviting. When Realtors say cozy, they mean minuscule."

"Yeah, I guess you're right. It's a two bedroom."

LuAnn ran a hand over her face. She had to get her focus back. She'd agreed to the B&B idea partly because of what it could mean to Tess and Janice. She needed to give them another vision, something to look forward to. "We should plan a trip." The tiniest smidgen of gumption rose in her. "Someplace exotic."

"And unadventurous." Tess moved one finger. Probably as close to a gesture of agreement as she could muster. "Just white sand and spa treatments and fabulous cuisine."

"Right." LuAnn took a sip of lemonade. As the cold spread through her chest, it revived something else. Hope.

"Somewhere on the Mediterranean. Italy?" Tess suggested. "Greece?"

"Too many old buildings."

"Yeah, you're right." Tess pressed her thumb and forefinger against the bridge of her nose. "Bahamas? All inclusive?"

"Perfect. Any place without old buildings." And shifty Realtors. "And no more mysteries."

"Preach it, sistuh!"

"We still have one to solve." Janice, the fearful one who was also, oddly, the eternal optimist of the group, smiled in another attempt to rally them.

LuAnn waved at the air. "We'll find out soon enough. And I don't think we'll be surprised."

Tess nodded. "And the way gossip scatters over this town, we'll probably hear by the end of the day."

"The sale will be public record, and the whole world will know Charlotte Bickerton beat us out to open her very own modeling studio. With one model."

All sound ceased. Even the birds seemed taken aback, stunned into silence by her tirade.

"Let it out, Lu." Tess removed her sunglasses. Tess, the queen of eye contact.

Feeling like a bug under a microscope, LuAnn squirmed. "Fine. I admit it. I don't have warm fuzzies for the woman. Why didn't she just offer twenty grand over asking in the first place? Why all the silly games?"

"Do you think it all had something to do with you and Brad? Do you think she was jealous that you and Brad went out? I mean, almost went out. For dinner."

"Evidently she had no need to be jealous. Thelma made it sound like Brad would lie down in a mud puddle and let her walk on him to keep her cutesy little shoes dry." She jammed her lips together, took a tight breath. "Okay. I feel better. Now I'm going to go into my room and get on my knees and repent and ask God to forgive me and help me see her in a whole different light." She grimaced at her friends. "All that was my way of saying I don't think the mystery is a mystery anymore."

Janice patted her hand. "I'm really glad you got all that out, but I wasn't talking about that mystery. We need to find out about Howard Bickerton and why he wasn't who everyone thought he was."

"Leave that for Mr. Grimes to figure out. It's his family."

Tess sat up, life returning to her appendages. "And what about the key? If the key we found goes to the box someone brought to the salvage store..."

"No. Stop." LuAnn raised her hand. "It couldn't be any more obvious that we're supposed to move on. I need to find another Realtor, a woman, who can find a nice, quiet little place..." Her words trailed off when her two best friends—supposedly forever—jumped up and left her.

"I'll get the journal pages."

"I'll get my laptop."

LuAnn sighed and rubbed her temples. "I'll get the aspirin."

"Prudence. Her name is Prudence Willard." Tess pointed to an almost indecipherable scrawl.

"I wish we could have known you, Prudence." LuAnn, who had taken an aspirin and spent time on her knees, looked closer at the name. Beneath it, in uniformly slanted cursive, was the verse from Psalm 118 she'd seen earlier. "It is better to trust in the LORD than to put confidence in man." She laughed. "I could not agree more, Pru."

LuAnn picked up another page. Tess had laid them out in rows across the living room floor, arranged by date. This one was from December of 1856.

It appears it is not God's will for me to be a mother, and yet I cannot seem to extinguish the hope inside. To this end, the hope of a child, I decided I should write something about who I am and how I got to where I am now.

I was born to free Melungeon parents, an only child. We had a small farm north of here, along the Muskingum. My father grew corn. Acres and acres of corn. My mother and I tended chickens and, three times a week, walked the five miles to town to sell them. It was on one of those trips to town that I first realized we were different. Not black. Not white. Mother kept her head down when someone called us half-breeds. I glared at the man, wanting to spit at him.

Every Sunday we took the buggy to church. I remember singing "The Old Rugged Cross" and pondering it at a very young age. How did one find beauty in the rough, horrid cross on which Jesus died?

I remember playing with friends after church. We were all the same there, Melungeon children of so many shades of brown. It didn't matter. We played tag and Graces and Annie Over. So much laughter. And then one day—I remember it being a warm summer day, and I was feeding the chickens—two men rode up in a wagon and asked to speak to Papa. I called for him, and he and Mother came out of the barn. The men pulled out guns. They wrapped Papa in ropes and then did the same with Mother. I screamed and screamed and Papa yelled for me to run, but I was only eight years old and I couldn't leave them. They hoisted my parents onto the wagon and I jumped in with them. Papa tried to push me away, told me to run to the neighbors, but I couldn't leave them. The men laughed and talked about how much someone would pay for a stubborn little half-breed.

LuAnn set the paper down. At least a hundred and twenty years separated Prudence's abduction from her safe and happy way of life and something eerily similar in LuAnn's life. *What can I learn from you, Prudence?* She picked up the paper again, but Janice began waving another one.

"We have to show this to Brad."

"Email it to him," LuAnn answered.

"Listen." Janice tapped the page. "Before, she hinted at Bickerton not being who everyone thought he was. Here she's kind of spelling it out." She stepped in front of the window and held the paper in both hands. "'The new Mr. Bickerton has given me authority to hire builders to do the work. He does not suspect that I know the truth. He has no choice but to go along with the plan already in place before he arrived, though I don't think he has any leanings either way. His cause in life is himself and the same is true of his wife. If, in this venture, they will look good by being touted as generous and compassionate stationmasters, they will play the part. Ironically, we have that in common. We are, the three of us, all skilled actors.'"

Janice lowered the page. "She pretty much comes right out and says the real Bickerton is gone and this guy is pretending to be him."

"Why did Thelma go and have a stroke right now?" Tess asked. "I bet those two know more than they're letting on."

Janice nodded. "Very thoughtless of her. But wouldn't you think Brad could get his hands on something? There must be other people in the family who have done ancestry searches."

LuAnn wrinkled her nose. "Charlotte knows something, or at least her parents do. Her family came here from England in the 1950s to claim an inheritance. She didn't seem the least bit interested in her family history, but that doesn't mean she doesn't have access to records. One of you should call her."

"I will." Tess picked up her phone.

"Wait a sec." Janice picked up another page. "'December 5, 1857. C says Z refuses to speak. She says it is because of leaving home. I know two truths she does not know I know. One being that this precious little one talks my ear off when we are alone. It is hard sometimes, to remind myself he is not mine. Today we made pies together. Today he told me about his daddy's secret box, the one he kept all his letters and photographs in. He says he told C he keeps his toy soldiers in it. He keeps it under his bed. Today he gave me the key and I read another truth.'"

"Do you think…?" LuAnn picked up her phone and dialed the salvage shop and left a message for Harry, then turned her attention back to Tess and Janice.

"…call the dealership. We have to talk to Charlotte."

"Let's invite her over for supper so you can finish your conversation." Tess looked at LuAnn.

"Invite her over so she can gloat?"

"Let's just play dumb about the inn. You're a history teacher. Tell her you want to start a blog about local history."

Janice pointed at Tess. "That's actually not a dumb idea. When we finally find that perfect place for a B&B, a blog would be a fantastic way to draw people to the area."

She hated to admit the idea had merit, but it did. "Okay. Let's do it. I asked God to show me how to see the good in Charlotte, so this idea is no coincidence. I need to get beyond this yuck. I'm a bigger person than this, aren't I?"

"Yes, you are." Tess scrolled and tapped. "Got it." She pressed her screen and put the phone on speaker. Bart answered.

"May I speak to Charlotte Bickerton please?"

"She just left, I think. Lemme go check. Who should I say is calling?"

"Tessa Wallace."

He put them on hold, and they listened to an instrumental version of the Beatles' "Yesterday."

Janice started singing along, but was interrupted when Bart came back on the line.

"Hello, yeah, sorry. Char left. Hey, you're one of those ladies buying the old hotel, right?"

Tess shrugged. "Yes." No one expected her to explain that they were now the ladies who were *not* buying the old hotel.

"Well, hey, I might as well give you her phone number. She's pretty free with it, if you know what I mean, and she said she had lunch with one of you and it got cut short. Quite a commotion you had over at your place, huh? Wish those tree huggers would do something constructive instead of just making life hard for decent, upstanding business owners. Why don't they go plant some trees at the cemetery or invent a way to turn disposable diapers into energy, you know?"

"Well, Mr. Sandman, I guess it takes all kinds to make a world."

"Yeah, you're right about that."

Tess tapped her fingernails on her knee. "It's really nice of you to give me Charlotte's number."

"Oh, yeah, almost forgot." He rattled off a number and LuAnn wrote it down. "Have a nice day now."

"Thank you. You . . . too." Tess's voice faded on the last word. She set the phone down and picked up a page. "Charisse," she whispered.

"What?"

"Charisse. Charisse Dawson. What if Thelma wasn't talking about our Char or Charlie or Charlotte? What if she was talking about Charisse Dawson?"

LuAnn nibbled her thumbnail as what-ifs cascaded before her, becoming a landslide. And then one rose to the top.

What if the "he" who loved a Char wasn't Brad? And the thing that wasn't someone's fault wasn't buying the inn out from under them?

Janice answered the knock at the door, and Charlotte walked in. She wore a knee-length vermillion skirt with a filmy sleeveless ivory blouse. And ivory sandals. And an ivory purse. "It's so sweet of you to invite me." She glanced around and complimented Tess on the decor. "I want to hear all about the ideas you came up with for the old hotel. I have some plans I want to run by you."

The sweetness melted out of Janice's eyes. Tess's lips pursed so tight they turned white. It wasn't enough the woman stole their dreams? Now she wanted to poach their ideas too? LuAnn pasted on a smile and invited Charlotte to take a seat at the table.

"Something smells delicious." Charlotte spread her cloth napkin on her lap.

Tess poured ice water. "That's LuAnn's tortilla soup. We were going to open a soup café, you—" LuAnn's elbow accidently connected with Tess's arm. She didn't need to be giving all of their plans to the enemy.

Charlotte cleared her throat. "I know I should have asked you, but I couldn't find your number on my phone and I just thought that if we're going to talk about my family history, we should have someone here who really—" Another knock at the door.

With a glance over her shoulder at Charlotte, LuAnn strode to answer it. Bradley Grimes stood on the front step, holding out a bouquet of daisies.

Chapter Nineteen

For a moment, LuAnn was caught off guard by the easy way Brad slid into the chair next to Charlotte. But the man appeared clueless. Maybe he hadn't heard Thelma's desperate ER plea, calling him out as a con artist, a conniving fraud... all for the sake of love. LuAnn gave him the most genuine smile she could resurrect. "How is Saffron doing?"

"Totally recovered. She's going to class tomorrow. She and her mom want to thank you for acting so quickly." He touched LuAnn's hand. "You literally may have saved her life."

"How's Thelma, and how's Irene holding up?" Tess jumped in, probably sensing LuAnn's discomfort under the blue-eyed admiration.

"Irene's staying with a lady from her church. She's always been too scared to stay home alone. They're releasing Thelma in the morning."

"Good to hear." Janice set a full bowl in front of Charlotte. "Let's get started and then we have some questions."

When they'd all been served, Janice prayed and Tess picked up a file folder with the journal pages. Sticky note tabs stuck out along the opening like daisy petals. "I'm glad you're here, Brad. We thought Charlotte might have some information from her branch of the family that could shed some light, and I'm sure there are details you can add."

"I put a call in to my mum," Charlotte said. "It's midnight there, and she and my dad are still out playing euchre."

Tess opened the folder. "You already saw the place in the journal with the question mark next to Howard Bickerton's name."

Brad nodded. "And the reference to his being a liar."

"Look at this." She handed him the page with what appeared to be a family tree.

Brad squinted as he read. "I don't get it. What's with all the quotation marks?" He slid it over for Charlotte to look at.

Howard Bickerton and ? Bickerton = Zephaniah Bickerton
Stuart and Charisse Dawson = Romulus Dawson
"Howard" and Charisse "Bickerton" = Zephaniah Bickerton and Romulus "Bickerton"

"So Charisse was married to Stuart Dawson and they had Romulus, and then Stuart died and she married Howard and they had Zephaniah?" Charlotte's expression mirrored everyone's confusion. "No. Zephaniah and Romulus were too close in age for that to work in the time line. So Howard had a son and Charisse had a son, and they lost their spouses and married each other?"

"That's a possibility." LuAnn searched for another page. "But that doesn't fit with Howard not being who he says he is. And Margaret Ashworth said Howard and Charisse had twins. And what is this all about?" She handed Brad a page and pointed to the entry from October of 1857.

Brad read it out loud. "'For the sake of the cause and the children, especially the precious orphan boy, I have found a modicum of peace in my silence...'" He looked up. "Who's the orphan?"

"Good question."

Brad sat back in his chair. "This is insane." His cheeks ballooned as he exhaled. "There's an old family Bible. I haven't looked in it since I was in college, but there's a family tree going back to before the Bickertons left Britain. We could compare dates and maybe figure out when Zephaniah and Romulus were born."

LuAnn hated to ask the next question. "Which one are you related to?"

"Zephaniah. I think. And Romulus is the aunts' father. I think. Right now, I'm not even sure. But if we're going to figure this out without causing Thelma to have another stroke, we have to do it tonight. Who's in?"

LuAnn stacked empty bowls by the sink and walked to her bedroom to get a sweater. As she was walking past the bathroom, she heard Charlotte's voice. The bathroom door was partway open. She could see Charlotte's arm, hand on the doorknob.

"...that rundown building. Can't see what anyone would want with it. Right." Charlotte laughed. "Give my love to Sissy and hug Dad. Love you too. Bye."

LuAnn backtracked to her room and walked out when she heard the squeak of the bathroom door.

Charlotte groaned when she saw her. "I think I'm too full to go sneaking around like a CIA agent."

"Me too."

"I just talked to my mum. She's going to copy the family tree stuff she has and send it."

"Good." LuAnn straightened a picture on the wall. "We didn't get to your questions for us. You asked about our plans for the inn."

"I did. Like I said, I'm kind of an amateur decorator, just for friends so far. I wanted to offer to help, but Brad just said someone else is buying it. I'm so sorry."

"Thank you. We actually thought you might be the one who outbid us." LuAnn gave a "how silly was that?" kind of laugh.

"Me?"

"Brad calls you Charlie, right?"

"Right."

"I overheard a phone conversation between you and Brad. He said something about Mr. Townsend eating out of your hand, and at the meeting you asked if it would go to the highest bidder, so we thought—"

"Oh!" Charlotte's airy laugh echoed in the hall. "That. I was trying to drum up some competition. It was just a way to, well, I suppose I should be honest, an attempt to warm the man's heart toward me."

"I'm sure Brad's heart…I'm sure he appreciated it."

"Brad? Oh no. You thought we…" Her face pinked. "No, I meant Paul."

"Paul? Townsend?"

"Yes. I've kind of got this thing for him."

"Oh." The laugh that bubbled out of LuAnn was woven with relief and compassion. "Men are complicated, aren't they?"

"Some of them are." Charlotte nodded toward the kitchen. "Not so much that one."

"What one? Brad?"

"Yep." She winked. "I saw him looking at you tonight."

Not another one. "We're just friends." *Or maybe we can be now.*

"Well, isn't that a lovely place to start?"

LuAnn felt a belly laugh rising, and it burst out as she lifted her arms and hugged her other new friend. *Oh, Lord, I see the good in her. Thank You.*

A sliver of moon and a sky peppered with stars. A slight chill laced the breeze that drifted through the car windows as they drove, headlights off, up Irene and Thelma's driveway. Tess, Janice, and Charlotte sat in the back seat. LuAnn sat in front, next to Brad. "This reminds me of the scene in *The Sound of Music* where the von Trapps were escaping."

"Only we're not escaping," Brad whispered.

"I hope we will when we find what we're after." Janice stuck her head out the window. "You're sure no one else would be here this time of night?"

LuAnn glanced at her watch. Nine fifteen.

"All of their friends know they're not home. And all of their friends go to bed at eight." He parked next to the garage, the building that had clearly once been a carriage house. "No one would think it was strange that I'm here, but you guys are on your own if the cops show up." He snickered and got out of the car.

Inside, the women knotted together in the dark kitchen while Brad went through the house pulling shades and drawing curtains. When he came back, he led them to the library. "Let's start in the most obvious place. The Bible is about three inches thick and maybe nine by twelve. It's kind of a reddish-brown leather."

LuAnn counted the floor-to-ceiling shelves. Three walls, six book cases each. Maybe a thousand books. "They'd keep it in a special place, right? Not just stuck randomly on a shelf."

"We have to think like Thelma. Do you know where she keeps her most expensive jewelry? In a Mason jar in the bathroom. Her theory is that a thief would be looking for a secure, hidden place."

"Good thinking." Tess ran a fingertip along a white-painted shelf.

They each wandered to a different wall, leaving LuAnn standing in the middle of the room, staring at a coffee table. Large and low, the carved piece had a deep drawer on each side—one facing the floral couch, one facing out. "Okay if I look in here?"

"Go for it." Brad stepped next to her.

"This feels invasive."

"I know. But this is kind of my second home. They don't travel much anymore, but when they did, I used to stay here when they were gone, sometimes months at a time. I have my own room upstairs."

"That does make this feel a little less criminal."

"They have an office upstairs. All of their personal papers and financial things are there. We won't invade that room or their bedrooms."

"Good." She knelt in front of the couch and opened the drawer. Magazines, crossword puzzle books, pens, pencils, a magnifying glass. She crawled around to the other drawer, which was filled with photo albums. She did a quick scan of the spines, making sure the Bible wasn't hiding among them, then lifted them, one at a time, reading the labels. Each book represented a decade. They were arranged in order, oldest at the bottom left. The album labeled 2011-2020 was the second from the top of the pile on the right. On top of that sat an empty album labeled 2021-2030.

Brad grinned. "I love their optimism."

The oldest book was labeled Old Family Pictures. She sat on the floor and opened it. "Brad, look." On the first black page, a black-and-white portrait framed in cardboard with an oval opening was held in place with glue-on photo corners. A stern-faced man with a bushy beard stood stiffly behind a somber woman with giant curls hanging in front of each ear. She wore a long, solid-colored dress with a lace collar. And on her lap sat a little boy, blond hair combed severely to one side. He wore buckle shoes, bloomers, and a wide-collared shirt. In white ink below the frame, were the words *Howard, Charisse, and Zephaniah Bickerton.*

Brad joined her on the floor. “Maybe Romulus was having a play date with a friend that day.”

“Right.” LuAnn touched the frame. “A family with twins doesn’t have a studio portrait taken with only—”

The photo moved beneath her finger. The paper corners lifted from the black paper, leaving a crusty triangle of shiny glue where each had been. She picked up the picture and turned it over. Bumpy cursive written over two white-painted stripes said, *Howard Bickerton family, June 1856.*

“The year 1856 is before any of the journal entries mention Howard. That means this was taken while they were still in—” Brad’s finger landed on her lips.

“Shh.”

The women froze at the sound of the back door opening.

“Winnie! Hi!” Brad’s voice drifted from the kitchen.

Janice and Tess settled on the couch, and Charlotte nestled in a high-backed chair. The three of them, legs crossed identically, following Brad’s hushed command to “Look natural.” LuAnn stuck the albums back in the drawer, but before she eased it closed, an idea hit. She lifted four albums and handed them out to the women who appeared as relaxed as plastic mannequins. Taking the other wing-backed chair, she opened the photo book on her lap and pretended to be engrossed.

She didn’t need to pretend. Two pages in, she found a picture of the inn, labeled Riverfront House, 1861. The same shutters, same front door. A darker-skinned woman in a plaid dress held the reins of a spotted pony in one hand and a basket of flowers in the other. Beneath the basket stood a long-necked and rather regal-looking white goose.

LuAnn slid her fingernail under the edge. The photo popped away from the page. On the back was a name. *Prudence Willard. 1861.* With all of the restraint she could conjure, she handed the photo to Tess, whose eyes opened wide as she read the back.

"That's our Prudence!" Tess mouthed.

Janice copied the wide-eyed look of wonder.

LuAnn studied three more pages of old buildings, recognizing several of them. A picture of the bridge taken from the other side of the river had caught the corner of the inn in the frame. And then, on the next page, an enlarged photo of the house they were in right now.

In front of the house stood a man and a woman and two young boys, almost the same height, maybe six years old. One blond, one with dark hair. Close enough in age to be twins. Different enough in looks to have been born to different parents.

"…ready to leave." Brad walked in, Winnie right behind him. "We were just…" He spotted the photo albums. "Looking at old pictures."

"Hi, Winnie." The four of them greeted her in unison. It sounded like an AA meeting.

"Hi. Good to see y'all." She patted her hair. "Sure didn't expect to see anyone tonight. Here I am in my sweats. I just come to put fresh sheets on Irene's bed. I did Thelma's yesterday and I just got to thinkin' how you got to do the same for each, you know?"

Brad smiled. "There's a bit of competition between those two." He turned to Winnie. "As long as I was putting the mail in the house, I thought I'd invite the ladies in. I was telling them about this old family Bible that used to be around. LuAnn's a history teacher. I think she'd be fascinated by the illuminations. Do you know where it is?"

"Got to be in here somewhere."

Brad stepped aside to let Winnie enter the room, and when he did, LuAnn saw something that made her bite her lip to muffle the sound of a small gasp. She closed the book and walked over to Winnie. "Did you hear we got outbid on the inn, Winnie?"

"You did? Seriously? That's awful. I'm sad for you, and I'm sad for myself. I was counting on that job you promised."

"Did you ever get to see the inside of the inn?"

"Back years ago when it was an antique store. Seen enough to know it could be fixed up to be something real pretty."

"But you haven't seen it recently? It's a bit more run down."

"I imagine. Time takes a toll on all of us, don't it?"

"It sure does." LuAnn patted the cuff of Winnie's tan sweater. "But we're hopeful something else will come up." She tugged on Brad's sleeve and hoped Winnie didn't see it. "We might be looking for another building."

"Good to hear."

She nudged Brad. "Well, we should be going. It's getting late."

They said their goodbyes and left. Brad turned to her after they got in the car. "What was that all about? Do you turn into a pumpkin when the clock strikes ten?"

"Did you notice the buttons on Winnie's sweater?"

"I did," Janet said wistfully. "They were beautiful. I love wood buttons. That whole rustic look is so—" She stopped when LuAnn pulled an identical button from her pocket.

Brad looked at her incredulously. "You stole a button from Winnie? You're a pickpocket too?"

"I found this. At the inn. Winnie says she hasn't been there in years, but this came off the sleeve of her sweater."

Tess held out her hand for the button. "Remember how she said she was using essential oils for her knee?"

Janice nodded. "Eucalyptus."

"And peanut soup is her specialty," LuAnn added. "Guess we have ourselves a new suspect."

"Whoa. Slow down." Brad turned right out of the driveway. "I've known Winnie Washington for years. There isn't a deceptive bone in that woman's body. Besides, she doesn't have the kind of money to buy the inn."

"Maybe she's not the buyer," Janice interjected. "Maybe she has another reason to interfere with the sale."

"If all the weird stuff quits now that we're not buying it, we'll know something." LuAnn scratched her head. "I don't know what we'll know, but something. Either the buyer was our spooker or—"

"The spooks just don't like you." Brad winked.

"Or the spooks just don't want *you* to be the one making the sale."

"Touché."

Her phone rang. Odd for this time of night and not a number she recognized. Normally she wouldn't answer it, but nothing was normal these days. "Hello."

"Ms. Sherrill? This is Harry over at the Salvage Mall. Sure hope I didn't wake you. I just couldn't wait to share this. I think I found the metal box."

Chapter Twenty

LuAnn woke with a sense of anticipation. Harry had said he wouldn't charge them for the box. He simply asked to be present when they tried the key.

They would meet at the inn at ten a.m. Even though the bank had accepted an offer, Brad was still managing the property.

She propped herself against pillows in a room that wouldn't be hers much longer. Opening her Bible to Prudence's verse, Psalm 118:8, she read, "It is better to take refuge in the Lord than to trust in men." She read the next verse. "It is better to take refuge in the Lord than to trust in princes." She smiled. *I learned that the hard way, didn't I, Lord?* She'd put too many men on pedestals in her life, made them princes in her eyes. Her father, Phillip, Jesse.

Read the first part.

The words were almost tangible. As if they hung in the air above her and she could reach out and touch them.

She went back to the verses. "It is better to take refuge in the Lord." And again in the next one. "It is better to take refuge in the Lord." She stopped there and wrote the words, twice, in her journal. She'd been so focused on the part about not trusting men that she'd skimmed right over the beginning.

As the smell of fresh-brewed coffee wisped under the door and sunlight landed in broken patterns on the bed, something dawned inside her. She'd spend thirty-five years not trusting men. Had she spent all that time trusting God, seeking refuge in him? Or did the box of old lists and calendars in the closet symbolize a lack of trust?

She laughed out loud when the thought popped in her head that she could make a list of the pros and cons of being a compulsive planner. She closed her journal, bowed her head, and said a simple prayer. "Help me trust You."

After showering, she put on a pair of faded Capri pants and a T-shirt that had seen better days. This might be the last time she'd see the inside of the inn before who-knows-who did who-knows-what to it. She wanted to be free to explore, to walk the tunnel and climb the ladder or uncover another mystery.

Was the box the one Prudence spoke of? Would the key fit? And if so, what would they find inside? Letters and pictures? Truth?

She walked out, in search of coffee.

Tess poured a cup and handed it to her. "What's on our agenda after the box reveal?"

LuAnn opened the fridge and pulled out an orange. "What would you say if I told you I don't know and I'm good with that?"

"I'd say…hallelujah!"

Brad was already there when they arrived. He leaned against the bar, bouncing the key in one hand and looking puzzled. "I just talked to Paul Townsend. He said he never took the new owners through the building."

"Never?" Tess and Janice spoke at the same time.

LuAnn squinted at him. "He's *never* brought them inside?"

"Unless I misunderstood him, that's what he said."

Janice stared up at the fan over their heads. "They don't need to. They've been here a ton of times."

"Owners?" LuAnn followed the track of Janice's gaze. "Plural?"

"He said 'they.' I suppose it could be just because there's no gender-neutral singular pronoun. It doesn't necessarily mean there's more than one person. He's being ridiculously secretive about this."

Why? LuAnn thought of the people they'd crossed off their list that had some kind of relationship with Brad. Saffron. Charlotte. And the new one they'd added. Winnie. One of them must be lying.

"Hello?" Harry walked in, carrying a shoebox-sized metal box under his arm. "Haven't seen the inside of this place since it was an antique store. Lots of potential."

LuAnn gave a poor excuse for a smile. "For someone."

"Not you?"

"No. We were outbid."

"I'm so sorry. I could really see your vision for transforming it. Too bad." He set the box on the bar. "It rattles. Definitely something in it."

Tess picked it up and turned it over. The brass box was about ten inches long, five deep, and four high. The outside was embellished with vines and flowers.

"These are lotus flowers. My guess is it was made in India sometime in the mid-1800s."

"Makes sense that Howard could have brought this from England." LuAnn touched one of the delicate-looking blossoms. "India was part of the British Empire until 1947."

Brad lifted the key. "Who wants to do the honors?"

"Tess found it. She should be the one to use it."

With a noisy inhale, Tess took the key and inserted it. "Here goes. Let's pray we're unleashing truth and not evil."

"Go for it, Pandora." Brad gave a throaty laugh.

Tess twisted the key. A quarter turn and it stopped. Nothing happened. "Might have to admit I'm a weak woman and ask for help."

Brad flexed his fingers as if loosening them. "Make room." Left hand flattened on the top of the box, he grasped the key. And his phone rang. "Sorry." He pulled it out of his pocket. "Irene. Better take it."

"Hi, Irene. Sure, I can do that. That's a good idea. Glad he's there to help. Right. See you in a few." He slid the phone back in his pocket. "Help me remember to pick up Thelma's blood thinner prescription when we leave. I might forget it after we find a couple cool mil in the box."

Harry raised his finger. "Five-way split?"

"Deal." Brad wiggled his fingers again, then cranked the key hard to the left.

The key snapped in half.

LuAnn tried one last time to shake the end of the key out of the lock. "Bubble gum."

"Huh?" Brad tried the smallest blade on his jackknife. Again.

"Teacher secret."

"I have some!" Janice dug in her purse and came up with two squares of Bazooka. "Who wants to do the honors?"

Brad held out his hand.

"You have to chew until all the sugar's out." LuAnn tapped her fingers on the bar as he chewed. Tess and Janice joined her in a percussion trio.

"Rr grs rr rly annering."

"We're annoying? I'm sorry. Maybe if we add lyrics." LuAnn started the song and the rest of the Inn Crowd found their parts. "'Chew, chew, chew, chew your bubblegum…'"

Brad rolled his eyes as they belted the Ella Fitzgerald song. On their second round of "'First you pop,'" a massive bubble exploded on his nose, perfectly timed.

Harry shook his head. "You guys really should take this whole show on the road."

Hmm…As LuAnn drummed her nails and sang, she envisioned the Inn Crowd Plus One eating up the highway in their touring bus, playing to packed-out venues night after night. *Tess,*

Janice, LuAnn, and Brad blazed on marquees from one coast to the other. While the girls sang, the man chewed. And popped.

"Done!" Brad pulled the wad out of his mouth and stuck it in the keyhole. "This better work, Teach."

"Guaranteed. I've retrieved more than one nose ring from a sink drain with this technique."

"Really? And you gave up teaching?" Tiny sucking noises accompanied his squishing.

"Good enough. Pull it out."

He pulled. And the key bit came out, smothered in pink.

Harry laughed. "Who knew? I know a guy who can probably replicate that. I'll take you there now if you want."

"That would be great." Brad turned to LuAnn. "Would you mind—?"

"We'll get the prescription. You go find the guy. What about the box?"

"Take it. Meet me at the aunts' house."

"Will do."

"Oh, a word of warning. Leo is there."

"And we need to be warned because…?"

"Don't be surprised if he sweet-talks you into loaning him money."

Winnie was there to let them in. "Come on in and make yourselves at home. They're not home yet. Leo probably suggested they go out for lunch."

Stopping for lunch on their way home from the hospital? Didn't Thelma need to rest? She didn't need to voice her thoughts. The tone of Winnie's voice said she shared them. LuAnn set the brass box on the table.

"What you got there?" Winnie picked up the box.

Did she already know about it? Maybe there were stories about the Bickertons passed down through generations in her family. Zephaniah must have told someone about his father's box. Why hadn't he taken it with him when he left home, and why hide it at the inn and not at home? Prudence must have said something to someone. A deathbed confession maybe? "We found this at the architectural salvage store. The owner thought it was probably made in India."

"Very pretty. What's in it?"

Maybe you should tell us. Maybe the original contents had been removed decades ago. Maybe they'd open it and find nothing but newsprint. "We don't know. It's locked. We found the key, but it broke." She studied Winnie's face.

"Interesting. I just made Thelma's favorite cookies. Have a seat. I'll make us all some tea and fix a plate of snickerdoodles."

Hospitable or evasive? Winnie seemed the epitome of the gracious hostess. Nothing about her said saboteur.

They sat at the oblong table. LuAnn surveyed the spacious kitchen. The cupboards reached the ten-foot ceiling. Glass handles on the doors reflected light from the wrought iron fixture over the table. "How much of the house is original, the way Howard Bickerton designed it?"

"Pretty much all of it, far as I know. I've been coming here since I was a little tyke. The bathrooms were redone maybe thirty years ago. All the plumbing and electrical were replaced, and of course the roof a couple of times and new furnace and A/C installed, but all the woodwork is original. Every time I'm cookin' I like to imagine what this kitchen looked like back when it was built. Woodstove, I imagine."

"And gaslights. They were probably wealthy enough to have an icebox."

"Used to be an icehouse out back. Still there, actually, they just use it as a garden shed. The river never froze over when I was a girl 'cause of the power plants. Does now, since they took 'em out, partially anyways. Probably would have back then."

"Once the railroad came in, they could have gotten—"

The back door opened and a tall blond man with a tropical tan walked in, followed by Irene supporting Thelma on her arm.

"Winnie!" The man wrapped Winnie in a bear hug and lifted her off the ground.

"Leo James Martin, you stop that!" Winnie's giggle belied her admonition.

"And these must be Bradley's women." He stepped out of the way so his mother and aunt could shuffle in.

Leo helped himself to a handful of cookies. Janice took Thelma's other arm. "Where are we headed, Thelma?"

"Living room sofa for now. I'm not sick, so I'm not going to bed." She directed a glare at her sister.

Winnie bustled into the next room behind Tess, Janice, and Thelma. "Got pillows and blankets all ready for you, Miss Thelma."

LuAnn put her arm on Irene's shoulder. "Let's get you settled in. The recliner in the living room looks comfy. I'll make more tea and bring in the cookies."

"No caffeine or sugar for Thelma." Irene pointed to a cupboard. "There's decaf bags in there."

"I can have *some*," Thelma argued from the living room.

Irene shook her head at LuAnn.

Leo plopped onto a kitchen chair. "Any coffee made?"

"I'm not the one who needs to rest. I'm going to visit with my boy." Irene patted LuAnn's hand, then pulled away. "What's that?" She pointed to the box on the table.

"Looks like a piece of junk," Leo said, stuffing a cookie into his mouth.

LuAnn pulled out a chair for her. "The man who owns the architectural salvage store found it."

"Huh. Weird-looking thing."

"He said someone brought it in a few years ago. It came from Wayfarers Inn."

"Interesting." Irene picked it up and shook it. "What's in it?"

"We don't know. It's locked, and the key broke."

"Too bad."

"Brad's getting a new one made. He'll bring it here."

"Oh. Good. Curious thing." Irene pointed to the cupboard to the right of the sink. "Would you mind taking a glass of water to Thelma? Doctor said she was dehydrated so she's supposed to drink a lot, and not just tea. She won't take it from me, but maybe you can convince her. Stubborn old woman."

"I'll give it my best."

"I'm going out to get the mail."

"Irene, I can do that for you. Or..." LuAnn stared at the tropical son. No hint he'd gotten the clue.

"I need to limber up. Haven't been able to do my stretches for two days."

"Okay, if you're sure." LuAnn filled a glass and took it out to Thelma, who shot a look at the kitchen as she took it.

"I could put a squeeze of lemon in it if that would help."

"Might. Never have been a water person. If God wanted us to drink water He wouldn't have made sweet tea."

"Good point. I'll get the lemon." As she walked toward the kitchen, her phone rang. She didn't recognize the number, but the way things were going, she wasn't about to ignore it.

"LuAnn? This is Charlotte. My mum just sent me a bunch of stuff I think you and Brad need to see. I talked to him, and he said I should talk to you about meeting somewhere."

"We're just getting Thelma settled. Why don't you come here?"

"Will do. See you in five."

She set the glass on the counter by the sink and opened the refrigerator. As she did, she glanced over at the table, expecting to see Leo in the same slouched position.

But Leo was gone.

And so was the box.

Chapter Twenty-One

"Janice? Tess? Can you guys come here a minute?" LuAnn stood by the window, eyes glued to Leo's car. When they came in, she pointed at the table. "Leo took the box."

"It's no good to him without the key," Tess whispered.

"Unless he has another one." Janice walked out the door and stood on the step, hands on hips. "Where's Irene?"

"She went to get the mail."

"I see the mailbox. I don't see the midget."

"She wanted to get some exercise. Maybe she took a longer walk."

"On the highway?" Janice turned slowly. "I bet *he* took her. Leo stole the box and kidnapped his mom, and he's going to call and ask for ransom money any minute."

"His car's still here."

"Well...maybe hers isn't. We need to check the garage." Janice stepped inside. "I'll sit with Thelma. You guys go look."

"Oh, no you don't." Tess wagged a finger at Janice. "If anyone's going out there, we're *all* going out there."

"I have to wait for Charlotte." LuAnn shrugged. "You guys have fun. Yell if you see anything. Or anyone."

"Why is—" Janice stopped as Brad pulled into the driveway. "Saved by the Brad."

"And the Charlotte." Tess turned to LuAnn. "Why is she here?"

"Her mom sent some family tree info she said we'd all want to see."

Before Brad and Charlotte reached the back step, they were volleyed by rapid-fire information.

"The box is gone."

"Looks like Leo took it."

"And Irene."

Brad held up a hand. "Irene's gone? Or Leo took Irene?"

"Yes." The answer came in three-part harmony.

He turned to LuAnn with an expression that said, "Help!"

She gave him the rundown. "We were just going to go look in the garage to see if Irene's car is gone."

"You think Leo kidnapped his own mother?" Charlotte's flawless forehead pleated. "Why would he do that?"

"Who knows? Or maybe they just ran off. Maybe there's a gazillion dollars in the box and maybe Leo is the one who's been spooking us so he could buy the inn and find the box."

Charlotte held out a file folder. "I think you guys should read what's in here."

Brad offered a patient smile. "We will. But first we need to find my aunt."

"I think you should read this before you do."

With a shrug, Brad motioned for them all to head inside. "Let's powwow in the library."

Brad kissed Thelma's cheek and said he'd only be a minute. They had business to discuss.

Charlotte sat on the love seat, and Brad and LuAnn crowded beside her. Tess and Janice pulled the wing-backed chairs as close as they could.

With a flourish, Charlotte withdrew a paper from her folder and set it on the coffee table. A copy of a dark and grainy photograph. "This is Howard Bickerton's family, taken in 1854."

A bearded Howard stood behind a chair on which a blonde woman sat, cradling a baby. Next to Howard stood a young man, probably in his late teens.

"Who's that?"

"That is my great-great-grandfather, Matthew Bickerton. Howard and Marta's oldest son. The baby is their son Zephaniah."

"Wait. Marta? Not Charisse?" LuAnn glanced at Tess, whose eyebrows tented in sharp points.

"My great-great-great-grandmother, and Brad's great-great-grandmother, was Marta Bickerton." Char pointed at the email she'd copied. "Now look at this. My mother said it was in a sealed envelope and looked like it had never been opened. My parents found it back in the fifties in my grandmother's things. It's part of what prompted them to come to the States." She handed it to Brad. "It's from Matthew to his attorney, written in 1866."

Brad cleared his throat. "'Dear Mr. Cooper, In hopes of making amends with my father I traveled to America. It was my desire to lay all of our differences to rest and reunite with my little brother. I was eleven when my mother died—'"

"Marta died?" Janice's eyes sparked. "Hmm…"

Charlotte nodded and Brad continued. "'...and so very angry when I ran away and went to live with my uncle. My father could have forced me to come with him to America and often I wished he would have, but I understand now why he didn't and that is why I came, but what I find here on my arrival at the hotel he purchased is something so horrific and confusing I can barely find words. The man claiming to be my father is a stranger. I do believe the boy they call Zephaniah is indeed my brother, but it is hard to be certain as I have not seen him for nine years. The child is bright and seems content, though quite an introvert and afraid of strangers. I have not confronted the man, nor told him who I am. I gave a false name when I registered here. Mr. Cooper, I long to know the truth about my father and take my brother home with me, but I must be advised of my legal rights before I proceed. I cannot seek counsel here as I know not whom to trust. Please advise as hastily as possible. Sincerely, Matthew H. Bickerton.'"

The paper rattled in Brad's hand as he sighed. "Wow. Can't get any clearer than this."

Charlotte got up and started pacing. "Do you realize what this means, Brad?"

"I'm beginning to."

"Bradley! Cousin Charlotte!" Leo bounded in the room with long, heavy strides.

Brad stood, confusion etched on his face.

Leo hugged Charlotte and then Brad, giving the requisite three man-pats on the back. "What have you two been up—"

"Where's your mom, Leo?"

"Huh?" He stepped back, as if shoved by the accusation in Brad's voice. "I came in here looking for her. She's not upstairs." He tipped his head to one side, bleached hair tumbling across his forehead.

The guy was an incredible actor. LuAnn resisted the urge to clap.

"What's going on here?" Leo backed toward the door. "Some kind of secret meeting?" His laugh landed flat.

LuAnn stood. "What happened to the brass box that was on the kitchen table?"

"How should I know?" Leo held up both hands, palms up. "It was there when I went upstairs." He took another back-step toward the door. If they didn't do something quick, he was going to bolt. LuAnn slid her hand toward her back pocket, watching Brad do the same thing.

"Sure it was." Brad pulled out his phone. "Hand it over now or I'm calling—"

A ripple of thunder rattled the windows. Tess walked to the window. "It's getting really dark. We have to find Irene."

"What do you mean 'find' her? She's not lost." Leo rubbed the back of his neck. "What's going on, Bradley?"

"Your mom went out for a walk and didn't come back. And the box disappeared. But you know that part."

"How do you know my mom didn't take the box to look at it?"

"Take it where?"

"How should I—"

"I see her!" Tess pressed up closer to the window. "She's backing out of the garage."

"Where is she going?" Brad's gaze lasered into Leo. "Is she covering for you? She has all your life. Why stop now, huh? Get her to drive off with the box because who would suspect an old lady of theft, right? Brilliant as usual, Leo." He motioned for the women to follow him and pointed to Leo as he flew out of the library. "Don't you dare leave. We. Will. Find. You."

Brad barked orders as they ran out. "Tess and Janice, block the driveway. Char, stand by the back door." He pointed to the side of the garage. "Lu, come with me."

Following Brad, LuAnn squeezed through the narrow space between the doorframe and the moving car.

"Aunt Irene! Stop!" Brad grabbed the handle on the driver's side. The car kept moving.

LuAnn pounded on the window. "Stop, Irene!" Her palms squeaked against the glass as Irene sped up. As she backed toward the road, they ran after her.

"We know Leo took the box."

"We know he's the one who's been trying to stop us, and we know why!" LuAnn screamed at the top of her range.

The car skidded to a stop.

Irene fell into Brad's arms, sobbing. Her words were unintelligible as they helped her to the house. Leo stood by the door. "Mom, what's going on?"

"Don't...know. So confused. So confused."

LuAnn grabbed Brad's arm. "Stroke?"

"Could be. Thelma was babbling nonsense before the ambulance came."

Leo stepped forward, but Tess stopped him. "No deal. Can't give you the chance to coach her on what to say."

"What? Are you people crazy? She's my mother!"

Sidestepping Leo, they took Irene into the house and settled her in her recliner. Janice knelt in front of her. "She's not making sense, but her speech isn't slurred and there's no evidence of paralysis."

Tess held Irene's wrist. "Her pulse is fast but strong and regular."

"Maybe we just need to let her rest." No sooner had the words left LuAnn's mouth than Irene's snores joined Thelma's, both increasing in volume as if the sisters were competing.

The front door banged open in a gust of wind. LuAnn ran to shut it. Why was it unlatched? She looked around. "Where's Winnie?"

"Good question." Brad called up the stairs. No sound but the pounding of rain.

LuAnn eased over to Brad and leaned close to his ear. "We may have the wrong suspect."

"I think you're right."

The door burst open again, and Winnie walked in with the mail and a dripping umbrella. "What in the world? What's wrong with Irene?"

"She's just upset." Brad glared at Leo and Winnie. "I think we should all go into the library and have a little chat."

"I'll bring tea." Winnie slid out of the damp sweater with the missing button.

"No, Winnie." LuAnn put a hand on her arm. "This time we just need you to bring your alibis."

"Me? Why would you think I would do a thing like that? I have no interest in buyin' that building, even if I had the money. I was lookin' forward to working for you all. Why would I interfere like that?"

She had a strong point. And if she was guilty, she was hiding it like a pro. LuAnn reached in her pocket for the evidence she'd retrieved from her purse and held it out in her flattened palm.

"My button. Where'd you find that?"

"At the inn."

"Well, I live across the street. Maybe it fell off when I was out walkin' my dog."

"*Inside* the inn."

Winnie's lips parted, but not a word came out.

Tess leaned toward her. "Did you know about the brass box?"

"I'd never seen it before you brought it here."

"But did you know *about* it?"

"No."

The woman looked traumatized. LuAnn picked up the picture lying on the coffee table and handed it to Leo. "Do you know who these people are?"

"No clue." He stood in the doorway, arms crossed over his chest.

"This is Howard Bickerton, his wife Marta, and their sons Matthew and Zephaniah."

"Cool. What's that got to do with me?"

Charlotte walked toward him. "Where have you been the last two weeks?"

"New York."

"Do you have proof of that?"

"Sure do." He pulled out his phone and swiped to his Facebook account. Picture after picture showed him with a woman with brassy blonde hair. At Times Square. Rockefeller Center. The top of the Empire State Building. The inside of a posh hotel room. Candlelit dinner on gold-rimmed plates. The posted dates started in mid-May and ended yesterday.

Brad joined the huddle around Leo's phone. "You can afford all that, Leo?"

"Nah. My woman can. She owns an IT company. Gotta find a rich woman, Bradley."

Tess stepped away. "The pictures could have been faked."

"You people are certifiable." Leo opened his wallet and dug in his pockets, producing a claim check for baggage checked at LaGuardia, a receipt from Gramercy Tavern, and a ticket stub from *Hamilton*.

All eyes turned back to Winnie.

"I don't have no Facebook or receipts, but I was helpin' get ready for a rummage sale at my church every day this week. You can call my pastor and all the ladies in my Bible study and ask—"

A low, mournful wail reverberated through the room. Haunting, chilling, and all too familiar.

All eyes turned to Janice, who stood behind the piano, blowing on the Civil War bugle.

Chapter Twenty-Two

Brad tried the bugle, then set it down. "That's it. Definitely. But who in the world—"

The sound of the front door opening sent all six of them running into the living room.

Irene, wearing Winnie's sweater, slipped out the open door. Brad charged ahead, grabbing her, gently but firmly, by the shoulders. "Where are you going, Aunt Irene?" He spoke softly as he guided her back to the recliner.

"I don't…know. Where am I? Who are you?" Dazed eyes bulged behind the magnifying lenses of her too-large frames. "Who am I?" Her hands trembled, a tremor jiggled her chin. "I don't remember what I'm doing or who I—"

"She's fakin' it." Thelma tossed a wadded napkin at Irene. "That's enough, sister, fess up. The jig's up, as they say. We lost."

The shaking stopped. Clarity returned instantly to the pale-blue eyes. Pink rose in her cheeks and her lips contracted into a tight circle, reminding LuAnn of the tied end of a balloon. Irene was clearly about to pop. A knobby finger jutted at Thelma. "You stay out of this. You wreck everything. I had this under control. Just like when we were kids and you ratted me out every time we played hide-and-seek. And you still can't get over that Fred fell in love with me and not you, and you never like it when I—"

"Mom!" Leo tried to quiet her but the little woman was having none of it.

And then the tight angles of her lined face seemed to dissolve, and she began to sob. "I did it…for you, Leo. All for you." She sank onto the recliner. "You've never been good at working. So much like your father. It's not in your genes."

"Mother."

"I did it for you. I wanted you to have something when we were gone, and I could no longer send you an allowance. If they found out, there would be nothing."

"Mother!"

"Thelma?" LuAnn addressed the woman who looked like she didn't know if she should still be mad or let herself feel sorry for her sister. "Do you know what this is about?"

A noisy sigh vibrated paper-thin lips. "She wasn't there. I never should have told her."

"Told her what?"

"Oh, what difference does it make? Irene and I can spend the rest of our days in the poorhouse, and Leo can go sponge off somebody else."

"Aunt Thelma. That's not fair. I—"

LuAnn waved him away.

"I was six when my great-grandfather died. He was a hundred and four. So many years to live with…" She took her glasses off and cleaned them on her blouse. "I was there when he told us everything. On his deathbed. Years later, I might have dismissed it as a nightmare, but my father confirmed it all." She closed her eyes and rested her head on the back of the couch. A long pause followed, interrupted only by the ticking of the grandfather clock. "My great-grandfather's name was Stuart. Stuart Dawson. He came with—"

"Wait. This is your great-grandfather on your mother's side?" Leo ran a hand through his blond waves. "Because Mom said—"

"Hush. You know nothing. I am talking about our father's father. His name was Stuart Dawson."

"Then how did—"

"He was a builder. Howard Bickerton took him on as a partner, even though he had nothing to contribute but his skills. Howard was a very wealthy man. His wife and father had died, and he was left with a fortune. And a son."

"*Two* sons," Charlotte muttered.

Thelma glanced at Charlotte but kept talking. "Howard had this house built while he was still in England and set up a bank account here."

"So you're not even related to—"

Thelma silenced Leo with a fierce stare. "Our great-grandparents and their three-year-old son came to America with Howard and his four-year-old son. Howard, being a lonely widower, showed interest in Charisse, my great-grandmother, and Stuart, of course, defended her honor. It turned to blows on the night their boat docked across the river. Stuart wanted to take Charisse and their son Romulus and return home, but Howard wouldn't let him out of the partnership. They fought and my great-grandfather won. Howard left, never to be heard from again."

"He left his son?" Janice gripped the front of her sweater, covering her mama heart.

Thelma nodded. Irene looked at her, eyes wide with what appeared to be surprise.

"Then how—" Leo paced, stopped in front of his mother and then his aunt. "Then he pretended to be Howard after that?"

"Only to keep the work going," Irene added, mopping her tears with the tissue Winnie handed her. "The inn was a station on the Underground Railroad. If the truth had come out, that all would have stopped. It was for a good cause."

"And the truth was in the brass box." Tess laid a hand on Irene's.

"Maybe. Our father said there was a box, and it was hidden at the inn. He had searched and searched for it. His uncle told him about it when he was a very old man but didn't tell him where it was. He just said the truth was in the box."

LuAnn took Thelma's hand. "So it was you and Irene who hid Prudence Willard's journal in the room under the inn?"

Thelma drew a ragged breath. "Yes. We'd found it in grandfather's desk years ago, and when all this started with selling the inn, we thought we'd put it somewhere where no one would ever find it. We couldn't bring ourselves to destroy it—so many risked their lives for its existence."

Janice sat on a needlepoint-cushioned chair next to Irene. "Did you hire Winnie to scare us out of buying the inn?"

All eyes turned to Winnie, who stood with eyes and mouth wide. "Why would I—"

Thelma shook her finger at Irene. "She's your ghost! She's the one scaring you."

"That's ridiculous. That's not possible." Brad rubbed his temples.

Winnie's empty laugh cracked the silence. "I guess maybe I did have a part in it, after all." Winnie directed sharp words at Irene. "All that time you told me to keep an eye on the inn and tell you when people went in and out so's you could help these ladies. And all those calls from Saffron tellin' you Mr. Brad's schedule..."

Brad's eyes appeared in danger of falling out of his skull. "You had people spying on us?"

"Oh, don't go making it sound so dramatic." Irene made a *pfsh* sound, lips sputtering. "I just needed to know when the ladies were there."

"So you could scare the life out of us." Janice pulled her hand away from Irene's.

"Who helped you?" LuAnn asked. "You couldn't have done all that alone."

"You think." Thelma gave a rueful laugh. "We've been crawling through that tunnel since we were toddlers. If it weren't for this hip of mine..."

"But, the scarf." Brad sat next to Thelma. "It was up on the fan. She couldn't."

"Gripper Grabber. It extends to ten feet."

LuAnn put a hand to her forehead. "And the receipt I found at the inn?"

Irene laughed. "That was my idea. I found it in the inn and decided to send you all on a little goose chase."

Winnie, hands planted on her hips, sank onto a chair. Her pointed gaze stayed on Irene. "You wore my sweater."

"You left it here."

"Where is my earring? There was a gold hoop earring in the pocket and it's gone."

"We found it, Winnie. I have it," LuAnn said. Another clue accounted for.

Brad folded his hands and bent down. LuAnn wondered if he was praying or counteracting lightheadedness. "You sold your car."

"And your clothes and jewelry," LuAnn added. It was all starting to make sense.

"Did you put the offer on the inn?" Brad voiced the question forming in LuAnn's head.

"It was the only way. I've hunted for that box since I was in my twenties and my father told us about it. It had to have been hidden in the walls, and if the ladies started renovating it was likely they'd find it. We have the house and some stocks but not enough cash on hand for a down payment. We—"

"Irene," LuAnn interrupted, "you stood up for us at the meeting."

"A ruse, all a ruse. To throw you off and deter anyone else who might be interested."

"What would all that history stuff matter, Mom? All that happened a long time ago. Those people are long dead and nobody cares what—" Leo stopped pacing. His mouth opened.

As the magnitude of the truth washed over him, he grabbed the back of his mother's chair. "This means I'm not…actually… an heir."

"The box isn't in her car." Tess shook raindrops off her hair. The pouring had stopped, but the trees were still dripping. "I checked everywhere." She set Irene's keys on the kitchen table.

Winnie put a plate of cookies next to the keys. Brad took one. "Winnie, I am so, so sorry."

"Mr. Bradley, if you don't stop apologizin' I will be forced to send you to your room. If I was you, I would have thought I was guilty too."

LuAnn poured coffee. They were all feeling the need for something bolder than tea. She tried to eavesdrop on the hushed conversation in the other room between Thelma, Irene, and Leo, but couldn't hear any of it.

LuAnn asked Winnie for the sugar and opened the cupboard she pointed at. On the shelf above the salt, pepper, and sugar were several bottles of essential oils. She picked up the eucalyptus. "What do they use this for?"

"I use it if I get a cold. Did you know you can use it to get stains out? Irene spilled spaghetti sauce on her cloth purse and wouldn't you know it got it right out."

Tess laughed. "Is Irene a big fan of peanuts?"

Winnie's eyebrows dipped toward her nose. "Don't know why you're askin', but yes, she is. With her low blood sugar, she always carries a bag of peanuts with her for snackin'. She likes 'em best in the shell. Fresher, she says. Too much work if you ask me."

Janice walked in from the back hall. "Look what I found in the bathroom." She held up a copy of Dante's *Inferno.*

Brad shook his head, something he'd been doing a lot in the last hour. "I still cannot believe that little woman—"

"What?" Irene stood in the doorway, Thelma and Leo behind her. "You can't believe I would do everything in my power to protect my son and our family's reputation?"

Tess and Janice pulled out chairs at the table, and the sisters sat.

"We have a plan," Irene announced, looking at Brad.

"For what?"

"We are moving to Seattle."

"You're *what*? Seattle? Why in the world would you do that?"

"The daughter of a childhood friend lives there. She has a large house and has often invited us to come."

"Irene, that doesn't make any sense. Why would you leave Marietta and all of your friends?"

She stared at him, her dried-apple face twisted in confusion. "Where else could we go?"

"Why are you talking about going anywhere?"

"Because the house is yours. It was never ours. We are a third generation of liars and deceivers. We have cheated you and your brother out of a lifetime of happiness in this house. And oh"—she turned to Charlotte—"our father lied to your parents when they came. They had a right to be here and we..." The tears began again. "We should probably go to prison but I hope you won't send us—"

"I don't want the house."

"What?"

"I don't want the house. The past is in the past. You two can stay here for the rest of your lives, and there will be no more talk of Seattle."

Thelma's hand flew to her mouth. Irene jumped up like a woman no more than seventy and threw her arms around Brad's waist. "What can we do to thank you?"

"All I want from you is a withdrawal of your offer on the inn so these ladies"—he winked at LuAnn—"can get moving on their dream."

LuAnn took a moment to process what he'd just said before addressing the little woman clinging to him. "There is just one more little thing, Irene. Where did you hide the box?"

Tess wiped cobwebs off the box they'd found right where Irene had put it—under the front porch. Janice yelped as a tiny striped spider skittered across the aunts' kitchen table. LuAnn smashed it with a napkin.

Brad brandished the shiny new key like a saber, then handed it to Tess.

Janice backed away from the table. "What if the whole thing is full of spiders?"

Tess shook her head. “Then we will all scream and run.” She slid the end of the key into the keyhole. “Déjà vu.” Three quarters of a turn and the lock clicked.

“I have to go lie down.” Thelma pressed her hand against her chest.

“I’ll come with you, Thel.” Irene grasped her sister’s elbow. “Not sure either one of us needs to be here for this.” The two shuffled into the living room. Leo’s eyes tracked their departure. He seemed to be questioning whether he had the courage to stay.

“Lu, you open it. You found the secret room.”

LuAnn wiggled her fingers as Brad had done hours ago and reached for the box. The hinged lid stuck, then opened with a loud groan.

Just as Prudence had recorded, the box was filled with letters and several daguerreotype photographs. “Let’s each take something out.” LuAnn lifted the top envelope—a letter addressed to the same attorney Matthew had written to.

My dear friend,

I write this missive with a heavy heart. I find myself in the awkward position of needing to dissolve the partnership you so skillfully crafted. The four-week journey that brought us to Ohio has revealed character flaws in my partner and his wife I could never have imagined existed in people who seemed, upon meeting them, to be made of the finest character, possessing the kind of integrity this venture required.

You are familiar with the story of Joseph in the Holy Scriptures. Think on Joseph's reason for fleeing Potiphar's house, leaving his cloak behind, and you will understand what has transpired. You know me, Saul, and know that I would never betray the memory of my dear Marta. I did nothing to encourage these advances and now find myself in the most awkward of situations as Mr. Dawson has been falsely apprised of my intentions toward his wife by his wife.

I have asked the Dawsons to return to England, at my expense, and have advised them that you will have monies waiting for them to begin a new life. However, this generous offer has been met with an anger the likes of which I have never encountered. The man has threatened my life. If they do not leave, it may be that Zephaniah and I will need to flee.

All I long for is a chance to continue in this country the legacy of freedom my father began. Moving into the house Marta and I designed together will be difficult, but it will be a place of new beginnings for my son and me.

Should news reach you of some tragedy striking me down, you will know the truth. I implore you to protect my sons and make sure Matthew and Zephaniah are well provided for.

Yours sincerely,
Howard

Brad stood, hand cupping his chin, index finger tapping his mouth. "I have a feeling my aunts left something out of the story." He turned on his heel. The women followed him.

Thelma and Irene sat on the couch, holding hands. Pale faces looked up. Thelma's hand fluttered against her chest. "Wh-what did you find?"

"We found that you apparently failed to mention something about Howard's disappearance."

"That's in there?"

Brad just stared. They all just stared.

"Oh... I have feared this day my entire life. I wish I hadn't been there. I wish I hadn't heard."

"What did you hear, Thelma?" Winnie's gentle voice slowed the flurry of Thelma's fingers.

"She made him do it, but he did it out of love. You must understand that. She had... a wandering soul, he said. He did it because he loved her."

LuAnn leaned in. "Did what, Thelma?"

"My great-grandfather... sh-shot... Howard Bickerton... in the back... and dumped his body into the river."

CHAPTER TWENTY-THREE

Tess signed the last paper and slid it to Janice who signed it and passed it to LuAnn. LuAnn wrote her name with a flourish and pushed the paper across the table to Paul Townsend. He signed, stacked the papers, and smiled. "This has been some ordeal, ladies, but you are now the proud owners of Wayfarers Inn."

When the cheering stopped, Janice hummed a note. Tess and LuAnn joined in harmony. "'I'm in with the Inn crowd. I go where the Inn crowd goes…'"

Brad stood, shook Paul's hand, and hugged the women in turn. "Lunch is on me, everyone. I hear the Ahi Tuna with wasabi aioli at Austyn's is divine."

Tess looked at Janice. "Oh, remember, we have that thing."

"Right. That thing. We have to go to that place and meet with those people."

"And do that thing."

"At noon, right?"

"Right. Can't be—"

Saffron poked her head in the door. "Phone call for one of you." She looked from LuAnn to Janice. "It's your brother-in-law."

"Oh. I have my ringer off."

Paul handed his phone receiver to Janice, whose countenance faded like a melting ice cream cone as she talked. "You're sure. No mistake? Okay. Bye." She looked up at Tess and LuAnn, face ashen. "The masonry guys who were at the inn to give us an estimate found something that didn't show up in the inspection. There's a crack in the foundation that's going to take some major work. And when I say major, I mean more than we can possibly afford."

The last envelope lay on her desk. The one from her mother's only confidant. Eleanor Zimmerman was the daughter of the woman who owned the diner LuAnn's mother had worked at for forty-two years. Eleanor was bedridden now, weak from the cancer she'd valiantly fought for more than a decade. LuAnn had called her when her mom died, and they'd cried together. Eleanor said then that she would send a letter with "some things your mom would want you to know."

She couldn't explain why she hadn't opened it sooner. She'd wanted to be moved and settled and ready to tackle her past. This was anything but settled. They'd spent the past three days talking to their bankers and investment brokers. Tess's son had suggested they start a crowd-funding page to cover the cost of the foundation repair. All in all, it had been a pretty bleak way to start out as business owners.

Maybe something in Eleanor's letter would lift her spirits. Why did she assume it would be bad news? She slid a letter opener under the flap and said a quick prayer. A small silver key tumbled onto her lap. She picked it up and stared at the number engraved on it. 317. What was it for?

The letter began, "My dear Lulu," and talked about how much Eleanor would miss her weekly chats with LuAnn's mom. It went on to talk of shared memories—their favorite customers and the ones who complained about everything and never tipped. And then it took a turn.

> Please forgive your mother for not being able to tell you everything. She was sworn to secrecy for so long that I think she just couldn't ever find the words. She left it up to me to decide whether or not to give you the key to the safe deposit box I've kept for you. I always thought you should know. Please forgive me too, for my part in this, and please know we did it to protect you, to keep you from being hurt.

LuAnn set the letter down and picked up the key. She could have been reading an entry in Prudence's journal. She picked up the key, set it down again, and began to read.

> Your father was a hero, LuAnn, though he was never recognized as one. He witnessed the murder of one of his supervisors by a very cruel and very powerful man. He wasn't sure if anyone knew he'd seen it. He could have kept silent. Your mother begged him to, but he couldn't. He was a man of integrity, and he felt a duty to protect others from this man, so he went to the authorities.

The mob found out and you and your mother were in danger. That's why you had to leave. The FBI gave your father a whole new identity. Your mother didn't know where he was for more than twenty years. That's when he sent the letters he'd been saving for you. By then, he had remarried and had other children. I think that was the real reason she never felt she could tell you.

The key is for a safe deposit box at Midtown Bank. In the box you will find things I hope will be healing and not hurtful.

Honey, your father has been dead for more than a decade. I'm so sorry to be the one to tell you. I wish I could be there to hold you in my arms like I did when you were little.

Your father loved you so much. You will feel that in his letters, and you will feel it in another way too. In the box you will find a savings account book. With the interest that has accrued over all these years, you will be able to travel anywhere you want or build the house of your dreams or do whatever God leads you to do.

LuAnn rested her head on her arms and sobbed…tears of loss, grief, bitterness, uncertainty…and, after a while, thanksgiving.

LuAnn pinched the metal nose strip on her dust mask and swept a pile of dirt and dehydrated bugs to the center of the room.

Tory walked in and grabbed a screwdriver from the toolbox on the bar. "Two more minutes." He waved as he walked out again.

Janice stopped wiping down the bar and lowered her mask. "This is actually happening."

A loud crash shook the mirror Tess was cleaning. "There goes the first wall."

The front door swung open again, and Brad strode in. "We're ready. Be warned, though, there's a pretty agitated crowd gathering outside."

"No." Janice dropped her rag.

LuAnn let the broom handle fall against the wall. "Not again. Please not again."

"They'd better not—" Whatever Tess was going to say was forgotten when Brad laughed.

"Let's see if you can talk them down, Abe. Another emancipation speech, maybe." He put his arm around LuAnn's shoulders, and the four walked out together.

The mass of people clustered around the front door cheered. LuAnn stood in shock, staring out at strangers who had become like family in the course of one crazy month. Charlotte and her mother. Maybelline. Saffron minus the boyfriend. Winnie. Bart Sandman. Paul Townsend. Marla Still. Margaret Ashworth. Joe. Marv. Pastor Ben. Even Leo. But the people LuAnn was the most touched to see were the two little women standing in the center of the crowd. She hugged Thelma and then Irene. "Thank you for coming."

Irene dabbed her eyes. "Here I thought I'd be spending the rest of my days behind bars."

LuAnn laughed. “Here at the inn we believe in grace.”

“You certainly do, my dear.”

“There’s one thing Tess reminded me of. A man called her one morning, somebody with a deep voice—”

“And said”—Irene lowered her chin and took a loud breath—“sometimes the past is best left in the past.” The entire crowd swiveled toward the low, booming voice. Irene lifted her chin and smiled an elfin smile. “But not in this case.”

A bugle tooted, a musical sound coming from the instrument that had once wrought fear. Kip took a bow when he’d finished and swept his hand toward the draped project he’d helped Tory complete.

LuAnn wrapped one arm around Tess and the other around Janice as they turned toward the old brass lantern, back home again, hanging next to the front door. With a flourish, Tory unveiled the sign that read:

OPENING SOON—

WAYFARERS INN BED & BREAKFAST & SOUP CAFÉ

A Place Where Old Friends Gather

And Strangers Become Family

Dear Reader,

I am so honored to introduce our Secrets of Wayfarers Inn series to you. Writing *Family Secrets* has been such a joy. LuAnn, Tess, and Janice seem like old friends now—the kind you can confide in, cry with, and not care if they catch you with your hair in a towel and a clay mask on your face! I hope you'll feel as comfy with them as I do and soon think of yourself as an honorary lifetime member of the Inn Crowd.

The highlight of my research for *Family Secrets* was a trip to Marietta, Ohio, the richly beautiful setting for this series. Walking the cobblestone streets, touring historic homes, spending a relaxing afternoon with my hubby onboard a sternwheeler boat on the Ohio River, lunching at the Levee House, and having tea (and a delish gluten-free pumpkin cookie!) at Jeremiah's Coffee House . . . all combined to make me fall in love with this picturesque riverfront town with all its secrets and stories from the past.

I pray that, as you read this, you will be inspired by the courage and compassion of LuAnn, Tess, Janice, and our historical character, Prudence Willard. May we strive together to be the hands and feet of Jesus.

Becky Melby

About the Author

Wisconsin author Becky Melby and her husband have four married sons and fifteen grandchildren. When not writing, reading, or spoiling grandkids, Becky may be found plotting and brainstorming on the back of their Honda Gold Wing or traveling the country with their camper.

Connect with Becky at: beckymelby.com or on her Facebook Author Page at: facebook.com/Becky-Melby-Author-Page-147542291976020

A Closer Look at . . .

The Levee House

The original inspiration for Secrets of Wayfarers Inn came from a riverfront building that, until recently, housed the Levee House Café. The redbrick structure at 127 Ohio Street, built in 1826 by Colonel Joseph Barker, who was the first master builder/architect of the Northwest Territory, has a colorful past—and probably a few secrets that have yet to be discovered. Originally built for Dudley Woodbridge as a dry goods store, over the years it served as a hotel, barber shop, tavern, brothel, and an automotive shop where Studebakers were assembled.

The historical building is most known for a "crime of passion" that occurred in the 1870s, when a young man, embarrassed by his father's frequent visits to the upstairs rooms, snuck in and ended his family's shame...with an axe! Those with active imaginations think the father's ghost still wanders about the building. (Watch for a cozy-mystery version of this story coming up in this series.)

In 1977, this historic building was condemned and doomed to simply disintegrate, along with its secrets, until local architect Harley Noland recognized its potential. Harley had even more vision than LuAnn, Tess, and Janice—for when he stood in the basement, he could see blue sky through the gaping holes in all three floors! Harley restored the upper floors for apartments and opened the Levee House Café on the main floor.

Harley Noland also snatched up another opportunity when the local trolley business came up for sale. His Marietta history tours started at the Levee House—where one of the waitresses posed as a lady of the evening and peeked out of an upstairs window, waved, then ducked inside and screamed. To complete the vignette, another character, dressed in black and wielding a massive axe, would hop on the back of the trolley and run up the aisle, terrifying tourists—much to their delight!

In 2004 the effects of Hurricane Ivan were felt in Marietta when the Ohio River crested at 44.97 feet. Much of the downtown area was shut down for over a month. Water filled the first floor of the Levee House and much of the renovation work had to be redone. But the people of Marietta are resilient and soon were back in business.

As of this writing, the building that housed the Levee House, and now serves as our fictional location of Wayfarers Inn, again stands vacant. However, LuAnn, Janice, and Tess invite you to come explore Marietta and its history and stroll down the riverfront, with its gorgeous view.

Something Delicious from our Wayfarers Inn Friends

Winnie's Creamed Chicken and Biscuits

Biscuits: (Easier than the ones she made with yeast starter!)

2 cups all-purpose flour
3 teaspoons baking powder
1 teaspoon salt
⅔ cup milk
⅓ cup vegetable oil

Creamed chicken:

¼ cup finely chopped onion
¼ cup butter
¼ cup all-purpose flour
½ teaspoon salt
⅛ teaspoon pepper
1½ cup milk
½ cup chicken broth
2 cups chopped cooked chicken
1 cup fresh or frozen peas
1 tablespoon minced fresh parsley

Instructions:

1. Preheat oven to 450 degrees Fahrenheit.
2. In a bowl, combine flour, baking powder, and salt; add milk and oil.
3. Stir until the dough forms a ball. Knead in the bowl ten times until smooth.

4. Roll or pat dough into a six-inch square about one inch thick. Cut into six rectangles or use biscuit cutter.
5. Place on a lightly greased baking sheet. Bake 10–12 minutes or until golden brown.
6. While the biscuits bake, sauté onion in butter until tender. Stir in flour, salt, and pepper until smooth. Gradually add milk and chicken broth; bring to a boil.
7. Reduce heat; cook and stir for 1–2 minutes or until thickened.
8. Stir in peas, chicken, and parsley and cook for 2–3 minutes until heated through.
9. Split biscuits. Top with creamed chicken.

Read on for a sneak peek of another exciting book in the series Secrets of Wayfarers Inn!

River of Life

by Kathleen Y'Barbo

July 1
Marietta, Ohio

"Quilts!" Tessa Wallace made an abrupt right turn into the newly renovated quilt shop. Though breakfast at the tea-room next door had been the first item on their agenda for today, she just couldn't help being distracted by a look inside the new quilt shop. "Look how beautiful! This was definitely worth the wait."

It had just been a few weeks since the Sassy Seamstress had reopened one street over from the inn. Tess and her two best friends had been dying to go beyond just peering through front windows filled with stacks of fabric, quilts hung on antique ladders, and the most adorable handmade accessories.

However, they'd made a pact not to go see what the new owner had done with the place until they could all go. With the repairs going on at the inn as well as all the other demands on their lives, they hadn't found a day to go together until today, the first day of July.

Today was meant to be a respite from all of those repairs and demands. Before they left this morning, they'd agreed there would be no discussion of the inn today, and then with pinkies interlocked they sealed the promise.

So instead of thinking about how the lovely items she saw here and there would fit into the decorating scheme of Wayfarers Inn, Tess distracted herself by concentrating on the many changes that had been made to this building. The previous owners—two sisters in their eighties—had not spent much time improving the condition of the interior or adding to the inventory in the past few decades.

The result was a hodgepodge of fabric dating from the seventies and eighties, mismatched how-to magazines and craft supplies, and the lingering smell of live bait they sold to tourists who rented boats at the docks nearby.

Tess couldn't recall the last time she'd visited the place, but then she had never been much of a crafter. Or a fisherman.

She inhaled. Somehow the aroma of bait had been replaced by the loveliest fragrance. Unless she missed her guess, that was Yankee Candle's Market Blossoms, her favorite. Because the candles filled any space with the fragrant scent of blossoms and berries, Tess had already packed away two of them to use in her new rooms at the inn once she moved in.

She glanced around the inviting space, allowing her attention to rest on the goods so artfully arranged on shelves and tables around the room. A lovely soundtrack of dulcimer music played softly, and a television behind the counter was silently showing an episode of the Arts & Entertainment Network's *Quilt Mysteries* series. A stack of the series's episodes on DVD rested nearby.

The restful atmosphere was exactly what they hoped to accomplish at the inn. Perhaps she should ask the name of the dulcimer music. It would be lovely to have that playing downstairs as guests come in.

Oh. No. Not today.

Tess returned her attention to the colorful fabrics standing at attention on the shelf to her right. Truly, she hadn't expected to find anything on their visit to the Sassy Seamstress, although she had thought perhaps to see if the new owner did alterations or made curtains and slipcovers.

Between the calorie-laden, hurry-up-and-eat meals and sweet treats they had been consuming on the run and the fact that half of the vintage furniture they had found to go into the inn would need recovering, a good seamstress who could let out skirts as well as cover windows and parlor furniture would be invaluable.

Tess had pulled out a bolt of fabric in a lovely shade of gold with burgundy and green dots when LuAnn Sherrill caught up to her and shook her head. "Don't you think this would make fabulous pillows for my new sitting room?"

"Oh no you don't," LuAnn told her as she looked at the price per yard on the end of the bolt. "We have a plan and a budget, and we absolutely cannot deviate from either. I don't care how beautiful... oh! Look how pretty."

Her nearly reformed list-making friend tucked her three-ring organizer back into her purse, now distracted by a beautiful quilt in red, white, and blue that Tess's grandmother would have called a hen-and-chickens pattern.

Tess thought briefly of her own list, a bucket list she and her late husband had created together on their last anniversary. Theirs had been a long and loving marriage, but not nearly long enough. After four years, she still missed Jeffrey dearly.

Tess still hadn't had the courage to unfold the list she kept in her wallet and begin checking off the items they had agreed to do together. Someday she would. She smiled as she returned the bolt of fabric to its place on the shelf. Indeed, someday when she was ready and when reading that masculine scrawl didn't bring back fresh pain.

But for now the Lord had certainly provided a remedy for that pain in the form of two best friends who likely had no idea how very much they helped to heal her heartbreak when it rose up. Three best friends for life, they were, and their motto said it all: "We will never be boring or bored and we will never act our age."

So far that had meant being there for each other during happiness and heartbreak, pregnancies and adoption, full houses and empty nests. She tucked those memories back into her heart and smiled. Yes indeed, despite the loss she would never get over, she was a blessed woman.

Still, from a business standpoint, Tess knew all too well the odds of turning the Wayfarers Inn project into a profitable venture. With the Lord's help—and with plenty of elbow grease—they would beat those odds.

In the meantime, even if they never had a paying guest—perish the thought, of course!—the fact Tess would be living in a lovely old inn made her happier than anything had in recent memory. She had a purpose again, even if that purpose on most days was to rein in LuAnn's endless additions to plans and lists and to convince the third member of their trio that there was nothing to fear but fear itself.

As if on cue, the third member of the Inn Crowd, Janice Eastman, joined her, her smile broad. "Oh Lu, that is just gorgeous. Wouldn't it look beautiful in the parlor at the inn? It's the perfect thing for the Fourth of July."

"I think so too," LuAnn said as she turned back one corner of the quilt to inspect the lining. "I can't decide whether to hang it from the railing, hang it from the wall, or just drape it over the back of one of the sofas. If we were up and running and could actually put a float in the town parade, I'd say this quilt should have center stage." She turned toward Tess. "What do you think?"

"I think both of you need to remember that there are neither railings nor sofas to drape anything over this Fourth of July, and anything hung on those walls will either get painted over or covered in whatever dust the contractors are kicking up. However, if you want to climb into the back of my son-in-law's red pickup truck and ride down the street behind the Marietta High School band wearing that quilt, I can certainly make that happen. The rest of it, not so much."

"Party pooper," Janice said with a laugh.

"May I remind you that we all agreed this afternoon would be a break from discussing the inn?"

"Well, of course," LuAnn said with a shrug. "But this is just so fun and pretty."

A blue-eyed young woman in her midtwenties, her dark hair tied up in one of those messy buns Tess's daughter, Lizzie, favored, stepped from behind a quilted curtain at the back of the store. She wore stylish jeans and sneakers and a red T-shirt that said *A clean house is a sign of a broken sewing machine.* A name badge in the shape of a spool of thread proclaimed her to be Wendy.

Something about Wendy seemed vaguely familiar.

Marietta, Ohio
July 1, 1859

"There will always be a need, Wife," Jason Willard said. "Let someone else take over now. Our son deserves a mama who's living and not one who gave her life to save someone else."

"Please lower thy voice, Husband," Prudence said gently as she focused on the swaddled babe sleeping in her arms instead of looking up at the husband she knew had only her best interests at heart. "I've only just got him settled and neither of us wants to hear him fuss again so soon, do we?"

As if he knew they were speaking about him, Moses opened his eyes to look up at Prudence. Her heart lurched. What a beautiful boy he was. Fat and happy most of the time with only the slightest complaint when he thought he might be missing a meal.

Born the day of the great Marietta fire back in May, little Moses was already a full month and a few days old. The child was his father made over in every way but one: he had his mama's eyes.

She had seen those eyes on the day he cried his way into the world and had known this one was strong. This one would live.

So while Jason went off to town to stand alongside the other men and do what he could to stop the flames that were taking building after building on that cold day, Prudence stayed home and held her son, wrapped in the quilt dyed blue for loyalty and red for freedom, while she prayed. Prayers of gratitude mingled with pleas for those in the path of the blaze.

Jason had come home in the early hours of the morning, his clothes smelling of smoke and ash dusting his face and hair. Nearly three blocks of buildings were lost to a blaze started by two young fellows bending lead in a barn. She added a prayer for those two as she tucked her husband into bed, then fitted herself against his side to attempt whatever sleep Moses would allow.

Prudence smiled at her baby boy and traced the dimple in his chin. Someday he would be a man who did great things, this much she knew in her heart. Like Mary in the Bible, this mama held tight to the promise the Lord gave her regarding her son and said nothing to anyone, not even Jason.

"Prudence," Jason said, his voice softer this time but still full of the concern she knew came from a place of deep love, "thou hast not answered me."

She looked up now, shifting Moses to her shoulder to rub his tiny back as she regarded her husband with what she hoped would convey the respect he deserved as head of this household. "To my recollection, thou hast not asked a question."

He would, though, and Prudence knew it. Though Jason's injuries made him unable to fully participate in the moving of the parcels, as those they aided along on their journey on the Underground Railroad were called, he would have been doing the same work alongside her if he could.

Oh, but he did worry. About her, and now about their son.

Prudence faced him now, her heart soft toward this man God had given her and yet knowing that with one word Jason could put an end to the work that meant so much. It was his right to do so, but she prayed now that he would not exercise that right.

"Do not thee worry," she told him with a smile. "Thou knows it has been months since I've done anything but help with the quilting. What harm can come of that?"

Jason traced the line of her jaw with his knuckle, his smile matching hers, and then rested his palm atop hers on their son's back. "My love," he whispered, "if thee were any other woman, I would agree."

Her smile faltered. Did he know?

She returned a happy expression to her face. "Thee wouldn't have it any other way, would thee? Perhaps thee wishes to have married a more docile creature."

Her dear husband paused, his gaze seeming to search her face as he appeared to be considering the question. "The truth?"

"Always," she said even though she was not certain she wanted to hear it.

"Then no," he said gently, "I would not have it any other way, but not because it is easy for me that thee are not a docile creature." His fingers tenderly traced the length of her jaw. "But because this is the way God created thee, and it is thee I love just as thee are."

"And I love thee, my husband, with all that I am," she said. "But there are times when things would be much easier had He made me different than I am."

"That I do agree," Jason said. "But much as it would be simpler, what about all of those on the other side of the river who need thee?" He shook his head. "Need us," he corrected. "What do they know of easy?"

"Indeed thee speak the truth," she said.

"And thee has a plan," he told her as he stepped away. "Should I ask what that plan might be or accept that thee and the other ladies from church are merely gathering on this July evening to make a quilt for a good cause?"

Prudence stepped back into his embrace. "Oh, Husband," she said as she rested her head against his strong, broad chest, "that is exactly the plan, and the cause is one thee and I would stake our lives for. So what is a little quilting with friends, some of whom are new friends and some old?"

"It is a worthy cause indeed," he told her. "So be sure thee take that goose with thee."

She looked up at him and laughed. "Whatever for?"

He shook his head. "With all the noise she makes at the slightest whisper, who better to alert thee to additions to thy quilting circle, wanted or unwanted?"

So he did know.

Prudence reached up on tiptoe to kiss her husband lightly on the cheek. "The Lord will protect us all, goose or not," she said, "but I wager Patience will do her part for the cause."

A Note from the Editors

We hope you enjoy Secrets of Wayfarers Inn, created by the Books and Inspirational Media Division of Guideposts, a nonprofit organization that touches millions of lives every day through products and services that inspire, encourage, help you grow in your faith, and celebrate God's love in every aspect of your daily life.

Thank you for making a difference with your purchase of this book, which helps fund our many outreach programs to military personnel, prisons, hospitals, nursing homes, and educational institutions. To learn more, visit Guideposts Foundation.org.

We also maintain many useful and uplifting online resources. Visit Guideposts.org to read true stories of hope and inspiration, access OurPrayer network, sign up for free newsletters, download free e-books, join our Facebook community, and follow our stimulating blogs.

To learn about other Guideposts publications, including the best-selling devotional *Daily Guideposts,* go to ShopGuideposts .org, call (800) 932-2145, or write to Guideposts, PO Box 5815, Harlan, Iowa 51593.

Sign up for the Guideposts Fiction Newsletter

and stay up-to-date on the books you love!

You'll get sneak peeks of new releases, recommendations from other Guideposts readers, and special offers just for you . . .

and it's FREE!

Just go to Guideposts.org/Newsletters today to sign up.

Guideposts®

Visit Guideposts.org/Shop or call (800) 932-2145